I0720729

JUSTICE FOR BOONE

BADGE OF HONOR: TEXAS HEROES, BOOK 6

SUSAN STOKER

AUTHOR NOTE

There is no doubt that domestic violence is an ever-increasing issue in society today. One in four women will experience some sort of domestic violence in her lifetime. Read that again. One. In. Four. That number is WAY too high.

But domestic violence is not only a man-on-woman issue. It can happen to anyone, regardless of gender, race, ethnicity, sexual orientation, or income. Abuse against women is talked about and seen in the media and on television shows more than any other type of abuse, but the fact of the matter is that men are victims of nearly three million physical assaults in the United States each year.

Yes, men are abused, it's just not talked about as much.

This book is a work of fiction. It's not based on anyone I know, or any situation I've read about. But it *could've* been. Boone is a Texan, a cowboy, a big strong man, but because he's witnessed abuse in his childhood, he's sworn never to be violent toward a woman... and leaves himself open to the same kind of abuse he witnessed when he was a young child.

Sadly, without intervention of some sort, boys who witness domestic violence from a young age are far more likely to become abusers when they grow up, thus continuing the cycle of violence in the next generation.

Most domestic violence incidents are never reported. Speak up. Speak out, and make a difference for someone who needs help.

Perhaps the people who know the most about this type of violence are our police officers who deal with it day in and day out. Thank you to every officer out there. You're the front line to try to get help for those who need it the most.

PROLOGUE

HAYDEN YATES CLOSED her apartment door behind her with a sigh. She dropped her keys on the table next to the door and headed down the hall to her bedroom. The small two-bedroom apartment was sparse. She had some pictures of her parents in the main room, and there were a few pictures on the walls, but there weren't any typical girly things to be seen anywhere.

No frilly pillows, no flowers on the kitchen counter, no sweet-smelling candles on any surface. The apartment didn't smell like frou-frou air freshener. If someone looked in her kitchen, they'd find a lot of pre-packaged meals, canned soup, condiments, and some string cheese in the refrigerator.

Hayden ignored everything and made a beeline to her bedroom. Opening the door, she was already stripping off her uniform. The sheriff deputy's badge she wore was taken off and placed on her dresser, the bulletproof vest unvelcroed and left right where she stood. The utility belt she wore around her waist was unbuckled and dropped on the floor by the shower, where she left it without a thought.

She unbuttoned and unzipped her brown uniform pants, leaned into the shower stall and turned it on. Hayden blinked back her tears and hurried to strip off the rest of her clothes, leaving them in a pile on the tile before stepping over the tub and into the hot shower. She huddled under the water, letting it pound against her shoulders as her head drooped.

It'd been a hell of a few months. As many went, they were interspersed with bouts of extreme adrenaline-inducing fear and excitement, and hours of boredom and routine police work. But it was seeing the love between her friends—Quint Axton and his girlfriend, Corrie Madison, and firefighter Cade Turner and his girlfriend, Beth Parkins—that was doing Hayden in.

A few months ago, Corrie was a witness to a workplace shooting and the men behind it had kidnapped her to shut her up...permanently. Quint, along with Dax, a Texas Ranger, Cruz, an FBI Agent, Hayden, and other members of the San Antonio Police Department, had tracked down Corrie and raced to rescue her. Even though Corrie was blind, she'd somehow managed to escape her captors without any help.

When they'd realized Corrie had headed into the forest and probably climbed a tree to hide, Quint had straightened his shoulders and gotten to work finding his woman.

Then more recently, Cade, otherwise known as Sledge, had started a relationship with Beth, who, because of events she'd gone through before moving to Texas, was agoraphobic and struggling with using fire as a means to try to get control over her life. She'd been able to beat both issues back, but had the bad luck to be inside Cade's house when it was burglarized. Amazingly, she used her love for Cade to get her through the harrowing experience.

Hayden had never seen the kind of love her friends shared. Oh, she'd read about it in the romance books she secretly devoured, but hadn't thought it actually existed. Her own parents probably loved each other, but treated each other more like friends than lovers. Hayden had thought the kind of love she read about was something dried-up, sexually frustrated, frumpy romance writers dreamed up in their lonely heads. How wrong she'd been.

Hayden shakily brought her hands up to her hair and smoothed it back as the hot water continued to beat down on her. That kind of love had eluded Hayden her entire life. As a kid, a teenager, a college student, and even as an adult. She'd had her fill of boyfriends, even some she could've loved...if they'd given her half a chance. But not once had she evoked that kind of emotion from another human being.

Remembering how Quint had looked at her as she

was about to climb up a tree to rescue his girlfriend, and said, "Be careful," Hayden had gotten a glimpse of what it might be like to have a man be concerned about her. It had felt good to be worried about for once. But then Quint had finished his sentence. He'd said, "Be careful, she means the world to me."

Of course he'd been worried about Corrie and not her. She was Sheriff's Deputy Hayden Yates...no one worried about her. She could take care of herself. She *always* took care of herself.

That moment ran through her again and again. The relief she felt that Corrie was all right, as well as the pain of knowing she herself was but a second thought in everyone's minds.

Hayden took a deep breath and quickly washed her hair, and then poured some body gel over the shower poof and scrubbed her body. She rinsed and turned off the water. She grabbed a towel and briskly ran it over herself, hanging it back on the rack when she was done. Standing naked at the sink, she brushed her teeth and swished some mouthwash before spitting it out.

She strode out of the bathroom with large strides, which had been called manly on more than one occasion, and threw back the comforter on her bed. Hayden's bed was her safe place. The one place where she could always be herself. The sheets were one-thousand thread count and luxurious against her naked body. Her comforter was pink and flowery and was almost obnoxiously feminine.

Hayden snuggled down and held her childhood stuffed animal tight to her chest. It was a pink elephant that had seen better days. The fur had been worn off long ago and the stuffing had been replaced several times. Ellie the Elephant's trunk had been sewn back on awkwardly more than once and sat crooked on the once-fuzzy face. Hayden had never shown anyone her prized possession, knowing it wouldn't fit their perception of her. Tough. Competent. Tomboy.

She choked back a sob and buried her head in Ellie's soft body, thinking back on the last few months and everything that had happened.

Witnessing Cade and Beth, relieved to see each other after the break-in at his house. Beth had admitted that Cade was her "safe place," and the thought of him arriving to find her where she'd been hiding behind their house had gotten her through the ordeal.

Seeing Quint in her mind, and his obvious love for Corrie, his relief she was safe and the looks on their faces as they'd held each other tight after Hayden had helped her out of the tree.

Hayden's sad, lonely words rang out in the empty room, with no one to hear them but her.

"Just once, I'd like someone to be afraid of losing *me*."

1

———

HAYDEN SIGHED HAPPILY for what seemed like the hundredth time that day. The two weeks she'd been on paid administrative leave had seemed like a lifetime. Without her work as a sheriff's deputy, she had nothing...she was nobody. She lived for her job. Right or wrong, it was what made her happy and made her who she was.

She didn't regret returning fire at the man who'd pulled a gun on her during a routine traffic stop. It was just another one of the hundreds of calls she'd been on during her career, except this time as she approached the driver's door, the man pulled out a pistol and shot at her. Luckily she'd had enough training to act instinctively, narrowly missing being struck and firing at the driver even as she'd been falling to the side.

The firefight was over within seconds, with

Hayden's bullet hitting the man in the forehead, and killing him instantly. It had turned out the man had a warrant for murder...he'd killed his girlfriend over in Houston and was on the run.

Anytime an officer was involved in a shooting, administrative leave was mandatory. Hayden knew she'd been in the right, but it took time for the investigation board to do their review, which seemed to take longer than it had in the past, in part because of the intense media scrutiny that always followed anytime a cop was forced to shoot a civilian. She'd been lucky not to have been that close to a bullet many times in her career, but the wait to be able to return to work was never easy for her.

When Hayden had finally received the call saying she'd been cleared and was back on the shift schedule, she'd been ready. She wasn't used to taking so much time off. She'd gone out for drinks a time or two with Dax, Cruz, Quint, and their girlfriends. Hayden really liked Mackenzie, Mickie, and Corrie. Sometimes Laine, Mack's best friend who was dating another Texas Ranger, would come out with them too, but she hadn't been able to join them lately.

Hayden was close friends with quite a few men from other law enforcement agencies, which was somewhat unusual, but no one cared. They'd all met up at various conferences and worked together on cases that crossed jurisdictions. The men's girlfriends were funny, feminine, and not afraid to give their boyfriends hell. Every time they went out, Hayden always left with her sides hurting from laughing so hard.

One night, some of the guys from Station 7, the firefighters who were becoming more like brothers to her than merely coworkers, had joined them, and she'd laughed more than she ever had before. Cade had shown up for a while, but left early to spend the rest of the night with Beth, who was still working her way up to going out with friends. She was managing her agoraphobia, and Cade said she was getting better each week, but wasn't quite up for a night out.

Hayden also went out a couple of times with some of her fellow deputies from the sheriff's department, and some of the other local single law enforcement officers that she knew and liked. Stag nights out were a lot of fun, and much better than sitting at home. Hayden loved watching TJ, Conor, Calder, and some of her other unattached friends flirt and try to impress the ladies.

She knew she was "just one of the guys," and that was all right with her. Hayden wasn't attracted to any of the men she worked with, and they certainly weren't attracted to her. She'd never had such good friends, and she'd take friendship over love any day of the week.

She knew what she was and what she wasn't. And

what she wasn't was that feminine, pretty, or prone to need a man to take care of her. She never had been, and she never would be.

Hayden had a strong self-esteem, an independent streak, and genuinely liked who she was, but seeing the relationships her friends had with their girlfriends was sometimes enough to make her long for someone of her own. A man who might worry about her when she was on shift. Or who might take the time to bring her lunch while she was on break. Or who might appreciate the fact that she wasn't the kind of woman who needed them to send flowers or treat her with kid gloves.

"Dispatch to four-two-four."

Hayden was brought out of her semi-depressing thoughts by the voice crackling over her radio. "This is four-two-four, go ahead."

"Assistance requested at one thousand forty-three Hildebrandt Road for domestic incident."

"Ten-four."

Hayden leaned over and flicked on the lights and sirens on her vehicle. She was already on the southeast side of San Antonio and was closest to the scene. She accelerated and noticed absently how the cars on the outer loop actually pulled over to the right for once as she came up behind them.

"Dispatch, this is four-two-four. Do you have any other details on the domestic?"

"Call came in about thirty minutes ago. The woman calling in claimed she'd been visiting her boyfriend and he'd gotten upset with her and hit her. Six-two-seven and one-seven-four are on scene now and requesting backup."

"Weapons?"

"Unclear."

"Ten-four."

Domestic incidents were some of the most difficult calls Hayden and her fellow deputies—hell, any law enforcement officer—had to deal with. Emotions were most often high, and it was left up to the officer to determine what actually happened. Most of the time both parties claimed it was the other person's fault. Not to mention the fact there was always the threat of a weapon being involved. Abusers knew the laws were against them and would do or say whatever it took to keep from going to jail.

Domestic assault was one of the few misdemeanor offenses in Texas where a police officer could arrest a person on the spot, even without actually witnessing the incident. All the officer needed was probable cause, like a witness statement or some sort of evidence of injury, to show one person had assaulted the other.

Hayden wholeheartedly agreed with the law. She'd only been in law enforcement for ten years, but even in that time, she'd seen the law slowly erring more on the side of the victim. She'd witnessed way too many abusers getting away with violence against their partners time and time again. From her perspective, it was incredibly frustrating.

Dispatch typically tried to send deputies in pairs to any and all domestic incidents, due to the increased danger. Six-two-seven was Jimmy Phillips and one-seven-four was Troy Bruton. Hayden knew and respected both men, even if they tended to be a bit on the heavy-handed side. They very rarely gave warnings to speeders and Hayden knew they were part of the "good ol' boy" network. But, even so, they were good officers and Hayden was honored to have them at her back.

Hayden pulled off the interstate on Hildebrandt Road and raced toward the address on her laptop GPS. She continued to be pleasantly surprised when the cars moved to get out of her way. Finally, she arrived at the address, surprised to see it was a cattle farm. Of course, domestic incidents could happen anywhere, but this was the first time she'd been called to such a large, and obviously successful, cattle farm.

Even though Hayden had lived in Texas for most of her life, she'd never learned the names of the different kinds of cows. The only ones she knew on sight were the longhorns. There were large black-and-brown cows lazily milling around the fields surrounding the property.

Hayden pulled into the driveway of the farm, and passed under the beautiful wrought iron sign proclaiming she was entering the property of "Hatcher Farms." She parked her vehicle next to Jimmy and Troy's patrol cars, radioed her position into dispatch, then climbed out.

Hayden could immediately hear a hysterical woman screeching as she adjusted her utility belt and made sure her equipment—taser, pistol, handcuffs, and baton—were in place before she headed toward the house. She took a small moment to appreciate the beauty of the building she was about to enter.

It was one level, with a wraparound porch across the entire front of the house with several large windows which would let in the morning light. It had a gray metal roof and three dormer windows along the top of the house. There was even a porch swing lazily swaying in the warm Texas breeze. All in all, it looked like a fairy-tale house for a perfect family...but as usual, appearances could be deceiving, as the raised voice she could easily hear from outside attested.

Hayden didn't bother knocking, the door was open. She pushed open the screen door and entered into a large foyer. Jimmy was in a room on the left with a hysterical female, which explained the screeching Hayden heard as she exited her car, and Troy was in the room on the right with a man.

Taking the scene in at a glance, Hayden relaxed a bit, realizing the threat of danger at the moment seemed to be low. The man was seated on a couch with his head in his hands. He was obviously not a threat to any of them at this point. The woman was the one who would bear some watching. She was gesturing wildly and wasn't giving Jimmy a chance to get a word in edgewise.

She was a couple inches taller than Hayden's five feet six, with long blonde hair. She was beautifully made up and had on high heels, which accentuated her toned legs and small waist. The bracelets on her arms tinkled together with her wild gesticulations.

Deciding to start with Troy—Hayden wanted to get the lay of the land before she waded into the volatile situation with Jimmy and the woman—she strode into the room and greeted her fellow deputy.

"Hey."

"Deputy Yates. Good to see you," the other officer said easily as she entered.

"You too."

Troy turned to the man on the couch. "Stay here a moment, Mr. Hatcher. I need to speak with Deputy Yates."

The man, Mr. Hatcher, lifted his head and Hayden saw his face for the first time.

Good Lord, the man was beautiful.

There was no other word for it. She wasn't a woman to be bowled over by a good-looking man, but there was an intensity in this one she'd never seen before. He had a five-o'clock shadow, as if he hadn't shaved in a day or two. He had dark wavy hair, which was probably about two months past needing a trim, but seemed to work for him. His jaw was square, his nose was crooked, it'd obviously been broken at one time or another. He had a full set of lips that were currently set in a grim line.

He didn't look extremely large, even though he was muscular and obviously toned. Hayden couldn't tell exactly how tall he was, as he was sitting, but she figured he'd probably only be a couple of inches taller than her. She'd never been attracted to hugely buff men before, having seen enough of those types of physiques in some of the fellow officers she worked with, but this man seemed to be the perfect mix of muscles, height, and looks.

But as much as she was immediately attracted to him, it was the man's eyes that really caught Hayden's attention. They seemed to reach out and grab hold of her heart. They were sad and, if Hayden wasn't mistaken, frustrated. She had no idea how she could read that much into his brown eyes, but she could. The color reminded Hayden of the one and only doll she'd owned in her life. Her mom had bought it for her when she was around four. Hayden had named her Molly. Molly had a plastic head with the most realistic eyes she'd ever seen in a toy.

She'd had that doll for exactly two months before it had disappeared. It wasn't until she was in her teens that she'd found out her father had thrown it away.

Hayden threw off the distracting thoughts, knowing this wasn't the time to think about her dysfunctional upbringing, or the odd and inappropriate attraction she had for a suspect in a domestic incident. She concentrated on her coworker. She and Troy stepped to the side and kept their voices low so the man wouldn't hear their conversation.

"What have we got?" Hayden asked.

"Typical domestic as far as we can tell. The woman called nine-one-one and claimed that her boyfriend," Troy gestured toward the man on the couch with his thumb, "hit her and she was scared he was going to keep at her. She's got marks on her face and fingerprints on her wrist. Looks pretty cut and dried."

Hayden, never one to take anything at face value, asked, "What does *he* have to say about it?"

"Same old shit. He's claiming he never touched her, would never hit a woman, and he further explained that he broke up with her a month ago, but she's refusing to take the hint and leave."

"Really?" Hayden was surprised. That kind of thing should be pretty easy to look into, and if the man was lying about it, he wasn't very smart.

"Yeah." Troy continued. "He further claims that she hit *herself* to make it look like he did it, and that she'd been threatening to get him arrested if he didn't take her back."

"Hmmmm." This was a new one. Hayden had been on a few cases where it was the man who was domestically abused, but none of the men had looked like this

one. He didn't look like he'd take shit from anyone...
never mind a woman.

"What a crock of shit," Troy scoffed. "Look at him.
He's huge. He's definitely a threat."

Hayden looked back at the man sitting on the
couch, then looked into the other room at the woman
who was still carrying on. She stuck with her original
assessment. Average height for a man, strong—he'd
have to be if he worked on a ranch—and if he decided
to strike out at a woman, he'd easily do some damage...
he wouldn't have to put much power behind his hand
to make her bruise.

But at the moment, the man didn't look the least bit
threatening. He was muscular, yes, but from her
professional experience, he wasn't exuding any scary
vibes. Hayden had learned to be a pretty good judge of
character. She had to be. Her life depended on it.

"Let me talk to him. You know as well as I do sometimes a woman can either make them relax and spill
their guts, or rile him up more so we can see what he
really thinks."

"Great. That's why we requested dispatch call you.
I'll go in and back up Jimmy. Sounds like he's got his
hands full over there."

Hayden nodded at Troy and watched as he ambled
off into the other room. She went back over to the man
on the couch. She noticed that he'd been watching her
and Troy talk. He might not have been able to hear
what they were saying, but his eyes stayed glued to

them as if he was afraid they'd come back any second and put him in handcuffs. Even though she'd just lain eyes on the man, Hayden realized that with the way his eyes scanned between her coworkers and the woman in the other room, that not much escaped this man's notice. She couldn't underestimate him.

"Hello, my name is Deputy Yates." She held out her hand in greeting.

"Boone Hatcher." He shook her hand politely, then dropped it.

She stuck her thumbs in her utility belt and assumed a relaxed pose, trying to put him at ease...well as at ease as he could be in a situation like this. "Hatcher. You own this farm?"

"Yeah. It belonged to my father, and when he passed away, it came to me."

"I'm sorry about your father." Hayden tried to establish a rapport with the man. She'd learned over the years that getting right down to the questions was never a good way to start an interview. She had to establish some sort of trust, show the person she was human and not jump right into questioning them. "You're obviously very successful."

Hayden resisted the urge to squirm under his gaze. It was as if he knew exactly what she was doing. Finally, he responded, but Hayden had the feeling he was simply humoring her.

"Yeah, Hatcher Farms is one of the most successful breeding farms in Texas. We sell bulls, cattle, and semen all over the United States. It's a large operation, but one that's still family owned and operated."

Hayden decided to get to it. Boone seemed like a man who'd appreciate straight talk. "What happened here today, Boone?"

He kept eye contact with her. "I already told your partner what happened."

"But you haven't told me. I like to hear things for myself. Make my own decisions."

He heaved out a long breath, then spoke. "I worked late last night. One of the heifers was having a difficult birth. I came into the house and took a shower, and then heard something in the other room. I came in here and found Dana in the kitchen. She was making eggs at my stove. I didn't invite her here, we've been broken up for a month. She won't take no for an answer. We got into a verbal fight, and she didn't like hearing me tell her that we were over...again. She grabbed her own wrist and held on tight until she bruised herself, then she told me that if I didn't take her back, she'd make my life a living hell. She threw the bowl of eggs at me and when I didn't rise to her bait, she hit herself, then called nine-one-one. And here we are."

Hayden kept her face impassive while Boone was talking. It sure sounded far-fetched to her. "Okay, I'm going to go and talk to Dana and hear what she has to say. Sit tight...all right?"

She watched as any welcoming light he had in his

eyes faded away. "Yeah, you do that. I know how this is going to go."

"Sir—"

Boone waved her away and put his head back into his hands, every muscle in his body sagging in defeat.

Hayden backed away and headed into the other room.

She relied on her gut. Call it women's intuition, call it good cop sense...whatever it was, it had rarely let her down. And at the moment, every pore in her body was telling her Boone was telling the truth. As far-fetched as it sounded, she believed him. He looked her in the eye as he told his side of the story. He wasn't too specific, yet he wasn't too vague either.

Jimmy had gotten Dana to sit on a chair in the other room, but she was still crying and carrying on.

"Ma'am," Hayden interrupted Dana in a hard voice. She knew she had to try another approach with Dana. Using the "I'm your friend" technique wasn't going to work. "I'd like to talk to you for a moment...alone." She gave Jimmy and Troy a look, which they immediately recognized. They nodded and left without a word.

"Oh thank God, I'm so glad you're here. No one understands what it's like to be vulnerable like another woman."

Hayden kept herself from rolling her eyes...barely. She'd never been vulnerable—at least not how Dana meant it—in her life. The other woman's voice was saccharine sweet and completely fake. Hayden had heard it all the time growing up. She'd learned how to detect bullshit at an early age. Most of the time people just wanted something from her when they used that tone. Hayden knew exactly what it was that Dana wanted from her.

"Dana...right?"

"Yes. Dana Chapman."

"Ms. Chapman, can you please tell me in your own words what happened this morning?"

"I was making breakfast for Boonie when he lost it. I'm not sure why, but he grabbed my wrist..." Dana held out her arm for Hayden's inspection, showing her the light bruise forming there. "And when I asked him to let go of me, told him that he was hurting me, he let go but then backhanded me." Again, she turned her head so Hayden could see the small mark on her face. "Then he threw the eggs I'd been making for him at me. Luckily I was able to dodge them so they didn't get me all gross."

"How did you get into the house?"

"What?"

"How did you get into the house?" Hayden repeated easily.

Obviously taken aback that Hayden wasn't examining her wounds closer, Dana sputtered, "Boone let me in, of course."

"When?"

"When?"

"Yeah, when did he let you in?"

"Well, this morning."

"You didn't spend the night?"

"No, not last night. I usually do, but I was busy and couldn't come over."

"When was the last time you stayed the night here?"

Dana squirmed in her seat and Hayden knew she was going to deflect the question.

"I don't know what this has to do with anything. He *hit* me. He *hurt* me. I thought as a woman, you'd be on *my* side, that you'd understand. I know the law. I know you have to bring him in if there's any evidence that he assaulted me."

Hayden mentally rolled her eyes. Obviously Dana had done her research into the Texas laws. "I'm just trying to get all the information I can, Dana. When was the last time you spent the night?" She watched as Dana looked up and to the left.

"I think it was the night before last."

"Okay. And you came over for breakfast today?"

"Yeah." Dana again looked up and left. "He called me late last night..."

"What time?"

"What time?"

"Yeah, what time did he call you?"

"Oh, it was late...I think it was around midnight."

"Okay, so he called you..."

"Yeah, he called me and told me he missed me and asked if I'd come over for breakfast and...you know..."

"I'm afraid I don't know." Hayden loved this part of interrogation. Watching people walk themselves right into a slew of lies and then exposing them was actually fun.

"Sex. He wanted to fuck me. He calls all the time when he wants to stick his dick in me." Dana's voice was belligerent now, and she was deliberately trying to shock her. Hayden was obviously starting to piss her off. Good.

"Okay, so he called you at midnight and asked you to come over this morning. You came over. Did you have sex?"

"Huh?"

"Sex. Did you have sex this morning?"

"Well...uh...yeah. He couldn't keep his hands off me. As soon as I walked in the door, he attacked me."

"So you did it in the hall?" Hayden kept the smile off her face...barely.

"Well...no. We started making out in the hall, but he carried me into his bedroom and we went at it like bunnies in there. He couldn't wait for me to suck his dick."

"Did you guys use contraception?"

"Huh? What the hell kind of question is that?"

"I'm just trying to get to the bottom of this."

"Well, of course we used condoms! I mean, I know we're dating and all, but I don't fuck without one."

"You're not on the pill?"

"What kind of interrogation is this? No, I'm not on

the pill! It makes me bloated and I don't fit into my clothes."

"Okay, so he wasn't upset with you after you had sex?"

"No. He loves my body. Loves what I can do to his."

"Okay, so you got up afterwards and came out here to make breakfast for him?"

"Uh huh."

"And he came out of the bedroom and got mad at you, then hit you."

"Yeah." Dana's voice was stronger now. She obviously felt like she was back on solid ground again. "I was making him his favorite breakfast and he came in and got upset with me for some stupid reason, and he hit me."

"Do you need some ice for your face? I noticed you don't have any on it. It might make it feel better." Hayden's voice was soothing and complacent.

"Oh, yeah. That would be great. Thank you." Dana's eyes filled with tears as if she'd turned on a faucet.

Hayden couldn't help but be a bit impressed with the way Dana could control her tears. "I'm going to have one of the other deputies get some for you. I'm going to talk to Boone once more, then we'll get this all straightened out."

"You're going to arrest him, right?"

"Don't worry, we'll arrest the abuser for sure."

Dana smiled a genuine smile for the first time. "Good."

"I'll be right back. Sit tight."

Hayden got up and made her way into the hallway. "Jimmy, can you please go into the kitchen and get Ms. Chapman some ice? I need to talk to Mr. Hatcher again."

2

HAYDEN CALMLY WALKED BACK into the room where Boone was waiting. He'd turned his head so he could watch what was going on, but he kept it in his hands.

"Mr. Hatcher—"

"Boone. Please call me Boone. Mr. Hatcher makes me think you're talking to my dad."

Hayden nodded. "Fair enough. Boone, as you can probably guess, your version of what happened this morning differs greatly from Ms. Chapman's version."

Boone nodded grimly, but didn't further proclaim his innocence.

"I have a few questions for you, if that's okay."

He simply shrugged.

"First, when is the last time Ms. Chapman spent the night here at your house?"

Boone sat up, as if startled at the question. "What does that have to do with anything?"

"Please, just answer the questions. I know they don't sound like they're related, but just humor me. The quicker you answer, the quicker we'll get out of your hair."

Maybe it was the way she said they'd "get out of your hair." Maybe it was a feeling of inevitability that he'd be spending the night in jail. Whatever it was, Boone obviously decided he didn't have anything to lose by answering her. "She's never spent the night here."

"Never?"

"No. I didn't sleep with her much, but when I did, I always went to her apartment."

"How long did you date?"

"Probably only about two months or so."

"So, she wasn't happy with you breaking it off with her?"

Boone grimaced. "That's the understatement of the century."

"When did you break up?"

"A few weeks ago."

"Have you called her recently?"

"No."

Hayden assessed the man. His answers were quick and to the point. He looked her in the eyes as he answered her and didn't seem to be lying at all. "If we pulled your phone records, would they prove what you're telling me?"

"Absolutely." The word was low and earnest. "The

last time I contacted her was probably around two and a half weeks ago. She'd been calling and leaving me rambling messages, as if I hadn't told her I wanted to stop seeing her, that things between us just weren't working out. I called because I felt a little bit bad for her. I told her once more that we were done. If you do check my records, you'll see that she *still* hasn't gotten it through her skull that I don't want anything to do with her, because she continues to call me at least twice a day, and sends me a ton of texts. None of which I want or asked for, and none of which I've returned."

"How did Dana get into your house this morning?"

Boone blushed and looked away for the first time.

"Boone?"

"I didn't invite her, if that's what you're thinking or what she said. She probably just walked right in. I was exhausted when I came into the house after being up all night. I didn't lock the door behind me."

Hayden nodded, not bothering to scold him for that. It was obvious he knew he'd screwed up there. "What's your favorite thing to eat in the mornings?"

Boone cocked his head and looked at her again. Hayden could almost see the wheels turning in his head. His eyes bore into hers once more, communicating so many emotions she couldn't sort through them all. It was obvious he had no idea why she was asking him the questions she was, but to his credit, he didn't balk at the seemingly out-of-the-blue question, just answered. "Waffles."

"Hmmmm, and has Ms. Chapman made you breakfast before?"

"Yes."

"At her place."

"Yes."

"And did you tell her that waffles were your favorite breakfast?"

"No. It never came up."

"So, she never asked."

"No. She never asked."

"Thank you. You've been very patient. And I appreciate it. I need one more thing before I think we'll be done here."

Boone sat patiently and waited for her to continue.

"I'd like to take a look around, if that's all right with you. I won't touch anything, and I won't disturb anything."

Hayden held Boone's eyes. She wanted to tell him what she was thinking, but kept her thoughts to herself as she'd been taught. It was best for all parties involved. His dark brown eyes still held worry, but she couldn't see any deception in them. He finally nodded.

"Thank you. Will you show me around?"

Boone nodded again and stood up.

Hayden bit back a gasp. Good lord, he was tall. She'd totally messed up in her assessment of him earlier. She felt shorter than most people all the time. At five-six, Hayden wasn't very tall, especially for an officer, but Boone was easily over six feet. Hayden wasn't frightened of his height or strength, she'd taken men like him to the ground, both in training and during her job duties. She was more...intrigued with his power. She could totally picture him wrestling one of the cows she'd seen in the field on her way in, or helping a mama cow birth her calf.

The thought of how any woman would feel cherished and safe around him flickered in her mind before she forcibly shrugged off her inappropriate thoughts. Wrong place and wrong time.

She walked with Boone into the hall, keeping herself between him and the room Dana was in. Hayden told Troy she'd be in the back of the house with Boone and she'd return in a few minutes.

Boone led the way through his house, through the kitchen and into a large family room with another comfortable-looking couch, an easy chair, and a large television on the wall. They went by a guest bathroom and went down another hall that had several doors.

Boone opened the first to show her a guest room. Hayden walked through quickly, seeing nothing out of the ordinary in the room. They continued and he showed her the linen closet, a guest bathroom and then into his office. The room was light and airy, with a large window along one wall. There was a bookcase lining another wall of the room, completely stuffed with books.

Hayden wandered over, not being able to help her curiosity. She saw books on cattle and breeding. There were some on farming next to mysteries and thrillers. There was even a stack of old farming magazines. Interspersed in the books were picture frames. Some were of an older couple, and there were some of what had to be Boone as a child with his parents. There were a few pictures of Boone with a group of men at various times in their lives.

Hayden turned back to the door to see Boone leaning against the doorframe. He'd lifted one foot and it was resting on the toe of his other battered brown cowboy boot. His arms were crossed in front of him, and Hayden knew if he'd been wearing a Stetson, it would've been pushed back on his head so he could see her more clearly. He was one hell of a sexy man, and the fact he was a true working cowboy made him even sexier in her eyes. She'd always been attracted to men who worked more blue collar jobs than ones who might spend their days in an office.

She mentally shook her head. She was in the middle of an investigation here and had to keep her mind on what she was doing, not the gorgeous man waiting for her.

"Great. Moving on?"

Boone stood there, examining her as if he was trying to see into her soul for a moment, then simply nodded and straightened. "My bedroom is the only room left in the house."

They walked out of the office and headed down to the master bedroom. Once again, Boone stood at the door, giving her space to do whatever it was she was doing, while Hayden looked around.

The room was large, even with the king-size bed taking up a big chunk of the area. There were two windows in the room on perpendicular walls. There was a tall dresser next to one of the windows and a door next to the other. Hayden walked to the door and opened it. It was an enormous walk-in closet. There were shoes and boots strewn around the closet in no particular order. There were dirty clothes overflowing a hamper in the corner, which made Hayden smile a bit. Not surprising for a man who seemed to be as busy as Boone was.

There was a row of shelves on the wall that had stacks of jeans and shirts on them. There were also a couple of rows of button-down shirts hung up as well. Seeing what she expected to see, Hayden walked out of the closet and into the main room again. She looked back at the bed.

The comforter was a dark blue and brown with a southwestern design on it. The corners were tucked in tidily at the end of the bed and the whole thing was as neat as a pin. Hayden turned and went into the bathroom attached to the room and looked around.

It was a woman's dream bathroom. There were two sinks on a large counter. Boone's personal items were haphazardly lying on the granite next to one of them. Toothbrush, toothpaste, razor, shaving cream, and aftershave lotion. His bed might have been made, but this, along with his messy closet, was proof of his casualness when it came to housekeeping.

Hayden crouched down and opened the cabinet under the sink. She saw a small trash can and pulled it out, looking inside briefly. Seeing nothing interesting, she put it back and looked at the other items under the sink. There was a bottle of bleach, a couple bottles of shampoo, and some empty plastic bags, obviously there to replace in the trash can when needed. She stood up and looked at the shower. It was heavenly.

The shower was separate from the tub. It was bigger than any shower Hayden had ever seen before. The walls were lined with the same granite the counter was made out of. The shower head was huge, and she knew the water pressure probably felt awesome against Boone's shoulders when he'd had a hard day. The Jacuzzi tub next to the shower was oval shaped and deep, perfect for long soaks.

Hayden ran her hand over the towel hanging over the rack, then along the countertop, before looking back up at Boone. He'd entered his bedroom then followed her to the bathroom, but had still given her space to do whatever it was she needed to do, and hadn't interrupted her with the questions she could see swimming in his eyes.

"Thanks, Boone. I'm done here."

He didn't say a word, but merely raised his eyebrows and shrugged. He held out a hand as if to tell her to proceed him. Typically, Hayden wouldn't have turned her back on a man, or woman, accused of domestic violence, but she had a pretty good idea of what had happened in the house that morning. She wasn't in any danger from Boone. She'd bet her life on it.

"Come on, let's get this done." Hayden's words were strong and firm. While she enjoyed investigating, she really liked making sure the bad guy got what was coming to him.

3

———

BOONE WALKED behind the deputy sheriff stiffly. The last twenty-four hours had been a nightmare. Dealing with the difficult birth of one of his most expensive heifers was just the beginning. He hadn't lied to the officers. He'd been so exhausted when he'd come back into the house, he hadn't bothered to lock any of his doors.

And why would he need to? He had over thirty employees who he'd hand-picked and worked with for years. Boone was never alone. He had a state-of-the-art security system and had never had any issues the entire time he'd lived in the house.

Boone had known the first morning after he'd slept with Dana that he'd made a mistake. He'd fallen for her crap, hook, line, and sinker. She'd reeled him in and he'd thought she was a nice, sweet woman who was ready to settle down and have a family. But when he'd told her he had to leave the morning after they'd made love for the first time to take care of an issue that had come up on the farm, she'd freaked out. Crying, screaming, yelling...accusing him of using her, of not liking her, of anything she could think of. Boone had only taken her to bed two more times—two times too many—and had spent the rest of their "relationship" trying to extricate himself.

Dana was bat-shit crazy, but the problem was, she didn't show that crazy side to anyone. When they were alone, she'd hit him, yelled at him, threw things at him, and did everything she could to belittle him. Boone had ended their relationship, but for some reason, Dana wouldn't let him go. She showed up at the farm unexpectedly. He'd see her car following him when he was out doing errands. She'd even contacted some of his clients—God knew how she'd gotten the information about them—and told them what an awful person he was.

Boone was convinced she was the person who'd anonymously contacted the SPCA of San Antonio to report animal cruelty on his farm. They'd come out to investigate and found all of the accusations against him and his ranch unfounded, but it still stuck in his craw that he'd been accused in the first place. It was the kind of uncertainty he didn't need focused on his operation.

When they entered the front foyer of his house, Boone took a deep breath. He'd never thought Dana would stoop as low as accusing him of domestic abuse, faking her injuries, and calling the cops. As he watched the female deputy talk to her partners, it hit home that he could actually be arrested. He was exhausted and now pissed, and the last thing he wanted was to spend time in jail over something he didn't do—and would *never* do. Boone had no idea what the deputy had been looking for on the tour of his house, or if she even believed his recounting of what had happened that morning.

Surprisingly, in the midst of everything that was going on, Boone found himself attracted to the deputy. He couldn't really make out much of her body since she was wearing her uniform, complete with a bullet-proof vest and utility belt, with all of the things that cops carried with them, but he'd always been attracted to women who were quite a bit shorter than he was... Dana notwithstanding.

The deputy was fair skinned and he thought he saw a few freckles on her face. She had no problem meeting his eyes and he thought the way she bit her lip and furrowed her brow when she was concentrating was cute. All in all, he couldn't say exactly what it was that drew him to her like a moth drawn to a flame, but somehow he knew that she was a woman he'd like to get to know better.

At the moment, he certainly appreciated the deputy's no-nonsense tone and the fact that she seemed to actually be listening to him, and not assuming he was a girlfriend-beating asshole, as her partners obviously did. That went a long way toward making him like her from the start. From the moment she'd stepped into his house and met his eyes, he somehow knew she was his best chance at getting out of the shit-pile Dana had piled at his door.

Her questions were certainly odd, compared to what her partners had asked; they'd stuck to the facts. But Boone really didn't care as long as she saw through Dana's bullshit. He knew it wasn't likely though. The police were obligated to arrest the man if the woman showed signs of abuse.

He went back into the room he'd been in earlier, tried to tamp down his instinctive desire for the competent deputy, knowing this definitely wasn't the time or the place, and waited for one of the cops to pull out a set of cuffs and tell him to turn around.

"Will you wait here a moment? I need to talk to my partners," the woman he couldn't seem to get out of his mind asked.

"Of course." He watched as she walked to the large archway and motioned for her partners.

Hayden, Jimmy, and Troy stood between the two front rooms, making sure Dana and Boone stayed away from each other while they discussed their next steps.

"So, who wants to take Mr. Hatcher in?"

"Wait a minute, Jimmy. Boone is the victim here," Hayden said with certainty.

"What? Like hell," Jimmy returned. "She's got

visible bruises on her face and on her wrist. The law says we have to take him in."

Hayden looked Jimmy in the eyes. "Do you trust me?"

"With my life," he said without hesitation. "You're one of the best deputies we've got."

Hayden felt better at his immediate response. "Then follow my lead here. I'm right. I know I am."

Jimmy nodded and Hayden looked at Troy. He'd tilted his head at her. When their eyes met, he spoke.

"You are one spooky chick, Hayden. I don't know what you've got up your sleeve, but I haven't known you to be wrong before. I'm in."

"Thanks, Troy. Just keep her covered...okay?"

Jimmy and Troy nodded and they all turned back to Boone and Dana.

"Mr. Hatcher, please come with me." Hayden motioned toward the room Dana was sitting in. Boone followed her and they all convened in the small front room.

Hayden got right to the point. She'd learned that was always much better than beating around the bush.

"Dana, you're under arrest for false accusations of domestic abuse and trespassing."

"What?" Dana shrieked and stood up abruptly, all images of the poor abused girlfriend cast from her as if she was a snake shedding its skin. "What kind of dyke cop are you? He *hit* me. I have bruises!"

Jimmy and Troy had come up beside Dana and

each took an arm in one of their hands, so she couldn't move.

"Okay, we'll start there, since you brought it up." Hayden walked over to Dana and took her hand in her own. "The bruises on your wrist are too small to have been caused by Mr. Hatcher." She circled Dana's wrist with her own hand. "Look, my hand fits these marks perfectly...you're only a few inches taller than me, but our hands are about the same size, aren't they, Dana?"

Hayden walked over to Boone. "Please hold up your hand, Mr. Hatcher." When he did, Hayden put her own palm against his, ignoring the jolt of heat that went through her arm and down her body at the feel of his warm palm against hers. "See the size difference? There's no way his hand made those marks."

Hayden dropped her hand and went back to Dana, asking over her shoulder, "Mr. Hatcher, are you right or left-handed?"

"Right."

"This mark is on the left side of your face. Mr. Hatcher is right-handed. If he backhanded you, he would've used his right hand and it would've been on the *right* side of your face." Hayden demonstrated, pantomiming a smack to a person's face with her right hand. "Also, if he'd backhanded you, as you claim, the mark on your face would've been more on your cheek than up near your eye. It also would've been a large red splotch, not the localized mark that you have. Ms. Chapman, I conclude that you must've hit yourself to try to make it look like Mr. Hatcher struck you."

"T-t-that's not true! *He* hit me."

Hayden ignored Dana's sputterings and continued, "And, Ms. Chapman, you said you've spent the night at this house as recently as a couple of nights ago. That's a lie. Mr. Hatcher has stated that you have never spent the night here, and you were not invited into his home last night or this morning. There is absolutely no evidence a woman has been in Mr. Hatcher's bedroom. There are no clothes in the closet, no feminine products in the bathroom, and no trash in the trash can that looks like it came from a woman's preparations in getting ready in the morning. Something like a cotton ball, Q-tip, or tissue."

"He won't let me keep any of my stuff here. I pack it all out every time I leave."

"Really? Even your trash? How unusual." Hayden's tone was deadpan. "Be that as it may, you claimed you came over this morning and had intercourse with Mr. Hatcher. You told me yourself that he used a condom. I find no evidence of this anywhere in the house."

"He flushed it." Dana was quick with the comebacks.

"Possible," Hayden continued without worry. "So where's the wrapper? It's not in any trash can that I could find. Flushing a condom wrapper would easily clog the pipes, and it's recommended right on the package not to flush the wrapper. And the bed, where you claim to have had sexual relations with Mr. Hatcher, is made up as if it hadn't been slept in last night."

Dana had nothing to say to that, her lips were now shut tight and curled up into a snarl. Hayden could see her lips turning white with the pressure she was applying to them.

"And you also claimed that you were making Mr. Hatcher's favorite breakfast...but you don't even know *what* his favorite breakfast is. Here's a hint: it's not eggs. There's only one towel hanging up in the bathroom, which happens to be dry, when you look like you recently showered and styled your hair, and there are absolutely no pictures of you and Mr. Hatcher together anywhere in the house, as there most likely would be if you were actually dating. Ms. Chapman, it's against the law to enter someone's home when you aren't invited and to make false statements to law enforcement. Not to mention accusing someone of something they didn't do."

Hayden turned to Boone. "Mr. Hatcher, I recommend you file a protective order against Ms. Chapman as soon as you can. And Ms. Chapman, Mr. Hatcher has told you, apparently time and time again, that he doesn't wish to date you anymore. That's unfortunate, but sometimes people just aren't meant to be. I suggest you move on and find a man who is more compatible with you. No harm, no foul."

Not surprisingly, Dana glared first at Hayden, then

at Boone, who was standing behind her. "You'll regret this!"

"Oh—and threatening others in the presence of law enforcement is ill-advised, especially when you're already being arrested. I suggest you don't add to your problems. Deputy Phillips, Deputy Bruton, take her to the station. I'll be there to make a statement shortly."

The other men nodded and Jimmy cuffed Dana's wrists behind her back and led her out of the house. Troy lightly slugged Hayden in the shoulder as he walked by and said in a low voice, "Good goin', Yates," and he followed Jimmy and a silently fuming Dana out into the sunlight.

Hayden turned to Boone. "I'm very sorry this happened to you. It wasn't right, and you shouldn't be treated this way."

"No, thank *you* for taking the time to really see what happened here. Those other two guys were ready to take me in," Boone said in an obviously relieved tone.

"It's unusual that we see a domestic violence case where the victim is male."

Hayden could see her words took Boone aback.

"This wasn't domestic abuse. I'm not being abused. Annoyed, yes, but not abused."

"I know it's not something you want to admit or think about, but men get abused in relationships all the time. They just don't want to acknowledge it, or are embarrassed they're in that situation. It's not manly or macho to admit it."

Hayden expected an immediate denial; she'd heard it every time she'd tried to convince a man that he was a victim.

Boone surprised her. "I hadn't thought of it like that before."

Hayden continued, seeing she was getting through to him. "Well, start. How many times has she yelled at you? Hit you? Thrown things at you? Pushed you? If you knew a woman whose boyfriend or husband was doing to *her* what Dana has been doing to you...would you tell her she's being abused? Would you encourage her to get out? To get help?" Hayden didn't give him a chance to say anything. "Of course you would. Why won't you see *yourself* as being abused then?"

"I can take care of myself."

"Of course you can," Hayden immediately agreed. "But that kind of behavior against you can eventually tear you down. It's not safe and it's illegal."

Boone was silent. Hayden sighed.

"Okay, think about it for a while. I *do* suggest you contact your attorney and get that restraining order. We both know it won't keep her away if she's determined to get to you, but it can help if and when she does break it. Keep your doors locked, and whatever you do, try not to be alone with her. If she's willing to hurt herself to get you in trouble, there's no telling what else she'll do."

"Good advice. Thanks."

"You're welcome. Can I ask something else?"

"Sure."

"How's the baby cow?"

"What?"

"The baby cow you were helping the mama cow birth this morning...how it is?"

Boone smiled at her. "She's fine. Healthy and strong."

"Good. Okay, I'm outta here. I have a ton of paperwork to do back at the office."

"Thanks, Officer Yates. I really do appreciate it."

"It's Hayden, and you're welcome." Hayden didn't know why she'd given Boone leave to use her first name. It wasn't like her—but she liked him. He was honorable, obviously hard working, he'd loved his parents, if the pictures in his office were any indication, and she was a good judge of character.

She held out her hand for him to shake and as their hands met, she once again felt the zing of awareness. Hayden pulled her hand back quickly, uncomfortable with the odd feelings coursing through her.

"Okay, well. Be safe."

Boone nodded at her and she turned to head back to her patrol car, convinced she'd seen the last of one Mr. Boone Hatcher.

4

———

HAYDEN COULDN'T HELP but notice her heart was beating a bit faster than was normal as she pulled down the familiar driveway of Hatcher Farms. It'd been a week since she'd been out there to deal with the domestic incident, and when the call went out for a deputy to investigate an act of vandalism at the property, she didn't hesitate to say she'd go and check it out.

For some reason, Hayden couldn't get Boone out of her mind. She wasn't sure why. She'd seen her share of good-looking cowboys over the years, so why this one was stuck in her brain was a mystery. Sure, he was easy on the eyes, but it was more than that.

Part of it was the mystery of why he'd put up with Dana doing the crap she'd done to him...but the other part was his absolute concentration on whatever he was doing at the moment he was doing it. She'd noticed it while she was there the week before. When he was talking to her, he was one hundred percent focused on her. When Jimmy or Troy was talking to him, he was focused on *them*. She could only imagine what he'd be like when he was helping his cows give birth, or cooking, or...

Nope, she wasn't going there.

She pulled up in front of the farmhouse and immediately saw why Boone had called the sheriff's department.

Every visible surface was defaced by ugly red paint.

The side of the barn nearest the house had words like "asshole" and "jerk." There was a big black pickup truck that had both headlights smashed out and more filthy words splashed across the sides. And the house...

Hayden sighed. Whoever had done this had spent quite a bit of time making sure the house suffered from the same wrath as the other property.

"You'll regret this," "asswipe," and "shitty fuck," along with random splotches of paint, were sprawled over the siding of the house. The first was exactly what Dana had said in front of three law enforcement officers, but without proof that she was the one who'd sprayed the words on his house, Hayden's hands were tied.

What looked like gallons of paint had been thrown on the porch floor as well. The swing, which Hayden had thought looked so comfortable and homey when she'd been there last week, was now covered in enough red paint that it actually dripped down between the slats of the seat onto the wooden boards beneath. The beautiful cushion had been torn to shreds and lay strewn around the porch, again drenched in the red paint.

Boone stood to the side of the stairs leading up to the front door, looking disheveled and disheartened. As Hayden walked up to him, he put a hand through his hair and looked up at her.

"Hey, Mr. Hatcher."

"Deputy Yates."

It seemed ridiculous to be on such formal terms with each other. "It's Hayden."

Boone smiled a small smile. "Boone."

"So...I see why you called."

Boone sighed. "Yeah. I was out of town last night purchasing a new bull. Got home this morning to this."

"Did anyone see or hear anything?"

"No, at least not the hands I've been able to ask so far. There are a few I haven't spoken to yet, they're still asleep."

"Okay, I'll want to talk to everyone who was around, just to make sure." Hayden paused. "Do you know who might have done this?" She thought she knew the answer, but she asked it anyway.

Boone simply nodded.

"Yeah." She paused before asking, "Did you file that restraining order?"

"No."

At the look on her face, he continued. "I know. I

know. I hoped after last week it wouldn't be necessary. That she'd see we were truly over and she'd move on. Guess I was wrong."

"I hate to be the one to tell you this, but I think you already know. She's not going to move on. I've seen this before. Unfortunately, things will probably get worse before they get better."

"Obviously."

Hayden didn't belabor the point. She figured it'd been made loud and clear. "Okay, let me get my camera and start documenting the damage. I'll write up a report and you can give it to your insurance company. Other than the obvious, was there any other damage? Are your cows all right?"

Boone nodded. "So far, this seems to be the extent of it. None of the cattle were in the barn last night, they were all out in the fields."

Hayden didn't move toward her patrol car. She impulsively put her hand on Boone's arm. "I'm sorry, Boone. Really. No one deserves this."

Their eyes met and Hayden swore she felt something pass between them.

"Thanks." The one word was low, and extremely heartfelt.

Hayden nodded and turned back to her car to get to work documenting the awful destruction of the beautiful property.

Boone watched as the deputy took pictures of

Dana's handiwork. He had no doubt it had been her who had done it, either. He sighed.

"That was a big sigh."

Boone tried to smile, but knew it was lame at best. He'd been following alongside Hayden as she took pictures for her report. "It's just that...I honestly don't know what I did to make her think we were more than we were."

"How'd you meet?"

Boone looked at the pretty woman next to him. She was even shorter than Dana, although Dana usually wore heels, which made her closer to his height. Today he could see that Hayden's hair was auburn. It fit her perfectly and made sense with the freckles across her nose. He'd never thought about it much, but suddenly he was extremely attracted to redheads, at least on the deputy, it was much more attractive than Dana's blonde hair ever was to him.

But with her size, Boone had no idea how Hayden was even able to do her job. He couldn't imagine her overpowering anyone, much less a pissed-off drunk or someone bent on defying the law. He'd bet everything he had that she was a natural redhead, though, because of her pale skin and those adorable freckles across her cheeks and nose. Boone guessed her to be in her early to mid-thirties, although it was hard to tell.

He also still couldn't really see the shape of her body because she was wearing her bulky utility belt and a bulletproof vest under her shirt. Her pants were typical uniform fare that didn't show much of anything. But Boone bet she was muscular. Seeing the way she moved and how she easily maneuvered around anything in her path, made it more than obvious she was in shape.

Boone also noticed how cute her nose was—it seemed to tip up at the end—and how full her lips were, especially when she licked them, making them shine in the Texas sunlight...when she suddenly loudly cleared her throat and looked at him expectedly.

Shit. She'd asked him something. Boone knew he was blushing but tried to ignore it. God, to be caught gawking like a teenager. He rushed to answer, hoping she'd ignore his faux pas. "She's the daughter of one of my buyers. He came to the house to examine a bull he was considering buying and Dana was with him. We chatted while her dad looked over the bull."

When he didn't continue, Hayden asked, "That's it?"

Boone shrugged. "Yeah. She asked if I wanted to go to dinner, and I said yes."

"*She* asked *you* to dinner?"

"Uh huh. Why?"

"You don't seem the type."

"The type to what?"

"To let the woman do the asking."

Boone was impressed Hayden had him pegged after only meeting him once before. "I'm not. But she took me by surprise. And she asked in front of her father."

"Ahhhhh." Hayden's response was knowing. "You didn't want to lose the sale."

Boone ran a hand over the back of his neck, embarrassed. "Something like that," he mumbled miserably.

Surprisingly, Hayden laughed. "Don't feel bad, Boone. Seriously. You couldn't have known she'd turn out to be psycho."

"Yeah, but even as I said yes, something told me I was making a mistake. I should've manned up and declined, or at least not carried it as far as it went."

Hayden got serious. "This is not your fault. Do not take this on yourself. You didn't ask for this, and you don't deserve this. Sleeping with her doesn't give her the right to hit you or to make your life miserable. No matter what you said, or didn't say, this is not normal behavior. Okay?"

Boone looked into Hayden's dark green eyes that held absolutely no hint of disgust. He nodded, more relieved than he could even admit to himself that she didn't seem to look down on him for the situation he was in.

"Can I ask you something though?" Hayden asked the question even as she turned back to photographing more of the vile words on his truck.

"Anything."

"Why are you allowing her to do this to you?"

"What do you mean?"

Hayden turned to him. Boone saw her bite her lip before taking a deep breath. Her words were quiet. "I'm not condoning anything here, you understand. But you're a big guy. You're one of the most masculine men I think I've ever met...but it's obvious she's hit you in the past. Last week you had a still-healing wound on your cheek. I even saw a gash on your arm, like you defended yourself against something. I'm not sure I understand why you didn't strike back, or at least protect yourself from being hurt by her. You wouldn't get in trouble for defending yourself."

"Maybe not, but it'd be my word against hers, and I know how that usually turns out. Look at last week...if you weren't there I have no doubt I would've been hauled off to jail. Besides, I don't hit women."

"I didn't necessarily mean—"

Boone cut her off and repeated, "I don't hit women. *Ever.* No matter what Dana does to me, I will not hit her. I won't strike back at her, I won't restrain her, I won't push her, I won't throw anything at her. There's absolutely no way in hell I'd *ever* hit a woman."

Boone knew Hayden understood something big was going on in his mind, but she was silent. Most women he knew would jump right in and reassure him or change the subject. Not Hayden. She kept her gaze on him and didn't say a word. It made him want to elaborate.

"My father built this farm from the ground up. He worked his ass off for this place. He had a best friend who was with him every step of the way. They got up at the crack of dawn and worked all day long. Both he and Chris were gone on buying trips a lot, and all my dad wanted was for this place to be a success. He was a great husband and dad, but he had tunnel vision and was loyal to a fault." Boone cleared his throat and then continued.

"Chris had a temper. I don't know how often he did it, but he hit his wife. More than once. When I was twelve, I saw him hit her so hard, her eye swelled shut and she couldn't see out of it for a week. Lizzy, as I called her, helped my mom at the house. I thought of her as my second mother. At one point, Lizzy thought she'd actually lose the sight in that eye. I swore then, seeing how much pain she was in and how she always made excuses for Chris, that I'd never hit a girl."

"Boone..." His name was said with such sympathy and understanding, Boone had to continue or he'd do something crazy—like yank her into his arms and bury his head in her neck and bawl his eyes out, as un-manly as that was. He hurried on with his explanation.

"Chris was always sorry. So damn sorry. Lizzy loved him and she always forgave him. I know they loved each other, but I never understood it. My dad never did anything about the situation, either. I heard him talking to my mom about it and he said they'd work it out in their own way. I know back then things were different than they are now, but it seems to me, love means taking care of, protecting, and supporting someone, not hurting them. I know it's not cool to let Dana hit me, but she will never egg me on so much that I'll lose my temper and hit her. Ever. I learned my lesson firsthand growing up."

"The world would be a better place if there were more men like you in it, Boone," Hayden said in a quiet, but utterly sincere, voice.

He opened his mouth to say...something...he wasn't sure what, but she continued before he could.

"With that being said, I'm sorry about Lizzy, but some women deserve to be hit. Shit, some women *need* to be hit. I'm not condoning smacking your wife or girlfriend around if you're upset, but in my line of work, I've hit my fair share of women, men, and even a few kids. Well, teenagers who have needed a good attitude adjustment. There are some bad people out there, Boone, and while I admire your convictions, I can't say the same thing."

"It's different for you."

Hayden smiled sadly at him. "Maybe."

"It is. Tell me about the last person you hit."

"I'm not sure—"

"Tell me."

Hayden sighed. How had she gotten into this conversation? If she wanted him to see her as a helpless female, the kind that men like him seemed to want, one who needed protecting, one who he might want to get to know better, this certainly wasn't the way to go about it.

She mentally shrugged. Oh well. She didn't think she had a chance to catch his eye anyway. After hearing his personal mantra, which was obviously set in stone, she'd known he was a good man. It was written all over him, from his head to his toes. She cleared her throat and straightened her shoulders. It wasn't like he was coming on to her; they were just having a conversation.

"We were called to do a welfare check. A neighbor called it in. She hadn't seen her neighbor's kids in two days, which was unusual. We went over there and found the two children, ages two and three, locked in dog cages inside the apartment. We were busy with trying to calm down and restrain the husband when the mother figured out she was about to get in deep shit. She ran over to one of the cages, opened it, and snatched up the little boy inside. She got in his face and threatened him, ignoring our demands to put him down. When she started shaking him, shaking him so hard his little head was wobbling back and forth uncontrollably, I didn't hesitate to coldcock her in the side of the head. I grabbed the little boy when she put her hand to her face and my partner threw her to the ground and held her there until I could assist him in putting the cuffs on her."

"Good for you."

Hayden didn't like remembering the scene and what she'd done, but she knew if faced with the situation again, she'd do everything exactly the same way—

well, except for letting the coked-out woman get her hands on her kid in the first place. "I won't hesitate to hit, punch, or throw someone over my shoulder, or even shoot them if I have to."

"As you shouldn't. It's your job. It's what you do."

"I'd do it even if it wasn't my job, Boone."

"Hayden, I'm not sure what point you're trying to make here," Boone said seriously, putting his hand on her shoulder lightly and looking down at her. "If I was a cop, I'd probably think the way you do as well. But I'm not. I'm just me. A cattle farmer trying to keep my dad's business up and running. It's a different world for me, Hayden. If I hit Dana back, I *will* go to jail, just as she wanted last week. I think she'll eventually get the point and leave me alone. I just have to deal with it until she does. Am I pissed you'd defend yourself? No. Will I defend myself against another man? Hell yes. But against a woman? No."

Boone wasn't sure he was getting his point across very well, but when Hayden nodded once, he let out a relieved sigh. He squeezed her shoulder and let go. "Okay. Did you get all the pictures you needed?"

He watched as Hayden got herself together, and then nodded again. "Yeah, I think so. I just need to get a few more of the house from out here in the yard, then I'll get out of your hair. I know you have a lot to do."

"Don't you need to talk to the employees who were here last night?"

"Yeah, but you can have them call me. Will that work?"

"Of course."

"Okay, I'll get out of the way and let you do your thing then."

"You're not in my way, Hayden."

She didn't agree or disagree. "Boone, you really do need to file that restraining order. I expect to see a copy at the sheriff's department today or tomorrow. Got it?"

Boone smiled. She really was adorable...like a little chipmunk chattering away at a dog from its safe perch high in a tree.

She narrowed her eyes at him as if she could hear what he was thinking. "Don't blow me off. Seriously. Who's the cop here?"

"All right. I still don't think it's necessary, but I'll do it."

"Good. And I know you think Dana will back off, but I'm not sure you're right. I *hope* you are, but I just don't see it happening. I've seen this time and time again. Besides, you're too much of a catch. You're obviously doing well for yourself, you're single, gallant; I'm assuming she thinks you're good in bed—"

Boone couldn't help it, he had to interrupt her. He put his thumbs in the front pockets of his jeans and smirked as he said, "I *am* good in bed."

Hayden smiled widely and shook her head in amusement, then continued as if he hadn't interrupted her. "You're conceited, but have enough charm it could be overlooked." Her grin faded and she looked him in the eye again. "You're everything a woman could ever want, Boone. She's not going to give you up."

Boone didn't know what to say. If he wasn't mistaken, he saw longing in the pretty deputy's eyes before she turned back into the professional law enforcement officer she was. She'd said he was everything *a* woman could want...but was she including herself in that statement? He didn't have to say anything as Hayden continued.

"Okay, I'll just take a few more pictures, then I'll be in touch with the report so you can get your insurance company a copy. This is going to cost a pretty penny to clean up. If anything else happens before you can file that restraining order, just call the station. Be careful, Boone. This isn't something to take lightly."

Boone took the hint, but filed in the back of his mind the intense and yearning look in her eyes when she'd said he was the kind of man any woman would want. "I've already increased security and I've doubled the staff that's on duty. The last thing I want is her escalating to trying to hurt the cattle."

Hayden nodded. "Good. I hope you have a better day, Mr. Hatcher."

"Thanks. It started off not so great, but in the last half an hour or so, it's gotten better. I appreciate your assistance today, Deputy Yates."

Boone watched as Hayden nodded at him, then strolled away. She took a few more pictures then climbed into her car and headed down his driveway. He narrowed his eyes as he watched the cloud of dust disappear as she pulled back onto Hildebrandt Road.

There was something about Hayden that made him want to pull her into his arms and hold on tight.

She didn't exude any vibes that she needed or wanted to be protected, but somehow he saw down to her core...to the woman that longed for someone to lean on. How he knew that, Boone wasn't sure, but she was intriguing, and it had been a long time since he'd wanted to dig deeper and see what was beneath a woman's surface. He was crazy to even be *thinking* about maybe seeing if he could start something with the pretty deputy when Dana couldn't get it in her head that they were over, but he couldn't let it go...let *her* go.

He'd visit with his attorney, make sure all went well with the restraining order documents, and then visit the sheriff's department to get copies of the reports Hayden had made about the vandalism to his property and Dana's shenanigans from the other day. He'd need those to submit with the restraining order...it was a great reason to stop by...and, if he was lucky, catch a glimpse of Hayden in the process.

5

———

HAYDEN WAS FINISHING up a report from earlier that day, a traffic accident that luckily didn't result in any deaths, when Jimmy called out from across the room, "Yo! Yates! That domestic guy from the other week is here to see you."

Hayden tried to tamp down the excitement she felt at hearing Boone was there. He probably just wanted a copy of the report regarding the damage to his property. "Tell him I'll be right there!" she yelled back.

Hayden took the time to save the report she'd been working on. She had just a few more things to do on it, but she'd already worked thirty minutes over her quitting time, which wasn't exactly atypical. She ran a hand over her hair, trying to make sure it was all still secure inside the bun at the back of her head. Feeling silly for even engaging in that small vanity, Hayden got up, grabbed her Stetson and the small purse she usually kept in her desk drawer, and headed to the front of the building.

She walked into the lobby and saw Boone talking with the secretary at the front desk. She stopped to admire him for just a moment. He was wearing worn jeans that fit him like a glove. His old brown cowboy boots were peeking out from the bottom of the frayed hems and his maroon button-down, long-sleeved shirt made the fit of his jeans look downright loose. She could see the muscles in his biceps flex as he moved. He held his black cowboy hat with his left hand and his right hand rested in the front pocket of his jeans. If *Vanity Fair* or *Texas Monthly Magazine* was there, they'd sign him as a model on the spot.

Boone looked up and spotted her, and if Hayden was the swooning type of woman, she probably would've fallen at his feet. As it was, she forced herself to nonchalantly walk toward him.

"Hey, Boone. How are you?"

"Good. I came by to get copies of the reports so I can turn them into the court for the restraining order."

"So you're doing it, huh?"

"Yeah, I thought about everything you said yesterday, and after what Dana did to my house, I figured it was the smart thing to do."

"It is. But remember, it doesn't mean she'll actually honor it."

"I know. I've seen enough news clips of assholes ignoring them to understand that."

Hayden nodded. She didn't need to go over all the things that could happen. She figured Boone understood. "Great. She'll probably be notified of the restraining order within a few days of you submitting it. I would suggest, if you haven't already thought about it, you get some cameras set up to watch your property."

"Already ordered. Actually, I'd been thinking about doing it before all this happened anyway. Some of the bulls and heifers on the property are worth quite a bit. Having cameras will actually help lower some of my insurance premiums."

Hayden nodded, feeling awkward now for some reason. "Okay, well, great. If you fill out a form there with the receptionist, she can get the copies for you. I wish you the best of luck. As bad as this sounds, I hope we don't meet again anytime soon." She thought she sounded flippant, but serious enough as she said the words. Truth be told, she wanted to get to know Boone better, but wasn't sure how to go about it. She'd had a few boyfriends in her life, but they'd always started out friends first. She couldn't even remember how they'd started going out, just that they'd be hanging out as friends, then somehow they were sleeping together. It was pathetic, when she thought about it.

"Actually, I was wondering if you wanted to go out for a coffee or lunch or something? I don't know when you have time off..."

The words came out of Hayden's mouth before she

thought about them. "I just got off now, believe it or not. I worked the late shift last night for one of the other deputies. Usually I work during the day, but we switched." She shut her mouth, knowing she was babbling.

"Great. So? Do you want to grab a bite to eat with me? Are you hungry?"

She wanted to. Oh, how she wanted to. "I need to change."

"No problem. Do you need to go home?"

"No, I've got clothes here." She stood there staring at Boone, neither of them saying anything for a moment.

Boone smiled in amusement. "Okay. Do you need help?"

Hayden shook her head ruefully. "No, sorry. I'll just...I'll just go and change and meet you back here?"

"Yeah. Sounds good."

Hayden turned and went back into the main station. She smacked herself in the forehead as soon as the door shut behind her, forgetting the admin area had a glass front and Boone could most certainly see her. She was such a dork. Standing there staring at the man after he'd asked her out.

She stopped suddenly. Oh crap. She didn't have anything she felt comfortable wearing out...even if it was just for coffee. She'd worn her usual tank top to work, knowing it was the most comfortable thing under her vest and uniform. She had about three extras in her locker, along with a pair of jean shorts, and that was about it. Shit.

Well, she'd vowed to be herself in the next relationship she got into, no matter what. And while she had no idea if Boone wanted a relationship, or just wanted to take her out for coffee to thank her, she would be herself. And that would be her in a tank top and shorts, darn it.

Hayden quickly changed out of her uniform and stuffed it in her gym bag to put in her car and take home. She took her hair out of the bun she always kept it in for work and ran a brush through it haphazardly. Her hair was thick, and it annoyed her most days. She liked the color but sometimes it almost felt as if it would be easier to chop it all off than deal with it day in and day out. She threw it up in a quick ponytail, rolling her eyes at how it curled up at the end since it'd been confined in a bun all night. A femme fatale, she'd never be.

She rushed out of the locker room, only to run right into another deputy named Brandon.

"Yo, Yates, where's the fire?"

"I'm off shift, headed out."

"With that cowboy in the front?"

"If you must know, yes."

"You look like a high school cheerleader."

Hayden rolled her eyes. So much for being sexy. "Whatever, Brandon. Don't you have any bad guys to process or anything?"

He laughed. "As a matter of fact, yes. Hey, the guys are going out tomorrow night. Wanna come?"

Hayden didn't take offense at being considered one of the guys. She loved hanging out with the other deputies when they were off duty. "Sure. Same place as usual?"

"Yup. See you then!"

"See ya!"

Hayden strode down the hall and back up to the front. She hoped she hadn't taken too long. What if Boone had left? What if he'd thought twice about asking her for coffee?

She opened the door and stepped into the lobby, relieved to see Boone still there. He'd stepped to the side of the reception desk, and was holding a large envelope, which probably held the reports he'd come to the station to get in the first place, and there were now two men talking to the secretary at the front. One of the men whistled as she came into the room.

"Well, well, well. You just get let out of the tank? Maybe you want to party with me and my friend here?"

It took a second for Hayden to realize just what the man was implying, but before she could put him in his place, Boone was in his face.

"I'm guessing you want to rethink your words. I do believe you just called a sheriff's deputy a prostitute. Besides being a dumbass thing to say to anyone inside a police station, or out, it was simply rude. I think you should apologize."

The man looked from Boone's unyielding pissed-off face, to Hayden, to the young secretary sitting behind the glass. She pointed up at a camera in the corner, smirking.

"Oh shit. Yeah. Uh, sorry. I was just kidding, but it was out of line. I didn't mean anything by it. Really."

Hayden rolled her eyes. God, had she ever been as young and dumb as this guy? She truly hoped not. She decided to ignore them.

"You ready to go, Boone?"

Boone hadn't moved from his position next to the younger man. He stood at least three or four inches taller than him, and was probably a good fifty pounds heavier as well. Hayden walked over to him and put her hand on his arm. "Boone. Come on."

He allowed Hayden to guide him away from the man, but said as he shifted sideways, "You're lucky you aren't in cuffs right now for solicitation. Think before you talk, man. And stop disrespecting women. It isn't cool."

Boone put his arm around Hayden's upper back and they walked out into the parking lot. He stopped outside the door and dropped his arm. "Sorry about that. God, what a dumbass."

Hayden giggled. Actually giggled. She couldn't believe it. She looked up at him. "It wasn't a big deal."

"Actually it was. I mean, you look amazing. Even in shorts and a tank, anyone could tell you're way too classy to be a prostitute."

"Uh, thank you?" Hayden decided to take his words as a compliment, even if they were a bit backward.

Boone scrubbed his hand over his face. "Damn. I screwed that up. Sorry. What I meant was, you look beautiful. That guy probably couldn't understand what someone as pretty as you was doing inside the sheriff's department. I know *I've* never seen a deputy who looks like you do."

"Uh...thanks again?"

Boone laughed at himself. "Shit. Okay, I'll stop before I dig myself into a hole I can't get out of. Sorry. Where do you want to go? Just coffee? Or do you want to eat something?"

"I could eat."

"Great. There's a small family-owned Mexican restaurant I know. They have a kick-ass lunch menu. Wanna chance it?"

"Sure, but...this place isn't fancy is it? This is all I've got here to wear."

"You're fine. Damn, you're more than fine, Hayden. Seriously. I wouldn't embarrass you by taking you to a restaurant you weren't dressed appropriately for. Trust me."

Hayden nodded. "Okay then. Sounds good. Give me the address so I can meet you there?"

"You don't want to drive together?"

Hayden took a deep breath, knowing she could piss him off with her words, but going forth anyway. "No. I'll meet you there."

Boone eyed her, then simply nodded. "Okay. No problem."

He rattled off the address. Hayden recognized the general area. "I'll follow you, if that's okay."

"Sure. I'll make sure not to lose you."

Hayden smiled at that. "Uh, Boone. I *am* a deputy you know...I'm sure I can manage to stay behind you without any issues."

He smiled sheepishly. "Yeah, sorry."

"Just don't break any laws...I might be off duty but if you run any stoplights, I won't be able to look the other way."

He chuckled. "I won't. I'm a law-abiding driver. Promise."

"Good. See you there!" She walked off toward her car, knowing Boone watched her the whole way.

Boone kept his eyes on Hayden as she walked toward a small gray Honda Civic.

Holy mother of God, he'd thought she was built under the uniform she wore, but he wasn't prepared to see her smooth, creamy skin in all its glory. He'd almost whistled when he'd seen her walk into the reception area, just as the stupid man in the waiting area had.

The black tank top she was wearing highlighted her small waist and her muscular arms. She was buff. Boone thought she might be able to out push-up even him. It was obvious she worked out. It looked good on her. She wasn't so buff that she looked manly or freakish, but her arms were cut. While he admired her arms, her chest was nothing to sneeze at either. She wasn't hugely endowed, but she was probably an average B cup. Boone had no idea how she kept those beauties hidden under her uniform. It had to be uncomfortable. But in that tank top of hers? Wow.

When he'd been able to take his eyes off of her upper half, her lower had him reciting statistics of his bulls to keep his cock from going hard and embarrassing himself. Hayden's legs seemed to go on for miles, and if he wasn't mistaken, she had freckles all over, not just on her cheeks. She wasn't wearing heels, but her calf muscles were prominent and her legs were as cut as her arms. He could easily imagine how it would feel to have her thighs squeezing his hips as he thrust into her. Crude, but so true. She literally had the kind of body women would kill to have...and the amazing part was that it was obvious she had no clue.

She had no idea whatsoever how gorgeous she was. She acted as tomboyish as anyone he'd ever seen, but her innate sensuality shone through loud and clear. Boone could just picture her lying back on his bed, her auburn hair spread out across his pillow as he kneeled over her.

As soon as his thoughts veered toward seeing her dark auburn hair against his white sheets, he cut them off. He shouldn't go there. He was taking her out for lunch. That was it. He had enough on his plate with Dana and his farm...but the thought of Hayden writhing in ecstasy under him as they made love, wouldn't leave his brain.

Boone got into his truck and waited until he saw Hayden behind him before pulling out to head to the restaurant. He wanted more than anything to get to know her—as a woman, not as a deputy responding to an incident at his farm. He had no idea if she wanted the same thing though, but he was going to do whatever he could to see if he could convince her to give him a shot.

6

HAYDEN SAT BACK in the booth and clutched her stomach. "Oh my God, I don't think I could eat another bite."

"You only got a taco!"

"Yeah, but I ate about a pound and a half of chips and salsa."

Boone laughed. "That you did."

"Hey!"

They both laughed this time.

Hayden bit her lip. "Thanks for this."

"For what?"

Hayden gestured to the table and the restaurant. "This. Taking me to lunch."

"You're welcome. You're fun to be around."

Hayden's smile stuttered a bit, but she forced it back. "Fun. Yup, that's me."

Boone reached across the table and snagged the

hand she'd put around her water glass. "Hey. What'd I say?"

"Nothing, Boone. Seriously. I've had a good time today. I have to get going, though."

Boone held on to her hand tightly, not letting go. "Hayden. What'd I say? And don't say nothing. It was something. I can tell when you're fake smiling. Now what was it?"

"You can tell when I'm fake smiling?"

"Yeah."

"How?"

"So you admit you were fake smiling at me?"

"Boone, seriously."

"See? Now *that's* a real smile."

Hayden couldn't help but laugh. She simply couldn't hold it inside. Boone just made her happy. He made her feel like a completely different person...a sexy female person not the competent, kick-ass sheriff's deputy.

Boone continued, "Now, what'd I say to make you lose that gorgeous smile of yours?"

Hayden looked at Boone. He was leaning toward her; she could feel his thumb brushing against the back of her hand. His eyebrows were drawn down in concern. If he was faking being interested in what she had to say, in why she didn't like what he'd said, he was a damn good actor. She decided to just be honest with him.

"I'm fun to be around. I'm the fun one. The life of the party. All the guys say that."

"All the guys."

He hadn't stated it as a question, but it was a question nevertheless.

Hayden continued. In for a penny, in for a pound. "Yeah. All the guys. Throughout high school. In college. Even now when I go out with everyone at the station. I'm the fun one."

"There's nothing wrong with being fun, Hayden."

She immediately nodded, agreeing with him. "I know."

"But it bothers you."

"Can we drop this?"

"No."

"Boone."

"Hayden."

She sighed. She hated having to spell it out to him. She felt like a dork. "I'm the friend. The good-time girl. The happy-go-lucky Hayden Yates. Not a woman. Not a date."

Boone didn't say anything, simply dropped her hand and scooted out from his seat in the booth. Hayden didn't have time to do anything before Boone had dropped himself onto the seat next to her. She scooted over in surprise, giving him room.

He put one hand on the back of the booth behind her head and the other on her upper thigh. His thumb rested on the hem of her shorts. Hayden felt the heat from his hand seep into her skin and she resisted the urge to squirm in her seat. She should've smacked his hand away, or rebuked him for being too forward, but the truth was, she liked his hand on her.

"Look at me, Hayden."

Hayden looked up into Boone's eyes. She felt surrounded by him. He was leaning into her and she had to tilt her head up to be able to see his eyes.

"You're funny, but that doesn't take anything away from your femininity. I don't know why none of those guys see you like I do, but I can't say I'm sorry about it, because it leaves things in the free and clear for me. I think you're funny. And compassionate. And you know how that guy responded when he saw you in the lobby of the station today?"

When Hayden nodded reluctantly, he continued, "He made an ass out of himself because of how hot you look."

At the look of blatant disbelief on her face, he lifted the hand that had been resting on the plastic behind her head and brought it to her face. He ran his knuckles down her cheek, then smoothed a stray piece of hair behind her ear. "You're beautiful, Hayden. Your legs are long and sleek, your curvy little body in this tank top had every man in this restaurant taking a second look as we walked in. And I'll tell you this right now, I can't wait to see if the freckles you have right here," he ran his fingertip over her nose, "are all over your body."

"Boone—"

He talked over her. "Even sitting close to you in this booth is making me have an embarrassingly masculine reaction to you," he nodded down to his lap, and the erection that strained against his jeans. He saw her glance down, then quickly bring her eyes back up to his in embarrassment. "So me telling you that you're funny takes nothing away from how pretty you are. Pretty seems like too tame of a word, but it'll do for now. Don't doubt yourself, Hayden. You might work with men, and they might see you in that light because of how competent you are at what you do, but trust me when I say they're seeing you through a whole different lens than I am."

Hayden knew her face was aflame. Lord. No man had ever spoken to her like this before. She wasn't sure she could believe Boone, even though he hadn't lied about having an erection. He was very healthily endowed if her quick glance was anything to go by. Embarrassed, she tried to deflect. "How can you tell if I'm smiling for real?"

Realizing he needed to give her some space, Boone leaned back and shook his head. "I don't think I'm going to tell you. I like having one up on you. I have a feeling I'll need it."

"Boone!"

"Hayden!"

She shook her head in exasperation.

The waiter came up at that moment and left the

bill on the table, telling them he'd be back for it whenever they were ready to pay. Hayden leaned over and picked it up to see what her half of the meal came to.

"What are you doing?" Boone growled.

"Seeing what I owe," Hayden said, studying the bill and not looking up.

Boone snatched the small piece of paper out of her hand. "You are not paying."

"What? Why not?"

"Because I asked you to lunch."

"So?"

"What do you mean, so?"

"Just that. So what if you asked me to lunch? I can pay my way, Boone. It's not a big deal."

"Hayden, I asked you to lunch. If I asked you to lunch, that means you aren't paying."

"So, if I asked *you* to lunch, I could pay?"

"No."

"No?"

"No."

"Boone, that doesn't make any sense."

"Hasn't anyone taken you out on a date before?"

"A date?"

"Yeah. What do you think this is, Hayden?"

"A thank you lunch?" Her words were soft and confused.

Boone rolled his eyes and sighed. Under his breath, he told the ceiling, "I'm obviously losing my touch." Then he looked back at Hayden and said in a normal voice, "Hayden, I asked you to lunch because I like you. Because the first time you touched my hand over a week ago I got a jolt so strong, I felt it in my toes. I came into the station today in the hopes I'd get to see you. I'm forty years old and I resorted to a lame excuse to come into your workplace to see you and ask you out."

Hayden smiled at him. "What would you have done if I'd said I was working, or if I'd turned you down?"

"I would've made up another reason to see you. I wouldn't have given up that easily, not when taking you out on a date was something I really wanted. But, Hayden, the point is, this *is* a date. And because it's a date, you're not paying."

"So if it *wasn't* a date I could pay?"

"No. Whenever we go out, I pay. Period."

"That's pretty cavemanish."

"Yup."

"Honestly, Boone, I can pay for myself."

"Give it up, Hay. Let me do this."

"Oh, all right."

Boone laughed out loud at her disgruntled capitulation. "You make it really hard to do something nice for you. Hasn't anyone taken you out before?"

"Not really, no."

Boone sobered. "I have no idea how that's even possible, but it's their loss, Hay. Their loss."

Hayden shrugged, but held the way he made her

feel close to her heart. She'd been honest with Boone. She was always one of the guys. No one thought to pay for her. And no one, not ever, had given her a nickname. She liked it.

"Okay, Mr. Moneybags, can you pay then? I have to get going." She hid the warm and fuzzy feelings Boone put inside her and tried to play it off.

"Yes, ma'am." Boone smiled at her. He gestured to the waiter and he came right over and took Boone's credit card and hurried away.

"So, when are we going out again?" he asked with a smile.

"That sure I want to go out with you again, are you?"

"Yup."

Hayden couldn't hold back her smile. "Well, the guys and I are going out tomorrow night...wanna come?"

"Yes."

"You don't even know where we're going."

"Doesn't matter."

"And if I said we were going to a strip club?"

"No problem."

"And if we were going shooting?"

"I'd bring my gun."

Hayden rolled her eyes. She should've figured a Texas cowboy like him would be comfortable around firearms and would have his own. "Fine. We're just going to this bar we always go to for some beers."

"Great. You want me to meet you there, or will you let me pick you up?"

Hayden considered it for a second. "I live in the opposite direction from your ranch." She tried to give him an out in case he'd only asked to be polite.

"Hay, I wouldn't have asked if I didn't want to pick you up."

She nodded and said softly, "Okay, you can come and get me beforehand. But don't be late. It's a pet peeve of mine."

Boone brushed her hair behind her ear once more. "I wouldn't dream of it."

The waiter came back and Boone signed the receipt. He scooted out of the seat and held out his hand to Hayden. She put her hand in his and he helped her stand up. He put his hand on the small of her back as they walked to the front door. Hayden had never understood why the women in her romance books always gushed when a man did that to them. But she got it now. She always thought it would feel controlling in some way, and maybe with another man, it would've. But with Boone, it felt comforting. He rested his fingertips against her back and applied just a bit of pressure. Enough for her to know he was there, but not enough so it felt like he was pushing her along. Hayden swore she could feel the heat from his hand soak through her tank top into her bones.

They stopped outside the restaurant and she gave him her address. "I just have to say this one thing."

"Sure."

"If you're planning on stalking me, taking me out, trying to get me drunk, then taking me home to tie me up, throw me into a dungeon under your barn, and rape me then kill me...it'll never work. I'll take you down before you know what happened."

Boone threw his head back and laughed. Hayden stood there with her arms over her chest, smiling, waiting for him to get control over himself. Finally, he put both hands on her shoulders and leaned in.

"Hay, I have no doubt if I moved even an inch in the wrong direction, you'd have me on the ground with your knee on my throat before I could even think about getting out of your way. And as sick as it makes me, the thought of you overpowering me makes me hard. I don't have a dungeon under my barn, and I have no plans to stalk you. But we can negotiate the taking-you-out, getting-you-drunk, and tying-you-up thing."

Hayden's smile died and she looked at him in confusion.

He took pity on her. He linked his hand with hers and tugged her toward their cars. "Come on, you have stuff to do. Let's get you home."

Hayden stumbled alongside Boone for a couple of steps before getting her stride back. She shook her head. He was such a goof. She'd never have thought it of him. For such a large manly man, he sure acted like a big clown sometimes. But she couldn't forget his serious side when he'd told her how much he liked her looks and when he said he'd always pay when they were together. He was absolutely fascinating.

"What time should I pick you up tomorrow?"

Boone had walked her to her car and they were standing by her driver's side door. "Around eight?"

"Eight it is."

"Just to warn you, it's going to mostly be the guys I work with there tomorrow night. I'll also invite some of my friends who are in other departments as well. Will it bother you to be around a bunch of cops?"

"No, Hay. As long as it's okay with you."

"It's good. But they'll probably give you shit."

"I'd expect nothing less. I'm looking forward to meeting your friends."

"Okay. Then I'll see you at eight."

Boone leaned down and Hayden held her breath. He kissed her cheek and straightened. "See you tomorrow, Hayden. I had a good time today. Thanks."

"Yeah, me too. 'Bye."

"'Bye. Drive safe."

Hayden didn't answer, but simply started her car and pulled out of the restaurant. Her last view was of Boone sitting in his truck staring after her as she pulled away.

7

———

HAYDEN WANTED TO CALL SOMEONE...BUT she had no idea who would be able to help her.

She was freaking out about her date that night with Boone. As she worked throughout the day, she tried to think about who might help her figure out what she should wear. She could call Corrie, Quint's girlfriend—she'd gotten to know her pretty well after helping her climb out of the biggest tree Hayden had ever seen—but Corrie was blind. She wouldn't be able to see her clothing choices to help her make a decision.

She liked Beth, Cade's girlfriend, but she didn't think the other woman would know anything about what she should wear on a date. Beth was a "computer geek," her words, and spent most of her time in sweats and T-shirts. She was fun to be around, and Hayden liked her, but she wouldn't be of much help in this case.

Dax and Cruz's girlfriends had said she could call them anytime, but Mackenzie and Mickie were so far out of her league, it wasn't even funny. Besides, Hayden didn't want to give the Texas Ranger or FBI agent anything to hold over her head in the future. They'd make fun of her for years if they knew she'd never been on a real date before and had no idea what to wear.

Hayden fit in better with the male deputies than the females, so she didn't feel comfortable asking them either. She sighed and finally decided not to worry about it. It was drinks at the same bar they always went to. She shouldn't be freaking out about it. She'd wear what she normally did...and if Boone didn't like it, it was his problem, not hers. She tried to tell herself that, but deep down she knew she was lying to herself.

The day went by surprisingly fast, especially because she hadn't slept that well the night before.

She hadn't had the nightmare for years, but last night it'd come back with a vengeance.

It was more of a memory than an actual nightmare. She was no more than four years old, sitting on a couch watching her father pace back and forth in front of her. She was wearing a ridiculously ruffled and frilly pink dress. It'd been a hand-me-down dress from a neighbor who had a little girl. They were moving and the family was trying to get rid of as much extra stuff as they could.

The dress had been worn by the woman's daughter

when she was a flower girl in a relative's wedding. Hayden had seen it sitting on top of the box of clothes when the neighbor had dropped it off. She'd grabbed it and immediately taken it to her room to put on. It was the most beautiful thing she'd ever seen and Hayden had loved twirling and dancing around her room in the princess dress.

Her dad had caught her though. He'd hauled her into the living room, made her sit, and was yelling at her as he paced. She was a disgrace to the family. If she wanted to be a prissy wuss, she had no place in his house.

Hayden always knew what was coming in the dream, but she never managed to wake up before it happened.

Her father hauled her up and roughly stripped the dress off of her. He made her stand there while he took out a giant pair of scissors and cut the beautiful fairy dress to shreds...all the while, telling her how pathetic and what a loser she was.

She'd woken up from the dream sweating and could feel the tears drying on her face.

Hayden knew her parents hadn't wanted a girl, and that she'd been disappointing them her entire life, but it was that one incident that made her realize at a young age that her father didn't really like her...not even a little bit.

Hayden had tried to be what her parents wanted after that. She played sports instead of going into dance. She wore jeans and T-shirts, instead of pretty girly dresses and blouses. She got straight As in high school in the hopes that her grades would make her dad proud of her. Nothing had worked. He'd treated her with the same disdain throughout her teen years as he had that one day when she'd sat on the couch as he'd harangued her.

It'd been an early morning for her, and she knew she'd never get back to sleep after waking up shaking and crying from the dream. So she'd gotten up, gone for a three mile run, did the pushups and sit-ups that she tried to make time for every day, had a large cup of coffee, then headed to the station to prepare for her shift.

Hayden was busy all day at work with calls, investigations, and paperwork. She made it home with plenty of time to stand in her closet, staring aimlessly at the clothes within. She'd made an effort after moving out of her childhood home, and getting away from her father, to try to purchase clothes that were more feminine, but most days, she simply felt more comfortable in what was familiar...jeans and T-shirts.

Finally, Hayden shook her head and grabbed a jade-green shirt that she hadn't worn in forever. It was more feminine than she usually went for, but Hayden figured being out with Boone warranted it. She wanted to make the effort. It was cut deep in both front and back with a wide scoop neck. The sleeves were three-quarter length and while it wasn't skin tight, it wasn't loose either. She paired it with a pair of low-cut jeans and her favorite cowboy boots. The boots were a bit too beat up to really match, but they were comfortable, and were the only type of heel Hayden was comfortable wearing.

She stared at herself in the bathroom mirror and tried to decide what to do with her hair. She should probably put it up. She always wore it up. Hayden didn't think the guys at work had ever seen her with her hair down. But Boone made her want to put in more effort than she usually did. She brushed out the thick strands until they were relatively tamed after being confined in her usual bun all day, and smoothed it behind her ears. She scowled at the ends, which curled up no matter what she did to try to make them lay flat. Shrugging, Hayden grabbed a scrunchie and put it around her wrist; she'd most likely put it up by the end of the night anyway.

She went into the other room of her apartment and paced. She wasn't one to be able to sit still very well, so she stalked back and forth from her small kitchen into the family room, then back into the kitchen.

What if Boone stood her up? What if she'd misunderstood what he'd wanted when he said this was a date? Shit. She probably shouldn't even really be going out with him since she'd investigated his case. It wasn't like her to ever want to date anyone she'd met during the course of her job. She should call him to...dammit. She didn't have his number.

Hayden looked at the clock. Seven forty-five. Crud. Fifteen more minutes. She paced back and forth and generally worked herself into a frenzy before the bell rang about ten minutes later.

Hayden stalked to the door, ready and worked up to tell Boone that there was no way they could go out tonight—or any night.

Boone could tell the second he saw Hayden that she'd talked herself out of wanting to go to the bar with him. He had no idea if it was him, having him meet her friends, or something more, but there was no way, after getting a look at her, he was going to let her back out now.

He knew her hair would probably be amazing, but he was so far off the mark as to what he'd imagined, it was laughable. She'd left it down, and the ends brushed the tops of her breasts. It was wavy and looked utterly unmanageable at the moment. Boone wanted nothing more than to shove his hands in it, tilt her head back, hold her still, and devour her mouth.

"Boone, I—"

He didn't let her get anything else out. He took a step closer and put one hand on her waist, and the other he rested on the side of her head, barely resisting the urge to tangle his fingers in her tresses and slam his mouth over hers. Instead, he leaned in and brushed his lips against her cheek then looked down into her eyes. "Good evening, Hay. You look beautiful."

"Uh...hi, Boone. Thanks. Um, so do you."

He smiled. She hadn't really even looked at him. She'd been looking at his feet when she opened the door, and when he'd kissed her, she'd brought her eyes up to his.

"Ready to go?"

"Well...uh...yeah. I guess so."

"Do you need a jacket or a purse?"

Hayden shook her head. "I have my money, ID, and cell in my pockets. I'm good."

Boone put a bit of pressure on her waist with the hand he still had resting there. "Great. Let's get going then."

"Okay. Yeah. I do need to grab my keys though."

Boone let go of Hayden enough so she could reach over to a key rack hanging over the small table inside the doorway. He backed up to give her room. She closed her apartment door and locked it. She pocketed her keys and turned to him, putting both hands in the back pockets of her jeans.

It was obvious she was uncomfortable, but Boone knew she had no idea by putting her arms behind her, she was thrusting her gorgeous tits toward him. He took a deep breath. Her absolutely unconscious sexuality was breathtaking. He held out his hand. "Come on, Hay. Let's get going. I believe I remember you saying you hated to be late."

He was pleased to see no hesitation in her actions when she put her hand in his. He led her to his pickup and opened the passenger door. "Need help inside?"

She looked at him as if he was crazy. "No." Hayden then proceeded to hop into the truck as if she'd been doing it her entire life. Boone would've complimented her, but he couldn't tear his eyes away from her ass in the tight jeans she was wearing. He shut the door behind her and walked around the back of the truck to the driver's side, taking the time to adjust himself inside his pants as soon as he was out of Hayden's view. Jesus, she was going to be the death of him.

He climbed into the truck and Hayden told him where the bar was that they were meeting all her friends.

"Did you get your truck fixed already?"

"No. The insurance company is covering a loaner until mine has been detailed and repainted. I refused to accept one of those small foreign jobs, and insisted on a black truck just like mine."

"And they agreed?"

"Well, since I work on a farm, I might have stretched the truth a bit and told them that I had to have the truck for work."

Hayden laughed. It made sense and she knew Boone could be charming when he wanted to. She changed the subject. "Any more trouble with Dana?"

The question wasn't unexpected. She was an officer after all. "No. I haven't seen or heard from her since last week."

"The restraining order was probably delivered

today. Keep on your toes, Boone. You never know what she's going to do."

"I will. Now...tell me who will be here tonight."

"Well, there will be a bunch of guys from the station. Brandon, of course, since he invited me, and you've met Jimmy and Troy...they were at your house last week. I think Juan said he was going to try to get there tonight as well. You haven't met him yet, I don't think. I'm also close friends with a bunch of guys from different law enforcement agencies across the city. We met at a conference and now we collaborate on cases when the need arises. Dax Chambers is a Ranger and Cruz is with the FBI office here in San Antonio. Quint Axton is with the SAPD. Those three will most likely bring their girlfriends, so I won't be the only woman there."

"Are you usually the only woman there?"

She shrugged, unconcerned. "Yeah. The other female deputies don't like to hang out on their time off. Two are married with kids and the other is...well, she's more of a girly girl...not like me."

Boone let that go for now. "Anyone else?"

"I invited Calder and Conor as well. Calder is a medical examiner for the city and Conor is with the game warden's office. The only one of our crew who can't be here tonight is TJ. He's with the highway patrol. I shot him a quick email this morning and he said he'd be out of town. He has friends up in the Fort

Hood area who are in the Army, who he used to know when he was in. I think he visits them on his time off."

"And you guys get together every week?"

"No, not really. And it's actually unusual that all of us can get off at the same time. Typically, it's only like three or four of us that end up hanging out. Having six out of the seven of us free on the same night is practically a miracle."

"I'm glad I'll get to meet them."

Hayden simply nodded as they pulled into the packed parking lot of the small bar. They had to park in a back corner of the lot, it was so full.

"Why's it so packed?" Boone asked as they got out of the truck.

"It's always like this. It's the best kept non-secret in San Antonio."

They laughed and Boone once again put his hand on the small of her back as they walked toward the front door.

As soon as they entered the dark, smoky bar, Hayden's name was called out from somewhere in the mass of people. Hayden waved airily in the direction of the voice and turned to Boone. "What do you want to drink?"

"Oh no, Hay. You will not be buying me anything to drink. Haven't we already had this conversation?"

"But Boone, it's just a beer."

"Nope. It's just nothing. You tell me what you want,

I'll bring it to the table. Just show me where you'll be and I'll be right there."

Boone smiled as Hayden rolled her eyes at him. "Fine. I'll take whatever's on tap. And we usually sit over in the corner, there..." She pointed toward a large window at the opposite side of the bar.

Boone couldn't keep his hands off her. He smoothed her hair behind her ear, enjoying the way she licked her lips nervously at his action. "Okay, I'll be there in a second."

Hayden headed off toward her friends and Boone watched for a moment as she greeted them. She fist-bumped a few of the men, and one slapped her on the shoulder as she sat down. He shook his head as he turned to the bar to get their drinks. How none of the men she worked with saw her as a desirable female was beyond him. But their loss was his gain, so he wouldn't complain.

Boone carried two pints of beer to the table and was glad to see nothing but welcoming smiles from the men and women around the table. He took a seat next to Hayden in the empty chair and put her beer on the table in front of her.

"Thanks, I appreciate it." She turned to the table and announced in general, "Everyone, this is Boone. Boone, this is everyone."

He gave a chin lift to the group and most of the men did the same. One of the women leaned across the table and held out her hand.

"Hi, I'm Mackenzie. It's so nice to meet you. I don't think I've met a real live cowboy before. I mean, I've met people who wear cowboy boots and hats and like to think they're cowboys, and Wes is technically a cowboy, but since he's a Texas Ranger I tend to think of him that way first, but Hayden tells me that you own your own farm and you have cows and bulls on your property. Do you ride them? And we're so happy to see Hayden has a date! I mean, not that she can't get a date or anything, but we've never seen her with a guy before, so that's cool, and you're hot, so that's even—"

Her words were cut off by a man, who Boone assumed was Dax. He held his hand over Mackenzie's mouth and shook his head lovingly at her. "What Mack here means to say is, nice to meet you."

Everyone around the table laughed and Boone smiled as Mackenzie blushed. Everyone was obviously used to her rambling comments. He turned his attention to Hayden—who was looking down at her clenched hands in her lap uncertainly. He sobered. Mack's words had obviously hurt her feelings.

Boone leaned down so only she could hear him. "See? Even Mack knows this is a date. And a date means you don't pay."

His words seemed to help. Hayden looked up and gave him a smile—a fake one; he couldn't see the small dimple in her cheek...the telltale sign she was genuinely smiling. But it was a start.

The conversation flowed around them. Boone

watched the interaction between the men, and between the men and Hayden. Everyone was relaxed and comfortable. He heard stories about how Hayden had single-handedly taken down a guy high on meth who was threatening the deputies sent to check out the situation with a knife. She'd literally charged him, put her shoulder in his gut and flipped him on his back. The other deputies then all jumped on top of the stunned man and disarmed and subdued him. Boone didn't like hearing the stories of how Hayden was in danger, but he understood it was a part of who she was and what she did for a living.

But Boone also noticed other little things throughout the night. Things that helped him understand Hayden a little more. The other men treated her just as they would a friend—a *male* friend. When Mickie's drink was empty, Cruz asked, "Ladies, anyone else need a refill?" and looked at each of the women, except for Hayden. When one of the other women needed to use the restroom, they all got up and went together, but didn't ask Hayden if she needed to go. It wasn't as if they were dissing her, Boone figured they honestly just didn't see her like he did.

Not only that, but when the women were gone, the men didn't temper their discussion as they had when their ladies were there. An intense conversation about whether the majority of the Dallas Cowboy cheerleaders' tits were real or fake ensued before the women got back from the restroom.

Hell, once, one of the men—Boone thought it was Juan—said to the three women sitting with their boyfriends, "I need a woman's opinion..." And he'd launched into a story about how the chick he was dating was acting weird and he wanted to know what they thought.

It was obvious the men around the table didn't see Hayden as female, and it completely and utterly baffled Boone. She was one of the most feminine women he'd ever met. Oh, some people would probably argue the point, but between her dainty facial features, the fact she was quite a bit shorter than he was, plump lips that he could imagine doing very carnal things to, and the subtle floral scent coming from her, she had his interest in a big way.

Sometime during the night she'd put her beautiful hair up in a ponytail. It swung down her back and Boone couldn't help but play with the ends as they brushed against his hand resting on the back of her chair. He wasn't sure if she noticed or not, but he couldn't keep himself from touching her if his life depended on it.

It wasn't until Hayden was halfway through her second beer that Boone noticed she wasn't enjoying it. Every time she took a sip, her lip would curl up...just a bit. The next time she took a drink, Boone leaned in. "Why do you drink that if you hate it?"

"What?"

"The beer. It's obvious you don't like it. Why don't you get something you enjoy?"

Hayden shrugged. "Everyone's drinking beer."

Boone looked around the table. What she'd meant was, all the *guys* were drinking beer. Mackenzie and Mickie had frou-frou drinks, and Corrie was sipping a frozen margarita. He pushed. "I can get you a margarita if you want."

"I'm fine."

"Hayden."

She turned to him. "I'm *fine*, Boone."

By the end of the night, Boone had a much better insight into Hayden's psyche. She worked with men, she was a female in a male-dominated field. She had to shoot as well as, or better than, they did, fight as well, and be as tough as, or tougher than, they were. She'd made herself blend in with the men as much as she could, most likely to protect herself. He got that.

What he didn't get was why not one of the other men saw through her bullshit to the tender woman underneath.

There had to be more to it though. There were women who worked in law enforcement all over the world. Many were married with children. What made Hayden put on this masculine persona, as if she was wearing a suit of armor?

No other woman he knew had ever had so many layers, and it was absolutely fascinating to Boone. He wanted to get to know her more. He wanted to be the one to strip off the armor she'd strapped so tightly around herself and find the true woman underneath. The glimpses he'd seen so far were tantalizing, and he wanted more.

The group started breaking up. First Jimmy and Juan left. Then Quint left with Corrie. Finally, the rest of them said they were headed home.

"Hey, it was supposed to be your turn to buy the rounds, Yates. How'd you get out of that one?" Brandon asked.

"Whatever! It was not. I bought last time; you always conveniently forget when it's *your* turn to pay," Hayden returned.

"That's what we get for letting the chicks crash our nights out. They always have to bitch about who pays for what." Brandon said with a grin, teasingly bumping Hayden's shoulder with his own. "Hey, Dax and Cruz, next time leave the women at home so we can talk about manly shit."

Everyone laughed, but Boone just shook his head in disbelief. If Hayden hadn't told him, he wouldn't have believed it. But seeing firsthand how just one-of-the-guys she was, was completely baffling.

The group eased out into the night and the other men and women disappeared into the parking lot and their vehicles. Boone didn't say a word, but led Hayden to his truck. He watched as she climbed into her seat and he quickly headed around the truck and got in on the driver's side. He sat there silent for a minute, trying to put together what he wanted to say, how to let her know how much he liked her and that he wanted to see her again.

Finally, he turned to Hayden. "I had a good time tonight, Hay."

She nodded, "Good. I think the guys liked you."

"How can you tell?"

"Well, because they were themselves. If they didn't like you, they would've been all polite and shit. But they weren't. They acted as they always did." She shrugged and concluded, "They like you."

"You fit right in with them."

"Yeah, we're tight."

"I suppose that comes with the territory."

"It does. I've saved Juan's life, and Troy has saved mine. We have each other's backs and that brings a bond that simply can't be broken. And even the guys I don't directly work with every day are important to me."

"How so?"

"Well, when Quint's girlfriend, Corrie, was kidnapped, she somehow ended up saving herself, even though she's blind. She walked into a forest and climbed the biggest fucking tree I've ever seen. When we found her, she was all the way at the top of the thing. Quint was too big to get up there to help her, so I had to step in. I helped her out of the tree and I know Quint is thankful for that."

"Wow, go on."

"Laine—she wasn't there tonight, she's with one of Dax's coworkers—she disappeared. It turned out she'd fallen into an old abandoned well on a property south of the city she was checking out—she's a realtor—and we all banded together to find her.

"And Mackenzie, Dax's girlfriend, was buried alive and actually died before they found her in a sealed coffin in the bad guy's basement. I wasn't on the op for that one, but I heard about it from TJ and Quint. And Mickie's sister was caught up in this motorcycle gang that Cruz had gone undercover in. Long story short, the sister ended up dead and it was a close call for Mickie."

Boone reached over and took Hayden's hand in his as she continued talking.

"Being a law enforcement officer is one of the hardest jobs in the world. Day in and day out, every single call could be a matter of life and death—mine, my partner's, or someone I'm going to help. Some days it seems like everyone I come into contact with hates me and would kill me on the spot if they could, but then other days I have interactions with people who are relieved and happy that I'm there. But whatever the job brings, I love it." Hayden looked up at Boone. "I can't imagine doing anything else. It feels good to help people, to see the light of relief in their eyes when I pull up. And without my partners and friends in the field, I wouldn't be able to do it half as well as I do."

"I understand. I'm proud of you, Hayden. You're

obviously good at what you do and your friends and partners respect the hell out of you."

"Thanks. That means a lot."

"Ready to head home?"

"Yeah." Hayden tried to hide a yawn and blushed when Boone smirked at her.

The drive back to her place was done in a comfortable silence. Boone pulled into a parking space and turned to her.

"I'd like to take you out again, Hay. I loved meeting your friends, and I'd like for you to meet mine, if you want."

She nodded immediately. "I'd like that."

Boone squeezed the hand he'd taken in his when they'd stopped. "I have to warn you though. It's going to be a different experience than tonight."

"What do you mean?"

"I mean, tonight you were just one of the guys. I'll be taking you to a country and western bar, where I can guarantee if I lose sight of you for one second, there will be ten cowboys willing and competing to take my place by your side."

Boone watched Hayden's brows draw down in confusion. "What?"

He leaned toward her and put his hand on the side of her head. His voice lowered seductively. "Hay, you're gorgeous. You have the type of body that was made for lovin'. The men you work with might see you as just another cop, but believe me when I say you are a sexy and desirable woman."

"Boone, I don't think—"

"I don't know why you can't see it, but that's okay. Because I can. And I'll be damned if anyone else is gonna snatch you up right in front of my eyes."

"No one is going to 'snatch me up.' You're being crazy. Did you drink more than I thought you did? Should you even be driving?"

"I'm not drunk, not even tipsy. And you're right— no one is going to snatch you up, because you'll be there with me. And another thing. You will not drink one beer the entire night. You hate it. I get that you want to be one of the guys when you're out with your colleagues, but when you're out with me, you'll drink what you like."

When she didn't say anything, Boone smiled at her. "Still want to go on another date with me?"

Hayden's voice was quiet and earnest. "Even though I think you're delusional, yeah, I think I do."

"Good."

They sat motionless for a moment before Hayden spoke. "I guess I should go in."

"Yeah, but I'd really like a kiss first...if that's all right with you."

She didn't say anything, just nodded and licked her lips in anticipation.

Boone took his time. He had a feeling this kiss would change his life. She'd pegged him right when she'd told him that he seemed like a man who did the chasing. He was enjoying the hell out of pursuing her. Knowing that he seemed to see something that others didn't, made it all the more special.

He put some pressure on the hand that was on her head and pulled Hayden to him. She put both hands on the leather seat next to her to keep her balance and tilted her chin up as she came toward him.

She closed her eyes at the last minute before their lips touched. He brushed his lips against hers once. Then again. Then the third time he licked her bottom lip. She opened for him and he didn't hesitate to respond to her invitation.

He surged into her mouth and felt her shudder under him as he took complete control of the kiss. He brought his other hand up to her head and tilted it even more, so he had a better angle. Boone felt her hands come up and hold on to his wrists as he continued to caress and learn her taste.

He drew back way before he was ready, but this was supposed to be a simple good night kiss. He wanted more. Way more. Boone thought Hayden might too, but he didn't want to rush her. She was a mass of contradictions that drew him to her like a moth to a flame.

He waited for Hayden to open her eyes. She did, and he nearly groaned when her tongue came out and licked her lips, as if gathering up every last bit of his taste he'd left on her.

"Wow."

Boone smiled and ran his thumb over her now damp lips. "Yeah, wow. Thank you for inviting me tonight, Hay. I had a good time."

"Me too."

Boone reluctantly sat back and reached in his pocket for his phone. "Can I have your number? I'll call and we can figure out when you have time to go out again."

"Uh, yeah, sure. That's probably smart in case something comes up." Hayden pulled her phone out of her own back pocket and they exchanged numbers.

"Stay there, I'll come around and walk you to your door."

"It's not necessary."

"It is to me."

Hayden shrugged and stayed put as he got out and came around to her side. He opened her door and she slid out of the truck. He grabbed her hand and they walked to her apartment door. She unlocked it and turned back to him.

Boone leaned down and kissed her lightly on the lips, not allowing himself to deepen it, then pulled back. "I'll talk to you later, Hay."

"Yeah, okay. I'd like that."

"'Bye."

"'Bye, Boone."

Boone waited until she closed the door and he heard the deadbolt latch. He walked back to his truck feeling lighter and happier than he had in months. For once he wasn't worrying about what Dana might be planning on doing next. All he could think about was Hayden, and how damn cute she was. He couldn't wait to learn more about her.

8

———

THE NEXT WEEK of work went by for Hayden as normal...as normal as it could for a sheriff's deputy. She'd received a few texts from Boone. They were all light, like asking how her day was going and things like that. But each one made her gut squeeze. She'd never had a guy court her before, and that's what this was feeling like.

Hayden rolled her eyes at herself. She was thirty-three years old, way too old to fall into the trap of getting all starry-eyed when a boy texted her. But since she'd never had it before, it felt good. Really good.

She'd asked Boone if he'd seen or heard from Dana again, and he'd said no, but Hayden wasn't sure if she believed him or not. It wasn't that she thought Boone was weak or less of a man for being...abused, for lack of a better word, by Dana. He certainly was strong enough to wrestle the steers on his farm when he needed to get them to do what he wanted them to do, and he was one of the most masculine, take-charge, in-your-face males she'd ever met.

But he'd told her point blank that he wouldn't defend himself against Dana if she decided to go crazy on him. And Hayden knew in her heart Dana hadn't given up. Boone was a hell of a catch. And if Dana was half crazy, as Hayden suspected, she was going to keep at him, throwing temper tantrums as if she were a toddler.

The only bad part to the week was her semi-regular phone call from her parents. Her mom had called to remind her about coming to dinner in a couple of weeks. Hayden felt horrible for the uncharitable thoughts she had about her folks, so she wasn't about to disrespect them outright by refusing to see them. Every month or so her mom made arrangements for her to come to their house and have dinner. Hayden had no idea how her parents felt about those meals, but they were excruciating for her.

Hayden never spoke with her dad on the phone; he didn't really like talking to her when they weren't face-to-face, but she knew he expected her to show up like a dutiful child.

Hayden put the impending dinner out of her mind for the moment. Tomorrow night, she'd be going out with Boone to the Cow Town Stampede. The only time she'd been inside the huge country-western bar was when they'd been called for a disturbance. She hadn't really been thinking about anything other than making sure all the patrons were safe, not to mention that she and her fellow deputies were safe, and getting the out-of-control drunk away from the building. He'd actually been a good guy; he'd just drunk too much, trying to drown his sorrows from his broken engagement that day.

Hayden was nervous about the outing. She'd be out of her league, and while she thrived on figuring out new situations when she was in uniform, being off duty in a new and uncomfortable setting was a different thing altogether.

She'd actually broken down and told Dax about her date with Boone, and how she was nervous about figuring out what to wear to the country bar. He'd obviously told his girlfriend, Mackenzie, because Hayden had received a call from Mack the day before. She'd offered to come over and help her get ready.

Hayden had almost declined out of habit, but remembered how she'd felt as she'd gotten ready for her first date with Boone. She'd wished for a girlfriend to help her figure out what to wear. So she'd accepted Mack's offer for help. She'd be over later that night to help her get ready.

Hayden had never really had many girlfriends growing up. She hadn't been allowed to go to birthday parties for her classmates, and sleepovers were out of the question. Hayden had never been invited to a high school dance while in school, but by that time, she hadn't even missed it. She'd been too busy trying to live up to her father's expectations...and feeling like she was failing.

Growing up as she had, she'd been robbed of the joys of teenage girldom. Hayden supposed she should be bitter about it, but she wasn't. She had a good life, a job that she enjoyed, and good friends. It was about time she tried to cultivate some *girl*friends for the first time in her life. There was no one around now to stop her.

Hayden got off work around six and rushed home. Mack said she'd be over at seven. She snarfed down a microwave mac and cheese dinner and stood in front of her closet trying to decide what Mack would think about her taste in clothes. Before she had much time to contemplate, her doorbell rang.

Hayden looked through the peep hole and, seeing it was Mackenzie, opened the door. Mack turned and waved at Dax, who was sitting in his car, waiting to make sure she got inside safely. Hayden again felt that tug in her chest at seeing the protectiveness Dax showed to Mack. No one had ever cared if she got inside wherever she was going after she'd been dropped off. She buried her jealousy deep, where it should stay, and welcomed Mack.

"Hey, Mack. Thanks for coming over."

"No problem! I'm thrilled you invited me. Seriously! You're really good friends with Dax, and any friend of Dax's is a friend of mine."

Hayden smiled at Mackenzie. The other woman was a bit older than her, but Hayden was a couple inches taller. Standing next to her, though, Hayden felt frumpy. Mack had the kind of curves all the guys Hayden worked with drooled over. Hayden was strong and muscular, and didn't have near the curves Mack did.

"I'm not sure this is going to work." The words came out unbidden and Hayden blushed at her uncharacteristic candor.

Mack didn't seem to notice, or at least she ignored, the panic in her voice. "Sure it will."

"I don't have any girly kinds of clothes."

Mack turned to Hayden and looked her up and down. "Hayden, I've seen how the guys treat you, and I think I've been guilty of following their lead, but believe me when I say—you're *all* girl."

Hayden scoffed. "Yeah, right. Look at me." She gestured to her chest and hips, then to Mack's. "And look at you."

Mackenzie didn't even pause. "And look at your hair compared to mine. You have beautiful, lush red hair—granted, you keep it up most of the time, but it's absolutely beautiful curled around your shoulders. I have stupid light brown hair that doesn't do anything I want it to."

Seeing she wasn't really getting through to the other woman, Mack tried again. "Hayden, you're really pretty. I know you don't see it, but I'm thrilled as all get out that Boone does. I saw the way he looked at you the other night. He couldn't take his eyes off you. You don't have the same size boobs as me, and your hips are narrower, but jeez, girl, your body is smokin' hot! The shot of you in my charity calendar was one of the most popular pictures. I think half of Dax's department has that calendar and I swear they all have it up in their offices...turned to your picture. Seriously, you don't have an inch of extra fat anywhere on you; you were made to wear short skirts and low-cut shirts."

Hayden rolled her eyes and ignored the calendar comment. She was so embarrassed that she'd agreed to be in the charity calendar and while she didn't think she was a troll, she didn't think the picture really looked much like her at all. "And I don't have either in my closet."

Mack ignored the eye rolling and said earnestly, "I'm not saying I'm the fashionista of the year, but trust me to help you find something to wear tomorrow night that will knock not only Boone's socks off, but every single guy at Cow Town. In fact, I'll make you a bet."

"What kind of bet?"

"I'll bet you that five guys—other than Boone—ask you to dance."

Hayden snorted in laughter. "That's a bet you're sure to lose. It'd be like taking candy from a baby if I made that bet with you. No guy, ever, has asked me to dance."

Mack crossed her arms over her chest. "So it's a bet then?"

"What are the stakes?"

"If I win, you'll let me take you shopping."

Hayden scrunched up her face in distaste.

"Yeah, that's what I figured, you hate shopping. I'm not ready to go to New York City and take on the fashion world, but I think I can find you some great stuff. Those are my terms."

"What if I win?"

"You decide."

Hayden thought about it. She knew there was no way any guy would ask her to dance. She'd been out before, and not one man had even looked her way once. She hated to bet on something like this, because she knew she'd feel like a loser, but she'd always had a competitive streak and she couldn't resist.

Shopping was her least favorite thing to do in the world. Hayden never knew what to buy, and she had absolutely no fashion sense. It was easier to pick up jeans and shirts and stuff at the big box store or online. Spending a day trying on clothes and acting like she knew what she was doing? Torture. But since there was no way she'd lose, Hayden felt safe agreeing.

"When I win, you have to sign up for my self-defense class for women I'm starting next month...and you have to get at least five others to come with you."

"Done." Mack's response was quick and firm. "And

so you know, I was planning on coming anyway. So thanks for the sucker bet."

The women smiled at each other for a beat before Hayden asked, "Drink?"

"Sure. What'cha got?"

Hayden went to her fridge. "Diet soda, water, iced tea and fancy flavored water." She shuffled some things out of the way and then said excitedly, "Oh, and I have some of those wine cooler things...watermelon flavor."

"Oh hell yeah, the watermelon one for sure! I'm not driving."

They both laughed and Hayden stood up with the drinks in her hand. She twisted off the tops and both women took large swallows of the sweet alcoholic concoction.

"Man, that's so freaking good," Mack said with a sigh.

"Um hum," Hayden agreed. Anything sweet and alcoholic was her favorite thing to drink. She might choke beer down when she went out with the guys, but thought the taste was absolutely disgusting.

"Come on, let's go see what we have to work with," Mack said.

"Don't get your hopes up," Hayden warned her with a laugh.

"I'm sure I can find something that'll work."

"If you mean jeans and T-shirts, you will."

Mack merely laughed and took another swallow of her drink. "Let's see what we can find."

Hayden followed Mack into her bedroom, knowing it would literally take a fairy godmother and a magic wand to find anything remotely sexy in her closet.

After two hours of laughter, and a couple more drinks, Hayden stood looking into the mirror on the back of her closet door and stared at herself in wonder.

It seemed that Mackenzie really did have magic up her sleeve, even without a wand.

After looking for around twenty minutes, and not finding even one skirt in the depths of Hayden's closet, Mack took matters into her own hands and made Hayden put on an older pair of jeans. Then she started hacking away until they were shorts. Really *short* shorts. Way shorter than anything Hayden was comfortable wearing. Shorter than the pair she'd worn the other day when she'd been out to lunch with Boone and the stupid man at the station thought she was a prostitute.

She'd tried to protest, saying only teenagers or hookers would wear shorts that showed as much as these were, and much more than she was comfortable with, but Mack had merely blown her off. The only consolation Hayden had was that her butt cheeks weren't showing...barely. Mack had dug around the closet and drawers until she'd found a blouse Hayden had bought on a whim a couple of years ago.

It was dark green and had small sleeves that draped over her shoulders to her upper arms. The back was cut low—low enough that there was no way

Hayden would be able to wear a bra. Not that she really needed one. Her B cup was small enough that she could go without, but not so small that if she wore a push-up bra, she wouldn't have nice cleavage.

The front of the flowy shirt was high cut, almost up to her neck, and the material was silky, shimmery, and didn't cling at all. There were no buttons or zippers or flounces, it simply draped over her body and left what was underneath to the imagination.

Hayden shifted uncomfortably in front of the mirror. She almost couldn't believe the person she was seeing reflected back was her. She looked...good. Feminine. Hayden couldn't remember the last time she felt this pretty.

"And you need to wear your hair down...well, at least partly. It's thick and I bet it gets really hot, and you'll be in a bar, but maybe just pull it back a bit away from your face, leave it down in the back. And shoes. You rocked those cowboy boots you were wearing the other night, but I don't think they'll work with this outfit."

Hayden turned and watched in amusement as Mack got on her hands and knees and sorted through her shoes. She had no idea what the other woman was looking for.

"Ah *ha!*" Mack sat on her heels and held up a pair of strappy sandals. They didn't have high heels, there was no way Hayden could ever wear anything with more than a two-inch heel, but she'd bought the shoes probably around the same time she'd bought the top she was currently wearing. They were black, open toed, and had straps that wound around her ankles.

"Try them on. I want to see the whole outfit!" Mack exclaimed.

Hayden did as requested, and again, looked disbelievingly at herself in the mirror. The shoes accented her strong calf muscles and the two inches they gave her somehow made her legs look even longer than when she was standing barefoot. There was a lot of skin showing, but as Hayden turned to look at her butt, she realized that she felt good. Really good.

"Oh my God. It's perfect!"

Hayden smiled at Mack, feeling excited about the next night now that she had something to wear.

"We are *so* gonna shop all damn day when you lose that bet!"

Hayden grimaced.

"Hey, I'll go easy on you, I promise." Mack laughed.

"What about earrings?" Hayden asked, bringing a hand up to her earlobe.

"I've got a pair I think would go great with your outfit if you wanted to borrow them. I think the green would match perfectly and they're dangly."

Hayden didn't even think. "Yes."

"You don't even know what they look like."

Hayden threw her arms out to encompass the room and the disaster of clothes strewn about. "Mack, look around. I'm a mess. I have absolutely no fashion sense. If you say they're perfect, they'll be perfect."

"Okay, awesome. I'll swing by the station tomorrow and drop them off for you."

Hayden turned to Mack, who was still kneeling on the floor. The feelings of gratitude and appreciation welling up inside her. She'd never had a friend to sit around with and try on clothes. "Thank you, Mackenzie. I appreciate this more than you know."

Mack stood up gracefully and hugged Hayden. "Me too. Seriously. This was fun. I hope we can do it again... and we will, once we go shopping and get you a shit ton of new girly clothes to wear that'll drive Boone out of his mind. I know this. Not with Boone, but with Dax. It's ridiculous how the man sees me naked every day. He knows what I look like, but the second I put on a sexy dress, he can't seem to control himself...and wants to take it off as soon as he can. So while men might like what we look like without clothes on, they love when we cover up our bits and tease them. Boone is gonna lose his mind when he sees you, just as every man at that bar tomorrow night will."

Hayden laughed, glad Mack had broken the intense atmosphere. "I still think you're wrong. You can dress me up, but I'm still me."

Mack didn't even hesitate. "And the *you* you are is gonna knock Boone's socks off. He'll be fighting off those cowboys tomorrow night."

Hayden rolled her eyes. "Whatever.

"Okay, take it all off and let's go and drink ourselves silly until Dax comes to get me."

"I have to work tomorrow."

"Yeah, shit. Me too. Okay, well, we'll just talk then."

Hayden nodded and carefully took off her clothes and put them on her dresser, ready for the next night. She put back on her sweats and a T-shirt, threw her hair back up into a ponytail, and the two women went back down to the living room. Before Hayden knew it, it was time for Mack to go.

Dax knocked on the door and Hayden let him in. He gave Hayden a chin lift before smiling lovingly at Mack as she scurried around the house, making sure she had all her stuff. Mack reminded Hayden she'd drop off the earrings and she left, Dax's arm around her shoulders and her arm around his waist.

Hayden watched as Dax opened his car door for Mack, then bent her back over his arm and kissed the stuffing out of her. It was as if they hadn't seen each other in months, rather than just a few hours. Hayden closed her door, giving them privacy—well, as much privacy as they could get in the middle of a busy parking lot.

She sighed and turned off the television. She made sure the doors were locked and headed down the hallway to her bedroom. She got ready for bed and checked that her service weapon was loaded and sitting on the bedside table. She snuggled under the covers with Ellie the Elephant and buried her face into the scruffy stuffed animal's belly.

She'd be going on a date with Boone tomorrow. A real date. She'd been out with men before, but they weren't what she'd really call dates…just precursors to sex. Hayden had known going in what the men wanted, and she'd wanted the same thing.

But Boone was different. Hayden really liked him, and that scared the shit out of her. So far it seemed he saw more than the tomboy cop, but only time would tell. Wearing the feminine, sexy outfit Mack had picked out for her was so far outside her comfort zone it wasn't funny, but at least she wouldn't run into any of her coworkers. The last thing she wanted was for them to catch sight of her all gussied up. She'd fought long and hard for them to see her as a competent police officer, and somehow she knew her short shorts, and backless shirt, would make them feel weird around her and possibly make them act differently.

Hayden fell asleep dreaming of the kisses she'd shared with Boone, and hoping she'd get more tomorrow night—and woke up with thoughts of Boone. The day was going to drag on, she knew it.

9
———

THE DAY HAD SUCKED. Hayden had been called as backup for a drunk and disorderly man. When she'd gotten there, the man, in his mid-twenties, was resisting arrest. Hayden hadn't missed a beat and had entered the fray. Three minutes later, and after getting kicked in the face by the man's flailing foot, he'd been subdued and stuffed in the back of Juan's patrol car.

Juan had thanked her for her help and had driven off with the protesting, swearing man.

The rest of the shift hadn't been any better. Some days were like that, more pissed-off people than ones who were thankful for a deputy's protection.

To top it off, Hayden was later than usual getting home because of a report she'd had to redo, which she'd somehow deleted entirely after finishing it. It was pushing eight-thirty and she'd just gotten out of the shower and dried her hair when her doorbell rang.

She threw on the ratty robe she hardly ever wore and rushed to the front door. After verifying it was Boone, she wrenched open the door, apologizing before it was open all the way.

"I'm so sorry, Boone. I'm not ready yet. Work was a bitch today and I just got home about thirty minutes ago. Come in and make yourself comfortable. I'll be out in just a bit, just give me about ten or fifteen minutes, okay?"

"What the hell, Hay?"

Hayden looked up at Boone in surprise. "Huh?"

He put a finger under her chin and lifted her head. "What happened to your face?"

"Oh." Hayden shrugged. "Part of the job."

"Have you put ice on it?"

"Ice?"

"Yeah, Hay. Ice."

"No. I haven't had time. It's fine. I'll just go and—" She didn't finish her thought before Boone moved.

He removed his hand from her chin and reached down for her hand. He grasped it in his own and towed her toward her kitchen.

"Boone, seriously. It's fine. This happens all the time. I have to finish getting ready."

Hayden bounced off of Boone's back as he stopped their progress toward her kitchen suddenly and without warning. "It happens all the time?"

Shit. Hayden nodded, but lowered her voice and tried to soothe him. "Yeah, but I'm fine. It's not a big deal. I bruise easily. It'll be better in the morning."

Boone started walking again until he got to the kitchen. He pulled out a stool. "Sit."

Hayden didn't say anything, but sat on the stool he'd indicated. She could've wrenched her hand out of his grasp at any point, but she didn't feel like Boone was any danger to her, and she'd been bemused. Hayden put her elbows on the counter and leaned on them as she watched him open her freezer, get out a tray of ice cubes, put a few into a dishcloth that was hanging on her fridge and twist it up. He walked over and sat on a stool next to her. He put his free hand to the side of her head and turned it toward him.

When she didn't balk or do anything to stop him, he held the makeshift ice pack to her face gently. When Hayden put her hand up to hold the cloth, he brushed it aside. "I got it."

Hayden wasn't sure what to say. She felt awkward and uneasy. This was so outside her comfort zone, she might as well be on another planet.

"How did it happen?"

Knowing what he meant, Hayden gave him a rundown of the encounter with the drunk man that day.

He didn't immediately say anything when she was done, but finally he nodded. "Does it hurt?"

Hayden shook her head and knew she had to

change the subject. "How're *you*? Any more drama with Dana?"

"No. I think she finally got the hint."

Hayden didn't disagree with him outwardly, even though she doubted the crazy lady had indeed given up. She'd looked into her eyes that day at Boone's house...Dana wasn't going to let Boone go without a fight. Hayden had seen it too many times. She let it drop.

Loving the feel of his hand on her waist as the other held the ice pack to her face, she asked, "So, who will I be meeting tonight?"

"My best friend, Tucker, should be there. He's a firefighter on the west side of the city. We went to high school together. He's a couple years younger than me. I think two of my employees will also be there, and we'll probably see some of the men I do business with and some casual acquaintances as well."

"Okay."

Boone, obviously reading her nervousness, reassured her. "They're going to love you, Hayden. Don't worry."

"Uh huh."

Boone smiled at her. He lifted the ice and leaned toward her to peer closer at her bruised cheek.

Hayden took in a breath. He was so close, all it would take would be for her to lean forward two inches and their lips would be touching.

"It looks better. I don't like it at all, but hopefully

the ice will keep it from turning too purple." He ran his fingers lightly over her slightly discolored cheek.

Hayden caught her breath at his touch. His hands weren't smooth. They were rough from working on the farm all day, but somehow the callouses on his finger sent heat straight down between her legs. She shifted on the chair. "I should probably go and finish getting ready," she said breathlessly.

"Yeah." But Boone didn't move.

"Boone?"

He didn't say anything, but leaned toward her again and kissed her bruised cheek, right where she'd been kicked in the face. But he didn't stop there. He absently put the ice pack on the counter and took her head in both of his hands. He kissed her forehead, her other eye, her nose, and finally, Boone settled his lips over her own.

Hayden couldn't stop the small, needy sound that escaped her as she immediately opened her mouth to take him in. She leaned forward and put her hands on his thighs as they explored each other's mouths. She vaguely felt Boone shift under her a second before he lifted his head from hers.

"God, woman. You make me want to forget taking you anywhere tonight...except to your bed."

Hayden was still lost in the kiss, otherwise she probably would've thought more before she spoke. "Sounds good to me."

Boone chuckled. "Oh no. I'm taking you out. I want

to show you off. But I'm not going to forget your finger-nails digging into my thighs anytime soon."

"Oh!" Hayden shook her head, realizing suddenly where she was and what she'd just been doing. She lifted her hands from his lap, realizing she *had* been flexing her fingers against him.

Boone put one hand over hers and brought it back down to his thigh. "I like it. I like knowing I can affect you like that." Seeing her blush, and more than charmed by it, Boone chuckled and took pity on her. "Go get ready, Hay. I was telling the truth about wanting to take you to bed, but I want to show you off more...at least right now. If you ask me later, I'll probably want to kick my own ass for taking you to the meat market tonight. I'll be fighting to keep you to myself the second we walk in."

Hayden dropped her hands from Boone and shook her head. "I don't know why you and Mack keep saying that. I'm just me. No one has taken a second glance at me before. Tonight's not going to be any different, no matter what clothes I put on to spruce myself up with."

Boone stood up from his seat and kissed Hayden on the forehead. "I'll enjoy watching you discover how many people find 'just you' irresistible."

Hayden rolled her eyes and got up, smoothing her robe over her legs, making sure she was covered. "Give me ten or so minutes?"

"Take as long as you need, Hay. We're in no hurry."

"Okay, thanks. I won't make you wait too long."

Boone nodded and watched as Hayden hurried down the hall, enjoying the sight of her backside as she disappeared.

Twenty minutes later, which was honestly about ten minutes before he expected to see her, Boone watched, speechless, as Hayden came out of her room.

"I'm sorry. I didn't mean to take so long. I couldn't get my hair right, and then I couldn't find the earrings Mack gave me just this afternoon." She stopped at the entrance to the main room and looked at Boone, who was staring wordlessly at her. "What? Do I look okay?"

Boone slowly walked toward Hayden, almost not believing he was seeing the same person he'd just been sitting with twenty minutes earlier. She was wearing shorts that showed off her muscular and toned legs. He'd seen her legs before, but her shorts tonight were shorter than when they'd gone out to lunch. He could see the definition in her thighs, and the vision of those same muscles flexing as she rode him flashed through his lust-filled brain.

The slight heels she was wearing only accentuated how long and sexy her legs were. He couldn't help but imagine what her legs would feel like wrapped around his hips as he pumped into her warm, willing body. He could even almost feel the heels she'd leave on her feet digging into his ass as he took her. It was inappropriate, but he couldn't stop the thought. Boone's gaze ran up Hayden's body to her hair. She'd left it down, mostly. It was pulled away from her face with a barrette that held some of the strands at the back of her head. There were large curls resting on her chest under her collarbone and he just knew it'd be flowing down her back as well. The green of her shirt looked fucking phenomenal with her red hair. His mouth actually watered at the vision standing in front of him. Suddenly he realized what she asked.

"Do you look okay?" Boone repeated, unbelievingly.

Hayden nodded, unsure.

Boone could tell she hated not feeling secure, but he was about two seconds away from hauling her into his arms and following through with his earlier threat to carry her down the hall and to her bed. His cock was so hard he was surprised Hayden didn't back away from him in disgust and call him a pervert. He licked his lips and said, "Yeah, Hay. You look great." The words were inadequate, but the blood in his dick was obviously making it hard for him to think straight.

Hayden turned away from him, saying, "Okay, Good. Let me grab my ID out of my wallet. Mack gave me a little purse thing, she called it a wristlet, to use tonight. I'll put my ID and some money in there and then I'll be ready to— Boone!"

Her words were cut off as Boone wrapped a hand around her waist and hauled her into him. He turned her so they were facing each other. He was taller than she was, even with the two-inch heels she was wearing. She looked up at him in surprise.

"Do you look okay? Jesus, Hay. I thought you looked absolutely stunning...then you turned around."

Boone ran one hand over her bare spine, and the other dipped dangerously low. Hayden could feel the pinky finger of his hand stop just below the waistband of her jean shorts. She inwardly cursed when she felt a blush bloom over her face. She'd actually forgotten how little material there was on the back of her shirt, but Boone's hands caressing her bare skin was a sure-fire reminder.

"You aren't leaving my side tonight. This is the sexiest fucking shirt I've ever seen. Demure and polite from the front, covering you from neck to waist, but pure sin from the back." His hands continued to roam up and down her bare back. He smiled when she broke out in goosebumps at his touch.

He moved one hand from her upper back, leaving the other low on her spine, skimming his fingers farther under her waistband. He put his knuckle under her chin and raised it. "Forgive me for my lame compliment earlier. You don't look great, you look absolutely stunning, Hayden. But it's not your clothes...it's you."

"Boone—"

"Yes, your hair is beautiful, and this is the sexiest shirt I've ever seen and it makes me think of nothing else but taking you out of it, but honestly? It's *you* I'm most attracted to. Your toughness, your loyalty to your friends and your job, and your determination. But I see more. I see the soft, squishy part of you that you try to hide from the world." Boone moved his hand from her chin and down the front of her shirt and rested it on the top swell of her left breast. "I sense a great hurt in you, here, deep in your heart. But it's that hurt that's made you who you are today...a woman full of contradictions who I want to get to know better."

Boone watched as her eyes filled with tears. "Don't cry, Hay. I'm not saying this to make you cry. I'm obviously bungling it. But yes, you look 'okay.' You look more than fucking okay."

She sniffed and pulled herself together before finally nodding and saying simply, "Good."

Boone smiled. She was so freaking cute. "Shall we go?"

"Yeah."

Boone didn't let go, but continued to look down at her.

"Boone? You have to let go of me if we're going to leave."

"This is a bad idea."

"What is?"

"Taking you to the bar tonight."

Hayden's brow wrinkled in confusion. "Why? I thought you wanted to go there."

"Because every man in there is going to take one look at you and want to see you sprawled on his sheets."

"Boone," Hayden protested. "That's not true!"

"It is. But you're with me."

Hayden started getting pissed now. She'd been feeling all soft and feminine, but now she was irritated. She forcefully stepped away from his embrace. "Boone Hatcher, this isn't cool. Seriously? You want to put a leash on me and parade me through the bar? Better yet, maybe you can just pee on me to make sure other guys know I'm your property."

"Hayden—"

"Maybe I should go back to my room and put on my uniform. Would that make you feel better? Wait, I have it: I'll just put on some sweats and an old ratty T-shirt and—" Hayden squealed as she suddenly found herself hanging off of Boone's shoulder as he strode into the living room. "Boone!"

Hayden knew she could get out of his hold, but shit, he was six-three and it'd hurt if she hit the ground from this high up. Besides that, she knew Boone wouldn't drop her. She decided to save her law enforcement tricks for a different time.

He got to the couch and leaned over, dumping her on her back with her knees hanging over the arm of the sofa, so her lower body was tilted up. He immediately crouched over her.

Hayden put both hands on his chest and pushed. "Jeez, Boone, was that necessary?"

"I wasn't kidding when I said I wanted to show you off, but I'm finding it hard to believe you're with *me*, Hayden. You're amazing. Not only because of your looks, but your personality. I'm a simple farmer. I'm comfortable with my ranch and my life. I know I'm not bad to look at, but I also know there are plenty of other men out there who are irresistible to women. I find myself wanting to punch any guy who even *looks* at you...and we haven't even left your house yet. I'm sorry for putting this badly, but I'm attracted to you. I want you. I want to bury myself so deep inside you, you don't know where I end and you begin. I've lusted after women before, but this feels like more. Much more. I know it's too early, but I want you to know. I need you to understand that I don't think this is a passing thing. At least not for me."

"Boone—"

"And the thought of other men looking at you, seeing all your sexy skin, makes me crazy. Maybe you should put on a pair of jeans."

"I don't want to be with any other guy. And I still don't think anyone else will even bother to look at me, no matter if I'm wearing shorts, jeans or a mini-skirt. Have you thought about the fact *I'm* concerned about other women eyeballing *you*? You say that you know you're 'not bad to look at,' but Boone, I have to say, you're six feet three of hot, sexy cowboy." She fingered the red button-up shirt he was wearing. "All I can think about is ripping this open and seeing your broad chest. And I know if *I'm* thinking it, so will other women."

Boone smiled down at Hayden, relieved that he wasn't alone in his lustful feelings. "How about we make each other a deal?"

"What kind of deal?"

"You keep other women away from me, and I'll keep the men away from you."

"Deal."

"Hell, Hay, you didn't even hesitate."

"Nope, you haven't been listening to me. I like you, Boone. I admire the fact that you own your own business. You work hard, you're tall and handsome, and you're jealous of other men even looking at me. The chemistry between us is off the charts...and something I've never felt with anyone before. What more could a girl want?"

She watched as his face turned serious. "I have baggage."

Hayden waved her hand in the air. "Dana? Pbsst."

"I know it's hard for you to understand why I let her do those things to me."

"It's okay."

"It's not, but that's a conversation we'll have another day. Right now, we have a night out to get to...if you still want to go."

"I still want to go."

Boone stood and put a hand out to help Hayden up. "Right. Then let's get going. And Hay?"

"Yeah?"

He leaned down and kissed her lightly on the lips. "You look absolutely amazing."

Hayden smiled at him. "Thanks. You too."

Hayden gathered her ID, some cash and her cell

phone and put it in the wristlet Mack had given her, not liking she couldn't bring her service pistol with her; she had absolutely no place to put it. Hoping she wouldn't need it, and feeling more naked without her pistol than she did in the shirt she was sort of wearing, Hayden locked her door behind her and put her keys inside the little purse as well.

They walked silently to the car, Hayden more than aware of the warmth of Boone's hand against the bare skin on her back. She shivered. She hadn't thought wearing a shirt like this through. She'd had no idea how much of a turn-on it'd be to have Boone touching her skin.

It was going to be a long night.

10

—————

Hayden sipped the screwdriver Boone had bought her and looked around the bar, not able to help scanning for trouble. She'd never been able to leave her job behind, especially not in a crowded bar like the Cow Town.

"Would you like to dance?"

Hayden turned to the voice and suppressed a grimace. At first, being asked to dance had been surprising and flattering, but after the fifth man, and after losing the bet with Mack, it'd gotten old.

Now it just seemed disrespectful. She was sitting with Boone at a bar table, they were sitting very close together, even holding hands, enjoying each other's company and the atmosphere, and every now and then a man would come up and ask her to dance right in front of Boone. She'd had enough.

"Look, cowboy. I have no idea what makes you

think it's okay to come on to me when I'm sitting here with my date. He's had his hand on me all night and I think it's pretty obvious we're together. So you coming over here to ask me to dance is just rude and presumptuous."

Thinking she'd delivered a pretty good smack down, Hayden was nonplused when the man laughed and clapped Boone on the back. "Pretty little wild filly you've got there. Enjoy the ride."

"Plan to," was all Boone said as the man nodded at him, tipped his hat at Hayden, and walked away.

"What the ever-loving hell, Boone? Enjoy the ride?" Hayden asked, scowling at the man at her side.

Boone leaned in. "You're in cowboy country, Hayden."

"Yeah? And?"

"It means they can ask, but I've got to be the one who agrees."

"Huh. So you're okay with them asking me to dance even though it's obvious we're out together? And they're asking *me* to dance, but *you* get to answer?"

"Yup."

"Okay, this is crazy. Did we somehow get transported back to the eighteen hundreds? I wish I was wearing my uniform. At least then they'd have some respect for me."

Boone put his hand on hers on the table and waited until she looked up at him. "They respect you,

Hayden. If they didn't, they'd just come up and grab you and pull you out to the dance floor."

"I want someone to try that. Just once. He'd find himself flat on his back before he knew what hit him."

"Bloodthirsty little thing."

"And another thing, why does everyone keep calling me little? That's annoying too."

"Because next to me, and a lot of the other guys in here, you *are* little."

"Humph." Hayden wouldn't admit it, even if tortured, but she loved that Boone saw her as little. It made her feel more feminine. Somehow her uniform made her seem taller than she was. She'd never had a problem with men calling her "little" when she was wearing it.

"Do you want to dance?"

Hayden looked up at the sultry words, and decided to take matters into her own hands. Enough was enough. "Oh good Lord." The slutty-looking woman standing next to their table was practically drooling over Boone. "No, he doesn't want to dance. He's mine. He's got his hand nearly down my pants, I'm almost sitting in his lap. He's fucking *mine*, so back the hell off already."

The woman rolled her eyes, but backed off. "Okay, jeez."

"Come 'ere, Hay."

Hayden stood from her perch on the bar stool and took the one step to plaster herself to Boone's side.

She'd never been the jealous type, but seeing the tall, skinny woman coming on to him while she was sitting right there made her blood boil.

She squeaked as he lifted her up and put her on his lap so she was sitting sideways over his legs. "There, now maybe people will leave us alone."

Hayden laughed and relaxed into Boone. One hand was on her back and he ran his fingers along her waistband, up her back, then back down to her waist. The other hand was draped over her thighs. He'd occasionally lift it to take a drink of his beer, but then he'd rest it right back on her bare legs again when he was done. Hayden put one arm around his shoulder and the other on his forearm resting on her lap and relaxed into his hold, loving how it made her feel.

"Hey, Boone. How the fuck did *you* catch someone like this?"

Hayden looked up at another tall man—another *hot* tall man. If she wasn't with Boone, she might have taken a second look at this guy. She estimated he was shorter than Boone, but not by much. He was wearing black jeans, cowboy boots that had seen better days, a black Stetson, and a black shirt that looked like it actually had snaps instead of buttons. He should've looked ridiculous wearing all black, but it made him look dark and dangerous instead.

"Hey, Tucker, how the hell are you?" Boone lifted his chin in greeting and shook the other man's hand.

As Tucker pulled the stool Hayden had vacated

closer, he responded, "Good. You know, same ol', same ol'."

"Hayden, this is my friend, Tucker Jacobs, but he goes by 'Moose.' He's the firefighter I told you about. Moose, this is Hayden Yates. She's a sheriff's deputy."

"Wait...Moose? Is that *you*?"

"Deputy Yates? Shit, I didn't recognize you at all!"

"You two know each other?" Boone asked, confused.

Hayden blushed. Yeah, she knew Moose, and a lot of the other guys who worked at Station 7. "Yeah. We've seen each other at calls. Sometimes when they get dispatched to people's houses for medical issues, they need law enforcement backup. I actually helped out one of the guys from his station a few weeks ago when there was a break-in at his house, and his girlfriend couldn't be contacted. Remember, I told you about Beth and Cade?"

"Shit. That's right. She's okay though, right?"

Hayden nodded. "Yeah. She snuck out of the house, even though she's fighting a wicked case of agoraphobia, and hid in the woods behind it."

"Damn."

"Yeah, Beth is amazing," Moose said with a nod. "I heard from Sledge that you kicked Detective Chambers's ass on that one training circuit the other day. He was extremely impressed."

"Thanks. I got lucky."

"I doubt that. Cade doesn't throw out empty

compliments. By the way...you look good, Hayden," the large firefighter said with a grin and a wink.

Boone scowled at his friend and tightened his arm around Hayden's waist.

The other man merely laughed and held up his hands in capitulation. "Hands off. I got it. No worries, I've already got my eye on a woman, I don't need to steal yours. Hayden, what are you doing with this reprobate here?"

Hayden laughed and squeezed Boone's arm. "He felt sorry for me and decided to educate me on what real cowboys and cowgirls do for fun."

Hayden was actually glad Moose was there. She didn't know him that well, but the fact he was a firefighter helped her feel a lot more relaxed. She felt more comfortable being around another person who worked in the service industry like her. She'd met a few people who'd come up to the table to say hello to Boone, but Moose was the first one she felt she could be herself around.

"Actually, she came out to the house when I had that last issue with Dana." It surprised Hayden that Boone was so honest.

"Ah. That bitch still giving you problems?"

"Not really."

"If you need help with that, all you got to do is say something. You know I'm there for you, man."

"I appreciate it, Moose. Thanks, but I've got it under control."

"Moose...can I ask a favor?" Hayden asked, knowing she was about to overstep her bounds, but she wanted to protect Boone as much as she could.

"Anything for a beautiful lady cop."

Hayden rolled her eyes, but continued. "I'm not condoning violence against women, but Boone won't defend himself against Dana. I get why, but she's crazy. She could hurt him." She stared at Moose, hoping he'd understand what she was saying.

"You know I don't work on this side of the city." Moose's voice was low and earnest. He got her.

"Guys..."

Hayden ignored Boone. She leaned forward but Boone's hand never left her body, she could feel his calloused fingers brush against the sensitive skin of her lower back as she moved. "Talk to your friends who work on this side then. Make sure they know what's going on. If she calls the cops, or sets a fire, or puts one finger on him, I want it documented that it was *her*, and not Boone, that did it."

"Done." Moose's response was immediate and heartfelt.

"Now, wait just a minute—"

Boone was again talked over when Moose told him, "I like this one, Boone. She's damn good at her job and anyone who wants to take that bitch down is okay in my eyes. Don't let her go. There's just something about a woman who works in a typically male field that is sexy as hell."

Hayden sat back and eyed the large firefighter. She didn't think he was really coming on to her, but there had been something in his tone that seemed... personal. Deciding she wasn't going to figure it out right this second, and wanting to enjoy her date, she leaned back and relaxed against Boone again. She picked up her drink and took a healthy swallow, squeezing Boone's arm as she did in reassurance.

"Another drink, Hayden?" Moose asked.

"Yeah, I think so. I'm not driving."

"Don't even think about it, Moose," Boone said in a semi-serious voice. "Mine. Got it?"

Moose laughed, knowing Boone was just messing with him...even if there was a bit of a serious edge to his words. "No worries. As I said, I've already got my eye on someone—and I've definitely got my work cut out for me with her."

Hayden hadn't looked away from Boone, and saw the irritated look flash over his face before it morphed into relief when Moose said he was interested in someone else. She ignored the fluttering in her belly at Boone's protective stance and his possessive words. "While you're getting me another drink, He-Man, I'm going to visit the little girls' room," she told him, needing a break from the lustful thoughts she was having about Boone.

"Make sure you use the one that says 'Fillies' and not 'Bulls,'" Moose warned, laughing.

"Yeah, think I got it. I might be a greenhorn, but I

do know the difference between a bull and a filly. Thanks."

Boone helped Hayden stand up, and leaned down to kiss her lightly. "I'll wait until you get back to go get our refills. Don't want to lose our seat."

She could taste the beer he'd been drinking on his lips and for once the flavor didn't disgust her. On Boone's lips, it was awesome. "Okay. Be back in a sec."

As Hayden walked away from the table, she heard Moose whistle low as she left. She merely shook her head in exasperation and kept going. The firefighter was totally going to embarrass her the next time she saw him in the field, but somehow it felt good to be seen as feminine for once.

She headed into the ladies' room, did her business, and was washing her hands when she was suddenly shoved violently into the counter.

Hayden reacted immediately and without thought, thanks to her training.

She whipped her leg around as she turned, knocking the legs out from under the woman who was standing behind her and who'd shoved her into the porcelain. No way was she letting some bar skank get the drop on her.

"Dana. I should've known," Hayden said, looking down at the pissed-off woman getting to her feet from the dirty bathroom floor.

"Stay away from him, whore! He's mine."

"You aren't allowed to be within two hundred feet

of him, Dana. You're in violation of the protection order just being in the same building. If you don't haul your ass out of here within ten seconds, I'm reporting you," Hayden threatened, knowing she was going to report her anyway.

Dana ignored the threat and put her hands on her hips and tried to stare Hayden down. "*You're* the one who needs to leave. Boonie's *mine.* I'm the only one who gets to suck his cock and I'm the only one he should be sticking his big dick inside of. He told me he'd never felt anything as hot and tight as my cunt."

Hayden tried to stay calm, even though the mere *thought* of Boone being intimate with the crazy bitch in front of her made her want to tear Dana's hair out then storm into the bar and ask Boone exactly what the *hell* he'd been thinking. The other woman was desperate and lashing out, reminding her that she and Boone had been intimate. Hayden knew Boone wasn't a monk, he'd had a life before they met, one which, unfortunately, included dating Dana.

Hayden tried to be reasonable. "I don't think you even really *like* Boone, Dana. Let him go. Find someone who loves you for who you are."

Dana didn't acknowledge her and continued her hate-filled spewing of ire. "*Boone* loves me for who I am and you'll regret it if you don't leave him alone. No one dumps me! *No one.*"

"That's it. I'm calling nine-one-one." Hayden reached to pull her phone out of her back pocket, and swore when she realized it was sitting in the little purse she'd left on the table.

Dana didn't say anything, just glared at Hayden and abruptly turned and left the restroom. Hayden followed her out and watched as she quickly disappeared into the crowd in the opposite direction from where Boone and Moose were sitting.

Hayden sighed in relief. The last thing she wanted was to have to mediate a showdown in the middle of the bar, but she would still report Dana violating the restraining order. She wanted every single violation reported, for Boone's sake.

She quickly walked back to the table, and saw two other men had joined Boone and Moose.

Boone held out his hand as she got near the table and Hayden took it. He leaned down and kissed her lightly, wrapping his arm around her waist and pulling her into his side before turning to the other men. "Hayden, this is Bub and Tommy, they work with me on the ranch."

Hayden held out her hand to each, understanding that the brief kiss and him locking her into his side was to show his employees she was off limits. "It's nice to meet you." Hayden had met quite a few men who either worked for or with Boone. Each of them were polite and had nothing but complimentary things to say about him.

"Same."

"You too."

Hayden turned to Boone. "I need to tell you something."

"Are you all right?"

"Yeah, of course."

"Can it wait until I go and get us refills?"

She grinned at him. He needed to know about Dana, but they were in a public place, she wouldn't dare do anything. She had time to tell him about his crazy ex. "Yes."

Boone smiled down at her again, then looked up at Moose. "You got this?"

"Got it."

"Got what?" Hayden asked, confused, looking between the two men. It was like they spoke their own coded language.

"He wants to go get refills, but doesn't want to leave you here alone. So I'm lookin' after you until he returns," Moose told her, taking a sip of his beer as if he hadn't just thrust them back into the wild wild west, where men could steal women and carry them off.

Hayden turned to Boone, hands on her hips and a frown on her face. "That's crazy. I'm perfectly able to look after myself, Boone."

He leaned in. "You might be able to take care of yourself in a dangerous situation, or when you have to tackle and subdue a drunk, but here, where every man in the place has been eyeballing you for the last two hours, waiting for his opportunity to put his hands on you, I'm not leaving you alone for a second, Hay."

Hayden rolled her eyes and waved a hand in the air at him. "Whatever, Boone. Just go. I'm thirsty."

He grinned at her. "Be right back." Then he leaned down and brushed his lips against the skin behind her ear and whispered, "Keep my chair warm for me, would ya?"

Hayden shivered at the warm air of his breath moving over her ear and nodded. Then scooted up on the chair Boone had been sitting in after he tapped her on the nose with a finger and left to go to the bar to get them refills. Loving the way he made her feel, Hayden pushed it down and turned to his friends. She didn't beat around the bush. She had just a moment to talk to his friends before Boone would be back. She wasn't going to keep what Dana had told her a secret from Boone, but she made the split second decision to tell him when they were home, not when they were out having a good time.

She turned on her serious-cop voice and looked each man in the eyes before she spoke to the group in general. "Look, I ran into Dana in the bathroom. She's bat-shit crazy and she's not going to give him up. I think you all know it, even if Boone is in denial. She already tried to get Boone arrested by hurting herself and saying Boone did it. You guys," Hayden looked at Bub and Tommy, "need to be alert and focused. If you see anything off at the ranch, call it in."

Hayden turned to Moose. "And I'm serious. Talk to your friends at other stations. I don't trust her to stay away. She's planning something, and I don't like it. I can talk to my law enforcement friends and the others at Station 7...the more people that are on the lookout, the better, as far as I'm concerned."

The men around the table nodded soberly.

"He won't defend himself against her. I don't know all of it—shit, you guys probably know more than I do —but because of that, he's opening himself up to being seriously hurt, or worse. I've seen way too many people on the job who swore up and down they could take care of themselves, only to end up on my friend Calder's table while he tried to figure out exactly how they died. Promise me you'll be on the lookout."

"We will. I've worked at Hatcher Farms since Boone was a kid. His dad was a great boss, but he ignored the abuse his friend was dishing out to his wife under his nose for years. Boone is better than his old man. He cares about every single person that works there, he wouldn't allow anyone under his watch to be harmed like Chris did to Lizzy, and I've never seen anyone so good with the cattle before." Bub's words were heart-felt and earnest. "And, unlike Chris, he'd never, *ever* hurt a lady."

Hayden nodded, liking how his employee defended him and feeling a bit better about the Dana situation, knowing these men would have Boone's back. The hair on the nape of her neck was standing up, and she'd learned never to ignore that feeling. Something wasn't right, but she couldn't see Dana anywhere and she had no idea what else it could be. She could see Boone at the crowded bar, but again, Dana wasn't anywhere near him.

Moose leaned closer. "I swear I'll do what I can to make sure he's covered."

"Thank you. Seriously."

"So...you're a cop, huh?" That came from Tommy.

Hayden smiled. She knew how to navigate *this* conversation. "Yup...been a sheriff's deputy going on ten years now."

They chatted about what she'd seen and the most extreme situations she'd been in, until Boone came back to the table. He had a beer and another screwdriver for Hayden. She scooted off the barstool and settled back into Boone's lap, at his urging, once he'd sat back down.

"Welcome back. Any issues?"

"What issues would I have getting two drinks?" Boone asked, with one eyebrow raised.

Hayden tried to shrug nonchalantly, not sure how well she was pulling it off. "None, apparently."

The five talked about nothing for another twenty minutes or so, until Hayden started feeling queasy.

"Hey, I think it's time I got home," she told Boone.

He looked down in concern. "You all right?"

"Yeah," Hayden reassured him, not feeling all right at all. "I just don't feel that good." She loved the way his hand lingered on her back and rubbed in circles, trying to make her feel better.

"Okay, no problem. It's late anyway. I'll see you guys later?" Boone asked his friends.

"Yeah, we need to get together more often," Moose told him.

Boone shook his hand. "Definitely."

He gave Tommy and Bub a chin lift. "I'm going to take Hayden home, but I'll be back at the farm afterwards. I'll see you guys in the morning."

Hayden liked that Boone wasn't assuming he'd be spending the night at her house, or that he'd be taking her back to his. Even though they had crazy intense chemistry, he was still taking things slow and not presuming anything. She liked that too.

"Sure thing, boss. See you later."

Boone helped Hayden stand—and frowned when she immediately doubled over. "Hayden?"

All thoughts of how impressed she was with Boone disappeared at the intense cramping in her stomach. "God, my stomach hurts. It must've been something I ate. I'll be fine." She tried to wave off Boone's concern. "Seriously, as soon as I get home and lay down, I'll be good."

Boone ignored her obvious lie and lifted her. Hayden would've protested, but it felt so good to be in Boone's arms, to be taken care of for once, and her stomach really did hurt. She wasn't sure she'd have been able to walk all the way to the car on her own.

Moose put her purse in her lap and Boone shouldered his way through the crowd to the door. They exited out into the cool night air and Hayden sighed in relief. God, it felt good to get out of the smoky bar.

Boone held Hayden against his chest, enjoying the feeling of her body against his. She really was a little thing compared to him. Her weight was akin to that of one of the calves on the farm that was a couple months old. She probably wouldn't like the analogy, but it was true. He hitched her higher and winced when she moaned.

"Hayden?"

"I wanna schleep on the foor."

"What, honey?" Boone leaned into Hayden so he could hear her better.

"The foor. Carpret is fluffy and crean."

"Oh shit." Boone's words were dismayed. She sounded way out of it and her words weren't coming out right. Something was seriously wrong. "Hayden, look at me." Boone shifted her in his arms. "Can you look at me, Hay?" When she met his eyes, Boone could see her pupils were dilated. She tried to put one of her hands on his face, but it fell uselessly into her lap before it reached his cheek.

"Where are the sows? They're so crute. Baby sows. I wanna see baby sows."

Boone opened the truck's passenger-side door and carefully placed Hayden on the seat. She immediately leaned to the side and continued to babble nonsense as she lay there. Boone took his phone out and texted

Moose, knowing his medical training would come in handy right about now.

Need you outside at my truck. Now.

Moose's response was immediate. *On my way.*

Boone reached in to Hayden and pulled her upright. "Come on, Hay. Look at me."

She rolled her head his way. Sounding completely lucid, which was scary since she'd just been slurring and jumbling her words, she announced, "I'm gonna puke."

Boone quickly stepped out of the way and helped Hayden lean over. She threw up all over the ground by his truck as Moose jogged up to them.

"What's up?"

"I think her drink was drugged."

"What?" Moose asked incredulously. "What the fuck?"

Hayden looked up at Moose. "Moosh! Your panchs are black and your shrrrt ish too."

"Jesus fucking Christ. How did this happen?" Moose asked, not saying anything about Hayden's random comment, leaning over to look more closely at her. The firefighter lifted up each of her eyelids as Boone answered.

"I have no idea. It had to have been that last drink I got her. She was fine before that."

Moose looked up at Boone. "She told us she ran into Dana in the bathroom. I don't know what was said, but I'd bet all the money I have, that bitch is somehow behind this."

Boone's fists clenched, but he didn't react outwardly more than that. "Dammit. When I was at the bar, some chick ran into me and almost fell. I put our drinks on the bar to make sure she was all right. She was really drunk and thought I was coming on to her. I quickly got her on her way again, but there was a minute or so where I didn't have eyes on our drinks. Dana wasn't anywhere near me, but she could've gotten someone to put something in her drink while I was preoccupied. *Fuck.* What do you think she was given? Oh shit, watch out, Moose!"

Hayden leaned over again and the men barely got out of way before she vomited once more. Boone leaned in and grabbed Hayden's hair, holding it back as she spit and gagged. She moaned and Boone's eyes narrowed in fury.

"Boo? I don't geel food."

It took Boone a second, but then he realized she'd just transposed the letters of the last two words. He ran his hand over her head gently. "I know you don't, Hay. We're gonna fix that."

"If I had to guess, I'd say probably GHB," Moose told Boone matter-of-factly as he pulled out his phone.

"So she wasn't roofied?" Boone asked in concern, looking over at his friend but not losing contact with Hayden.

"I doubt it. Rohypnol seems to act much faster. She

sat with us talking for at least twenty minutes before feeling any effects, and roofies typically don't make the victim throw up as violently as she's been doing. Vics usually pass out quicker than this...that's why it's called the date-rape drug. GHB can make someone speak improperly, throw up, and even sometimes hallucinate. In small doses, people use it to get a sort of high, but it can be very dangerous in high doses."

"Fuck."

"Yeah. She'll eventually lose consciousness and be out for a while, and she most likely won't remember a lot of what happened tonight, if anything. GHB is a lot like Rohypnol in that way." Tucker held the phone up to his ear and Boone could hear him talking to the cops. He leaned down to Hayden again.

"Hay?"

She looked up at him. "I don't feel goosh," she repeated miserably, tears leaking out of her eyes.

He ran his hand over her head. "I know, Hay," he crooned. "Don't worry. I'll take care of you."

"You will? No one's shaken mare of me before. I kin shake myself."

Boone understood what she meant just fine...and it hurt his heart. "I know you can. But tonight you don't have to. Okay?"

"Kay. Do you have Ellie?"

Her words were surprisingly clear. "Ellie?"

"Ellie. My elephone."

"No, but I'll get her for you."

"Home."

"Ellie's at home?" Boone wasn't sure who or what Ellie was...elephone didn't make any sense. But if she wanted Ellie, whoever or whatever that was, he'd do whatever it took to get it for her.

"Yeah. Wanna skate to home."

Moose hung up and said the paramedics were on their way, along with the cops.

Boone nodded but didn't take his eyes off of Hayden. "I'll take you home in a bit. Okay? The paramedics are gonna take a look at you first though."

Hayden rested her head back on the seat and Boone ran his hand down the side of her face. She was sweating and breathing fast as the drug worked its way through her body. God. Fucking Dana. It was one thing to hurt *him*, but to hurt someone else because of her delusions that they were still a couple? No fucking way.

"Kay. Boo?"

"Yeah, Hay? I'm right here."

"Like."

"Like?" Her speech was getting harder to understand. "What do you like?"

"You."

"I like you too, Hayden."

Her grand announcement was ruined by sudden coughing and more vomit that ended up in her lap and on his seat.

Boone sighed in relief at hearing the ambulance sirens in the distance. Thank God.

11

———

HAYDEN ROLLED OVER AND GROANED. She felt like complete shit. She had no idea why she felt so horrible. She opened her eyes and shut them quickly. Damn, it was bright. Was she hungover? She couldn't remember.

She squinted her eyes open this time and looked around.

What the fuck? Where was she? The room looked vaguely familiar to her, but she couldn't place it. Hayden sat up in a panic and looked around.

She was on a king-size bed and had been covered with a dark green fluffy quilt. She looked down and saw that she was wearing a large T-shirt with a cartoon cow on it. There was a speech bubble over the cow that said, *Think Chicken*.

Hayden was confused, and it almost hurt to think. She knew she didn't own a shirt like the one she was currently wearing. She wasn't wearing any pants, but had her panties on. Her feet were bare and her hair had been pulled back into a low ponytail on the back of her neck. She felt grimy and her mouth tasted like something had crawled in there and died.

Hayden moved her legs to the side of the bed and sat there for a moment, trying to get the energy to stand up and get out of there, wherever *there* was. She looked back to where she'd been lying—and saw Ellie the Elephant. She reached over and grabbed her precious stuffed animal and held it to her chest.

Oh my God...what the ever loving *hell* was going on?

Hayden heard a noise from across the room and looked up quickly, ready to do...something. She had no idea what, but she wouldn't sit around and be a victim.

"Hey, Hay. How do you feel?"

It was Boone. He was leaning against the doorjamb, legs crossed at his ankles, looking cool and relaxed, but when Hayden looked again, she could see dark bags under his eyes and the concern in them as he gazed at her.

"Confused."

Boone nodded. "I expected as much. Feel like a shower?"

"Uh huh."

"Okay, go ahead and jump in," Boone told her, gesturing to a door to the side. "There's stuff for you to put on when you get out and a new toothbrush by the sink. When you're done, come on out. We'll talk after you get something to eat."

"I'm at your house?" Hayden asked the question, but realized why it had looked familiar to her when she'd first opened her eyes. She recognized it now from that first day when she'd taken a look around trying to find proof Dana had been lying.

"Yeah."

Hayden eyed Boone. He hadn't moved, and was going out of his way to try to make her feel at ease. She wasn't sure it was working, but she appreciated the effort. He looked tired, and anxious, and he sure as shit wasn't relaxed.

"Hayden?"

She looked up. "Yeah?"

Boone paused and ran a hand over his head before he looked back up at her and asked carefully. "Do you mind if I give you a hug?"

Hayden could only shake her head. No she didn't mind. A hug sounded wonderful. She *needed* Boone's arms around her.

He came toward her slowly and sat on the mattress next to her. He reached out and carefully pulled her into his arms. Hayden melted into his embrace and wound her arms around his waist. Ellie fell to the ground, but neither of them seemed to notice.

Boone buried his head in the side of her neck and squeezed her tight. His arms easily wrapped around her back as he pulled her tightly into him. Neither of them said a word, Hayden because she was a big chicken at the moment. She was scared to death to figure out exactly what the hell was going on.

Finally, Boone pulled back. He framed her face with his big hands and smiled at her.

"Take your shower, Hay. I'll see you out in the kitchen when you're done."

He stood, leaned over and picked up her stuffed elephant, and held it out. Hayden took it, embarrassed. Boone ignored her embarrassment and leaned down to kiss her forehead. "Don't take forever."

Hayden glared up at him. He'd been so nice up until then. "I won't take forever. Jeez."

Boone only smiled at her and walked backwards to the door. "I'll get some food on."

"Boone?" Hayden called when she lost sight of him, feeling loathe to be away from him for some reason and trying to think of something to say to prolong his presence for just a moment.

He stuck his head around the doorjamb just as he was about to close it. "Yeah, Hay?"

Hayden grabbed a bit of the material of the T-shirt she was wearing and pulled it out as she asked. "Think Chicken?"

She loved the relieved smile that crept across his face. Relieved that she could make a joke? She wasn't sure. But he simply shrugged. "It's appropriate for a cattle farmer, don't you think?"

Hayden nodded and watched as he shut the door

behind him, and then she grinned. She was totally stealing his shirt. She got up on shaky feet and made her way into the bathroom. It wasn't exactly how she envisioned getting to spend time in Boone's wonderful shower, but she'd take it.

Twenty minutes later, she emerged with no better idea of how she'd gotten to Boone's house and what had happened the night before. She remembered being at the country and western bar, vaguely, but not much more than that. More alarming was the fact it was two o'clock in the afternoon. She'd about had a heart attack when she'd looked at her watch lying on the counter in the bathroom. The big black hole in her memory was more frightening than facing an armed thug bent on escaping prosecution.

She'd never done drugs in her life, she'd never had the urge to try them to see what the big deal was. She'd seen the way drugs destroyed people's lives, and she had no desire to even try the stuff. It was a slippery slope that too many people thought they could navigate with just one hit, one joint. Hayden didn't like losing control of her faculties and had stayed away from any kind of mind-altering substance...so she couldn't understand what was going on now.

There was also the question of how her precious stuffed animal had gotten to Boone's house, as well as how a pair of her jeans and a V-neck T-shirt—with a clean pair of panties and a bra—was waiting for her in

Boone's bathroom. Hayden didn't have a good feeling about it all.

She headed out the door and down the hall and put a hand over her stomach when it growled at the smell of bacon cooking. She entered the kitchen to see Boone at the stove turning pieces of sizzling bacon on the hot grill. On a plate next to him was two pieces of bread with lettuce and tomato slices.

"BLT, huh?"

"Yeah. That work?"

"Oh yeah. I love BLTs. But aren't you having one?" Hayden asked.

"Already ate."

Hayden nodded and pulled out a chair at the small table in the kitchen. She watched as Boone finished cooking the bacon and set a couple of slices on the sandwich.

"Mayo?"

"Ranch if you have it, please."

Boone nodded and reached into the fridge for the dressing. He put the plate down as well as the bottle of ranch. He went back across the room and grabbed a cold bottle of water from the fridge, and placed that in front of her as well

When Hayden didn't reach for the food, but merely eyed him, he told her, "Go on. Eat. Then we'll talk."

"You know you're completely freaking me out, right?"

"It's fine, Hay. Trust me. We'll talk after you get some food in you. I know you've got to be hungry."

She looked at him for another beat, then nodded. Hayden snarfed the sandwich down, thinking it was one of the best meals she'd ever eaten. She drank half of the water, and as Boone carried her empty plate to the sink, he told her to take the remaining water and go and sit on the couch. He'd be there in a moment.

Hayden wandered into the other room, trying to take as much of it in as she could. She'd been in his house before, of course, but this time she could take her time and satisfy her curiosity.

Boone's couch was dark brown leather. He had a coffee table in the middle of the room and a large television on the wall. There were two framed pictures on the walls, both of cows. There were a few more pictures in frames on the bookshelves along another wall, most likely of his parents. In one photo, a young couple was standing near the barn on the Hatcher Farms property. They had their arms around the other's waists and were gazing at each other with enough love that Hayden could almost feel it just by looking at the picture.

It was hard to believe Boone's dad could look at his wife like that, and allow anyone around him to abuse someone else.

In another photo, a little boy was standing between the couple; it was most likely taken a few years later, and he was looking at the camera smiling with the kind of unfettered happiness that only kids can have, and his parents were both looking down at him, smiling as well.

"Have a seat."

Hayden jerked in surprise, disgusted for allowing herself to be distracted enough to not hear Boone come into the room. That totally wasn't like her.

She sank down onto the surprisingly comfortable couch and balanced her water on her knee.

"Please, Boone. Tell me what the fuck happened last night. How'd I end up here? And did we...?" Hayden let the sentence trail off, feeling stupid for even having to ask.

"What do you remember?"

Hayden was afraid he was going to say that. "I remember being with you at the bar. Your friends were there..." She couldn't say what they'd talked about though.

"Do you remember seeing Dana?"

"Dana?" Hayden scrunched her eyebrows in concentration. Dana had been there? Nope. Nothing. She shook her head.

Boone leaned forward and rested his elbows on his knees, but kept his eyes on Hayden. "The two of you apparently had words when you went to the restroom." When no recognition lit in her eyes, Boone continued. "We don't know what was said, you didn't really say when you warned Tommy, Bub, and Moose to have my back."

Hayden shrugged and gestured for him to continue. She could tell he was irritated, but she'd do it again in a heartbeat. She'd wanted to get with his friends since he'd filed the restraining order. If she'd said something to them last night, all the better.

"Apparently Dana had been watching us, and wasn't too happy. She had to have paid someone to put something in your drink. I'm so sorry, Hay. I was distracted at the bar when I got our last round of drinks and took my eyes off them."

Hayden sat up straight and exclaimed unbelievably, "This isn't your fault, Boone. Seriously. And really? Dana spiked my drink? That fucking bitch!"

Boone almost laughed. Almost. There wasn't anything funny about what had happened to her. "I'm happy to see you almost back to normal."

"What did the doctors say? Did she roofie me?"

"Moose and the doctors at the emergency room said it was GHB."

"The emergency room? Jesus. I can't remember any of it." Hayden's face dropped, obviously not remembering anything about visiting the hospital.

"Yeah." Boone's voice dropped as well. "I got Tucker to come out and take a look at you and we called the cops. The EMTs took one look at you and brought you in. You'd puked three times, which actually helped get the drug out of your system faster than it would've otherwise, and your words were all jumbled up. You were in the ER until around three this morning. I took a look at your phone and saw you had Mackenzie programmed in. I called her, and got Dax. He was none too happy that you'd been drugged. Even though it was the middle of the night, he and Mackenzie went over to your place and got some stuff for you. When you were finally released, and the doctors assured me you'd be fine and you'd sleep off the rest of the drug, I brought you back here, got you comfortable...and here we are."

Hayden considered what Boone had told her. There was a lot there, none that she particularly liked. "Did they find Dana?"

Boone shook his head. "Yeah, but she said she had no idea what the cops were talking about. She had dozens of witnesses who said she was on the other side of the room. Apparently she was easy to identify because she'd been dancing with any guy who'd asked, grinding up against them on the dance floor. And since there was no proof she was the one who arranged for your drink to be spiked, they couldn't do anything."

"What about whoever spiked the drink? Couldn't that person be identified?" Hayden asked, frustrated. "What about cameras at the bar?"

Boone tried to relax, loving that she was herself again. Seeing the detective side of her come out relieved him and reassured him she was getting back to normal more than anything else she could've said or done. "No go. The owner said he's been having problems with bartenders and theft, so they were aimed behind the bar at the alcohol and the cash registers… not at the patrons."

"Well, shit. Even if the cops questioned everyone in the bar, there's no guarantee whoever did it was even still there. If he or she was smart, they would've left right after they did it. I'm sorry, Boone. Catching whoever Dana hired would've gone a long way toward making sure she was prosecuted and stayed away from you."

Boone nodded in agreement, but was amazed Hayden only seemed to care about his issues with Dana and not with what the woman had done to *her*.

Hayden looked up at Boone. "GHB, huh? Did I say anything weird?" She didn't like the small grin that crept across Boone's face. She totally had said something weird.

But he didn't elucidate. Instead, an intense look washed over his face and he said, "I was more concerned about the fact you couldn't stop throwing up."

"Oh Lord." Hayden put her face in her hands in embarrassment. "I'm so sorry."

"For what? For being drugged? That I allowed myself to be distracted and stupidly gave someone an opening to spike your drink? For me having a psycho ex-girlfriend? *I'm* the one who should be saying sorry."

"Thank you, then."

"Again, I ask, for what?" Boone asked, shaking his head on disbelief.

"Well, for everything. Calling the cops, staying with me in the hospital. Calling Mackenzie. Bringing me here...although I would've been fine at home."

"I wasn't going to take you back to your place and leave you there!" Boone's voice was horrified and even a little pissed. "You weren't even conscious. I can't believe you'd even think I'd do something like that."

"It's just that I—"

"I know what it's 'just.' You aren't used to anyone taking care of you. Well, I'm here to tell you, I'm going to take care of you whether you want it or not."

"I—"

"And another thing. I'm not happy you didn't tell me about seeing Dana in the bathroom."

He was on a roll, and while a part of her liked that he wanted to take care of her she couldn't let the last accusation go unchallenged. "Boone, I don't remember seeing her, but I probably had plans to tell you. I wouldn't keep something like that from you. Shit, if nothing else, you'd need to know she was lurking around. But, I'd probably do it the same way again. I'm assuming we were having a good night?" At his nod, she continued, "Right, so even though I can't remember, and that pisses me off because I *do* remember you looking really good last night and it was my first time on a date at a country bar, I was probably going to continue letting us have a good night and planned on telling you when we left."

Boone shook his head, his ire disappearing as if it

hadn't been there in the first place. "You're always thinking about others, aren't you?" He got up and sat next to Hayden on the couch. He put his hand on her leg and leaned in. "I can see I'll have to make sure I keep watch on you to ensure you take care of yourself. And if you don't, I'll have to do it for you."

Hayden decided to move on from the conversation. He wasn't serious. He'd get sick of her soon enough. She was too self-reliant for a nurturing man like him. "So Mack packed stuff for me?"

"Yeah." He let her change the subject.

"How'd she get in?"

"Dax talked to your landlord."

"Ah." Hayden didn't know what else to say. She was sure her landlord hadn't been happy about being woken up in the middle of the night, but a badge, especially a Texas Ranger badge, would've been plenty of motivation.

Boone leaned in and whispered into her ear, "And I have to say, I hadn't thought about it much, but if I had, there's no way we would've left your place last night. We never would've made it to the bar in the first place."

"What? Why?" Hayden tipped her head to the side to give Boone more room.

He kissed the sensitive skin under her ear. "I didn't realize you were bare under that shirt. I should've, since I had my hands all over your back, but I didn't notice you weren't wearing a bra. I was enjoying the feeling of your warm skin too much.

Until I got you comfortable in my bed, I had no idea."

Hayden inhaled and tried to shift away from Boone. He brought one hand up and held her in place with the simple act of putting it behind her neck and holding her still. They both knew she could break his hold in a second, but she didn't.

"And to answer the earlier question you didn't quite ask, Hay—nothing happened. There's no way I'd take advantage of you when you were as helpless as you were last night. When we make love for the first time, you're going to be completely aware of what's going on and you're going to participate fully. I want to see those beautiful green eyes looking up at me with passion and feel your legs tighten around me as I push you over the edge. You have no idea how badly I want to feel those long beautiful legs around me."

"Boone." Hayden's voice came out in a whisper.

"I was a gentleman last night as I helped you get comfortable, but I'll tell you, you are absolutely fucking beautiful, Hayden. Every inch of you is perfection. From your sculpted abs, to your perfectly sized tits, to your mile-long legs. "

"Uh, thank you."

"And I know there's a story behind Ellie...and I want to hear it. I want to know everything about you."

"Oh my God. Kill me now." Hayden refused to meet his eyes. How the hell Mack had known to throw her stuffed elephant into her overnight bag was beyond her. But she was mortified. What other thirty-three-year-old still slept with a stuffed animal?

Boone turned Hayden's head until she had no choice but to look at him. He kissed her briefly, then said, "I know you're embarrassed, but you shouldn't be. It's cute as all fuck that you sleep with Ellie. You're full of contradictions. Tough as nails on the outside, and an adorable, begging-to-be-taken-care-of little girl on the inside."

"I don't need to be taken care of."

"Um hmmm."

"Boone! I don't. I'm an adult woman who happens to be able to kick anyone's ass."

"Are you ready to face the cops?"

He changed the subject, but Hayden could tell he hadn't dropped it forever. Whatever. As long as he was moving on now. She was able to kick almost anyone's ass...as long as she wasn't drugged to her eyeballs, that is. Besides, she had no desire to talk about Ellie at the moment on top of everything else. "Yeah, no problem."

"They wanted to talk to you as soon as you woke up, but I wanted to make sure you had something in your belly first."

Hayden was still amazed Boone wanted to take care of her. It was a weird feeling. She nodded. She'd always been expected to take care of herself...even from a very young age. Her dad made sure she could do her own laundry and look after herself by the time she was seven or eight. The fact that he'd purposely put off the police until he'd fed her made her feel weird inside. A good weird, but weird nonetheless. "I'm ready. I need to talk to them as well. I want to know what they've found out and what the next step is in making sure Dana doesn't do something like this again."

"Great. I'll take you over there, then bring you back to your place when you're done. I think I remember you telling me you were off for the next day or so, right?"

Hayden tried to remember what her schedule was. She nodded. "Yeah, but I'll need to call the sheriff and let him know what's up."

"That's smart."

She smirked at him, feeling a little more like herself. "That's me. Miss Smarty-Pants."

Boone pulled Hayden toward him and kissed her forehead again. "As much as I love seeing your smile, I have to say, you scared me, Hay."

Hayden shifted until she could lean her forehead against his chest. It didn't feel weird...and that freaked her out. She wanted nothing more than to spend the rest of the day snuggled up with Boone...where she could be just Hay. Not Hayden Yates, bad-ass cop.

"Don't do it again," Boone breathed out softly.

They both knew she couldn't guarantee anything of the sort, since it wasn't her fault in the first place, but she nodded against him anyway. They sat there together for a long while, each reveling in the feel of the other.

12

———

HAYDEN COLLAPSED on her couch and shut her eyes. Damn she was tired. She'd just worked a twelve-hour shift where she'd had to deal with two car accidents—one with a fatality—two disturbance calls, two public intoxication calls, *and* she'd had to endure the teasing of Jimmy, Troy, and Brandon throughout the day about Boone. It was all too much.

She hadn't even bothered to remove her gear when she got home. She'd walked straight to her couch and crashed. She was dozing when her cell phone rang.

"Hello?"

"Hayden, this is your mother."

"Oh. Hey, Mom."

"I'm just calling to remind you that you're expected at the house for dinner tomorrow night."

Hayden repressed a sigh. She hadn't forgotten, but she'd pushed it to the back of her mind with everything else that had been going on. "I know, Mom. I'll be there."

"Good."

Hayden spoke before she really thought about it. "I'd like to bring someone with me...a man...if that's all right?"

There was a shocked pause before her mom responded. "I'll ask your father, but yes, I think that will be acceptable."

"Thanks. So...same time?"

"Yes, we'll expect you and your friend at seven."

"Okay, see you then."

"Goodbye."

"'Bye, Mom."

Hayden clicked off her cell and let her hand collapse to the couch, the phone still clutched in her fingers. She shut her eyes, trying to work up the energy and desire to get up and make something to eat. Knowing the monthly dinner with her parents was tomorrow just made her all the more tired. No matter what she did, no matter how hard she tried, it was never enough for her father. She couldn't live up to his expectations; she'd been disappointing him from the second she'd emerged from her mother's womb.

Her phone vibrated in her hand again. Without looking at it, Hayden wearily brought it up to her ear, not even lifting her head from where it rested against the back of the couch.

"Hello?"

"Hi. It's Boone."

"Hey. Everything all right?"

"Why do you always assume something's wrong when I call?"

His words were unexpected, but true. "I don't know," she admitted a hint of embarrassment in her voice.

"I know how we met, Hay, but I can take care of myself."

"I know you can. But it's been two weeks and Dana's been quiet. It's freaking me out. I keep expecting her to do something...grand, any day now."

"And drugging you wasn't grand?"

"You know what I mean."

"No, Hay, actually I don't."

Hayden sighed. She lowered her voice and shut her eyes as she tried to explain. "Boone, I've seen this before, okay? The abuser lays low for a while, letting his victim relax and think things are good. Then he strikes when she least expects it. Sometimes she gets away with just being beaten up again. Other times she has to be hospitalized. Still others, she doesn't get away at all and is killed."

"She's not going to kill me." Boone's voice was firm.

Hayden's was sad when she responded. "I've heard that before too. Then I have to watch as a battered and broken body is loaded into the coroner's van to be taken to the morgue."

Boone didn't say anything for a beat. Then, surprising her, he said, "You're tired. Have you eaten?"

Hayden sighed. "I *am* tired. It's been a hell of a day. I'm too exhausted to eat. I'm going to go to bed as soon as I hang up and work up the energy to get my butt off the couch."

"You hungry?"

"Yeah., but I'm more tired than hungry, and my bed is calling my name."

"I'll be over in a bit."

"Boone, seriously. I'm good. I'm just going to crash."

"Chinese or pizza?"

"What?"

"Do you want Chinese or pizza?"

Hayden could tell from his tone that he wasn't going to back down. Shit, she didn't fight it because she wanted to see him. "Pizza."

"Pepperoni?"

"No way. That's for wussies. Supreme meat lovers."

Boone chuckled and Hayden swore she felt it between her legs.

"My kind of woman. I'll be over in about thirty minutes. That enough time for you to unwind and get showered and changed before I get there?"

"Maybe."

"Maybe?"

"Yeah. Depends on if my butt has fused to the couch or not. I think my bones have melted into the cushions."

Hayden loved the sound of Boone's laugh. "Okay, well, if you've disappeared into the couch when I get there, I'll come in after you."

"Thanks, Boone." Hayden's voice was quiet and earnest and she wasn't talking about him pulling her melted body out of her cushions.

"My pleasure, sweetheart. Go get changed and comfy. I'll be by with the food before you know it."

"Okay. See you soon."

"Soon."

"'Bye."

"'Bye."

Hayden clicked off the phone for the second time that night and tried to muster the energy to stand. Finally, after almost dozing off again, she forced herself to move. She headed to her bedroom and stripped off her utility belt, her uniform pants and shirt, her bullet-proof vest, and finally her bra and panties, leaving them in a heap on her bedroom floor as was her usual. She staggered into the bathroom and turned on the water, letting it warm as she used the toilet and brushed her teeth.

Stepping into the hot shower felt heavenly, and Hayden almost felt normal again after she was done. She wandered into her bedroom and pulled a huge sleep shirt over her head, and a pair of what she called "fat pants." They were elasticized cotton pants that hung loose on her legs. She pulled on a pair of fluffy socks and wandered back down the hall to wait for Boone.

She was sitting at her small table when her doorbell rang. Making sure it was Boone before she opened the door, Hayden smiled at him standing on her doorstep holding two large pizza boxes and a six pack of the brand of bottled mixed drinks she liked.

"Hi. Come on in."

Boone smiled at her and stepped into her apartment as Hayden closed the door behind him.

"God, Hayden, you look exhausted," Boone said looking concerned.

"I told you, it's been a hell of a day."

"Come on, sit. I'll get the plates."

"Screw the plates. Just put the boxes on the table, we can eat out of them."

Hayden missed the gentle smile Boone gave her as she turned into the room and headed toward her table.

"If I have to wait any longer I might start gnawing my hand off, so it's better to just let me dig in."

"Wouldn't want you to hurt yourself," Boone said, chuckling.

Hayden loved how comfortable she felt with Boone. It was sort of like how she felt with the men she worked with...but not.

She nearly snorted. Of course it wasn't. She didn't want to jump any of the guys at the station and tear their clothes off, and that was really what she wanted to do with Boone. But she was following his lead.

While she might outwardly portray a self-confident, assured, independent woman who wasn't interested in the opposite sex—she'd been called a dyke on more than one occasion—the reality was that she'd simply repressed her sexual feelings because she was scared of rejection.

It'd become second nature to act macho and tough, but deep down she yearned for a true relationship just like the next woman. The vibrator in her bedside drawer got quite the hefty workout, not that she'd ever admit it to anyone.

Hayden watched as Boone put the pizza boxes down on the table and twisted off the cap to one of the drinks and placed it in front of her. He took the rest into her kitchen and put them in her fridge. He pulled out a bottle of water for himself and came back over the table. As he sat, he said, "Go on, dig in. Thought you were hungry?"

Hayden concentrated on the food and did as he requested. She picked up a piece of pizza that was loaded with sausage, bacon, hamburger, pepperoni, and enough cheese to feed a small third world country, and bit into it.

"Mmmmm," she moaned. "Jesus, this is so good." She glanced at Boone. He'd frozen with a piece of pizza held up near his mouth and was just staring at her. "What?"

"Uh, nothing." He shifted uncomfortably in his chair.

Hayden shrugged, and continued to eat her dinner. She knew she'd have to bring up dinner with her folks. She'd told her mom she was bringing someone with her, and by God, she'd better have someone with her when she went over there tomorrow night, or there'd be hell to pay. But now that she was sitting with Boone, she didn't know exactly how to bring it up.

Finally, Hayden leaned against the back of the chair and groaned. "*Why* do I stuff myself every time we eat together?"

"Because you always wait too long to eat and you're starved?"

Hayden glared at Boone. "That was a rhetorical question, Boone."

He laughed and patted her knee. "Come on, you're dead on your feet. Finish your drink and go to bed."

"But you just got here."

"Yeah, and I brought you dinner. You don't have to entertain me, Hay."

"But I want to."

Boone smiled hugely. "And I appreciate that, but you're exhausted. There'll be other times you can entertain me. Come on."

It was one more thing, in a long list of things, that made her like him even more. He'd left his house, gotten her food, gone out of his way to bring it to her, just to make sure she ate something. He wasn't expecting anything in return. He'd done it because he knew she was hungry and was going to skip dinner. No one made her feel as cherished as Boone did.

He stood then held out a hand and Hayden took it. He helped her up and Hayden realized once again how small he made her feel. He really was a huge man. At six-three, he towered over almost everyone, her included.

"Can we talk for a sec before you go?" she blurted out.

They stood next to the kitchen table, Boone still held her hand in his. He examined her for a moment before nodding. "Sure."

They went over to her couch and Hayden sat and Boone settled himself down next to her. Before she knew what was happening, he'd turned her until her feet rested in his lap and her back was to the cushions of her couch. She tried to sit up, but he gently pushed her back. "Relax, Hay. Let me do this."

Hayden lay back on her couch and moaned as Boone started to rub her feet. "Good Lord, I had no idea this would feel so good. Is there anything you can't do?"

She hadn't meant him to really hear her question, but he answered anyway. "I can't believe you've never had a foot massage. It's my pleasure to be your first." His voice was low and teasing, but the look in his eyes was scorching hot. "And to answer your question, I can do a lot of things, but successfully break up with Dana isn't one of them."

Hayden chuckled, even though it wasn't really funny. She lay on the couch, enjoying being able to zone out and feel taken care of for just a moment. Just a moment, then she'd go back to being super-Hayden. Finally, without looking at him, she blurted out what she needed to ask. "Every month or so I go over to my parents' house for dinner. It's expected of me. I know we haven't known each other very long...only about a month...and there's no pressure, but I asked my mom if I could bring someone with me tomorrow night, and she said yes. It's not going to be fun; my parents are... difficult at the best of times. I don't really get along with my dad and we don't have to stay very long and I'll owe you big, but—"

"Of course."

"Huh?"

"If you're asking me if I'd like to go with you to your parents' for dinner, the answer is, of course. I'd love to."

"Oh, okay. Great." Hayden inwardly sighed in relief. She knew she'd bungled asking, but thank goodness he'd agreed anyway.

"And, Hayden, we *are* dating."

She opened her eyes at that. Boone had stopped rubbing her feet and was merely holding them gently in his big hands. She could feel the warmth in his hands seeping into her bones and up her legs. It felt heavenly. "Oh, uh...we are? I didn't want to presume in case this was...a friends thing."

Boone smiled at her with a patient look on his face. "Yeah, we're dating. And while we are friends, I'm hoping we're more. I don't text women every day to see how they're doing if I'm not dating them. I don't drop everything with a flimsy excuse of bringing over dinner when I know full well my girlfriend is capable of making herself something to eat. I don't sit on a couch rubbing a woman's feet if I'm not dating her. And I certainly don't get a hard-on for a woman I want more than I've wanted any woman before in my life if I'm not dating her."

"Oh." Hayden felt stupid. Her heart was beating out of her chest and she could feel his hard length under her feet for the first time. How she'd missed it before, she had no idea...except she was an idiot. She wasn't sure what to say.

"Come here, Hay." Boone pulled her upright and Hayden shifted around until she was nestled into him. She carefully put one arm around his stomach and curled the other in front of her against his hard side.

"You haven't dated much, have you?" Boone asked carefully.

Hayden tried to sound mature. "Of course I have."

"Then you've been dating idiots."

Hayden had no comeback for that one, because he was probably right.

Boone continued, running one palm up and down her forearm resting across his abs, while the other played with her hair at her back. "I like everything about you, Hay. Your tough-as-nails spirit, your friendship with the men you work with, the way you melt into me like you're doing right now, how your voice drops when you realize it's me on the phone, how you let me take care of you when I know full well you can take care of yourself, how I know when you're honestly smiling and when you're fake smiling, how you worry about me, how you want to kick Dana's ass for me, how you sleep with the cutest stuffed animal I've ever seen, how sexy you look in both your uniform and in those short shorts, and even in what you're wearing right now. Seriously, I find you're full of contradictions and every single time I'm with you, I see a little bit more into what makes you, you. And I like what I see, Hayden."

"I like you too, Boone," Hayden said, not really knowing what to do with everything he'd just told her.

He chuckled, realizing she wasn't going to delve into his words...at all. "And that right there is why we're dating as well. You don't play games with me. You don't fish for compliments, you state what you're thinking, you don't beat around the bush. It's refreshing."

Hayden looked up at Boone. "I'm not good in bed, Boone."

"What?"

"Bed. I'm not good at it. I'm afraid I'm going to disappoint you. I don't think I have whatever womanly gene it is that makes me able to get off easily. None of the guys I've been with have ever been impressed with me. I can't—"

"Shhhhhh." Boone put his finger over her lips. "Again, we've already established that you've been dating idiots."

"Boone, really," Hayden mumbled around his finger, reaching up to remove it so she could warn him again. "You like that I tell you what I'm thinking, so I'm trying to do that here. I don't enjoy going down on a guy, the taste is weird and I gag way too easily. I don't even like it much when they go down on *me*. I'm awkward and don't know what to do so I usually just lay there. I've been accused of being a limp fish before..." Her voice trailed off awkwardly. "I just thought you should know."

Boone didn't say anything, but put his finger under her chin and lifted her head to his. "Close your eyes, Hay."

When she continued staring at him, he laughed low and rumbly, and repeated, "Close your eyes."

She did and held her breath. When nothing happened after a couple moments, she opened her eyes to see Boone's lips a hairsbreadth away from her own. "Boone?"

"Close your eyes and keep them closed. I'm right here. I'm not going anywhere."

Hayden was confused, but did as Boone asked. She squeezed her eyelids shut and took a deep breath, trusting him. She could feel his finger under her chin and his warm breath against her face.

Boone waited until Hayden's breathing evened out, felt her muscles against him relax, and then took the time to take her in. She would never be a poster child for femininity, but when her tough outer shell was peeled back, she was irresistible. Every time he did something for her, she melted. She obviously hadn't ever had someone do things for her simply because they wanted to...he was thrilled as he could be that he was the first. It was quickly becoming his mission in life to make sure Hayden knew how much he valued her and enjoyed doing things for her...simply because he could. Including her sexuality. He'd take care of her in the bedroom as well as out of it.

Boone had absolutely no worries whatsoever about Hayden's sensuality. Their chemistry was off the charts and Boone felt more desire for her than anyone he'd ever met. He had no doubt when they came together, it'd be out of this world.

With the masculine job she had and the clothes she wore most of the time, clothes that hid her body from the world, Hayden was the most interesting woman he'd ever met. She had no idea of her appeal and how much he wanted to take care of her, whether she realized she was being taken care of or not.

He leaned in and brushed his lips over her left eye, then her right. He didn't stop when she inhaled and her fingers clutched his shirt. He moved the arm that had been behind her on the couch until it hung around her shoulders and he shifted until he'd brought her even closer to him. His lips next kissed the tip of her nose and moved to her cheekbones. He kissed the apple of her cheek before shifting to her ear. Boone brought his free hand up and palmed the side of her neck, loving how she seemed to fit perfectly in his grip.

He ran his tongue lightly over the lobe of her ear, never staying in one place for long, but trying to worship every part of her. He sucked the lobe into his mouth for a moment before moving on. He moved her head so it was tilted even farther, giving him more room. He brushed her hair off her shoulder and blew on her neck as he moved down.

Smiling as goosebumps rose on her skin, he didn't stop. Boone licked the skin below her ear and rejoiced at the small groan that escaped her lips.

"Boone..."

"Shhhhh," he murmured as he continued. He worked his way back to her face, running his thumb over her bottom lip as he spoke. "You're beautiful, Hayden. I can see the pulse beating in your throat, your breathing has sped up, and the goosebumps on your skin have all given you away. You're more sensual than any woman I've ever seen. I'm guessing the assholes you've been with have just climbed on top and started thrusting. And I bet they only made a cursory effort at eating you out, and you could tell. So of course it wasn't good for you...and they blamed you." Boone made a disgusted sound in the back of his throat.

"When we go to bed, I'm going to take my time and worship every inch of you. Your toes. Your knees, your belly button, your gorgeous tits...there won't be anywhere on your body that I haven't caressed, licked, or kissed...and that's all before we make love. Hayden, it's a man's responsibility to make sure his woman is ready for him. That she wants him more than she wants to take her next breath. We'll take it slow. We'll do only what feels right to both of us. But I have no doubt whatsoever that you'll be anything but a limp fish, sweetheart."

Without giving her a chance to respond, Boone brought his lips to hers...finally. He licked her bottom lip, then the top one. When she opened for him, he fused their mouths together. They licked and explored, tongues dueling with each other. Hayden might have been docile as he spoke, but she was anything but docile now. Her hands gripped his T-shirt even harder and she tried to pull him toward her.

Boone shifted and pulled her across his lap until she was straddling him. She pulled her mouth off his and looked at him, then slowly leaned in until their lips touched again. Boone brought both hands up to frame her face and to hold her where he wanted her. He felt Hayden's arms go around him. One rested on his upper back and the other clutched the nape of his neck.

They writhed in each other's grasp until he couldn't think of anything but her taste, her lips, and how good she felt in his arms. Boone was hard as a rock, and he groaned as Hayden ground herself down on him. She rode his cock, even through both of their pants. It was the single sexiest thing he'd ever experienced in his life. They were both fully clothed, but he was as close as he'd ever been to coming...with just the friction of her frantic movements on him. It was probably his imagination, but Boone swore he could feel her heat through his jeans and her slacks.

Finally, knowing he needed to pull back or he'd throw her down sideways on the couch, rip her pants off and go at her right there—which he didn't want to do their first time—he tried to ease his mouth off of hers. Boone wanted what he'd told her earlier. He wanted to worship her body the first time they made love, not shove his cock deep inside her while they were still half dressed on her couch.

Boone tried to break the kiss but Hayden wasn't having any of it. She gripped him harder behind his neck and refused to give up his mouth. He smiled and tightened his grip on her face. He was finally successful in breaking their kiss, but he only moved back an inch.

"Fucking amazing, Hay."

"Mmmmmm."

His smile grew. "Open your eyes."

She did and Boone saw they were dazed and full of lust...but he also saw the exhaustion she'd been trying to hide from him all night.

"What time do we have to be there tomorrow evening?"

Hayden tried to get herself together. She'd never felt anything like what she felt right now in Boone's arms. She could feel his hard erection under her and she shifted in his lap, wanting to get closer, to rub her clit against his hard cock until she came. She leaned back and looked down between them and moaned. God, he was huge. She could see the outline of his erection through his pants and between her legs. If they'd been naked, all she'd have to do was lift up a couple of inches and—

"Hay. What time?"

She looked up at Boone and blushed. "Oh. Uh. Seven."

"Pick you up here at six-thirty? Will that give us enough time to get there? I don't know where your parents live."

Talking about her parents was enough to bring her out of her happy place where only she and Boone existed. She sighed and answered, "Yeah, that'll work." She unwound her arms from Boone and awkwardly rested them on his shoulders, feeling uncomfortable now that they weren't kissing.

"Hey, look at me."

Hayden looked into Boone's eyes and bit her lip nervously.

"Don't be embarrassed. We're dating. We're allowed to make out on the couch," he joked lightly.

Hayden smiled back, still discomfited, but trying to hide it. "Yeah."

"Come on, time for me to go and you to get some sleep."

Hayden nodded, because she *was* tired...and she needed some time away from Boone to process what had just happened. She awkwardly lifted her leg off of him and stood on shaky legs. Boone got up and grabbed her hand. They walked to her front door and he stopped before opening it.

"What's your schedule for the next week?"

Hayden tried to get her mind off of Boone's kisses, the heat between her legs, and instead on her work shifts. "I'm off tomorrow, then I have three days of regular eight-hour days, then two days of twelves. Then I'm off for two days."

"I want to take you out—on a real date—on one of your days off. That okay with you?"

Hayden looked up at Boone. How in the hell this gorgeous man was interested in her was beyond her at the moment, but she was going to go with it. "Yeah. That's more than okay with me."

Boone smiled. "No games. I love it."

"You already know how much I like you. I think I made it more than obvious back there on my couch."

She gestured to where they'd been making out with her head.

"I was right there with ya, Hay. I think I might have that couch bronzed." He grinned down at her. "I'll see you tomorrow at six-thirty." He leaned down and kissed her, putting his hands on the small of her back to steady her as she went up on her tiptoes to reach him better.

"Sleep well, sweetheart."

"Be safe driving home. Text me when you get there?"

"I don't want to wake you up."

"I sleep like a log. I'll hear your text and go right back to sleep. Promise."

"Okay then. I will. Lock up behind me."

"Always."

Boone kissed her one more time and took a step back, waiting until she had her balance. "Bye."

"Bye."

Hayden closed and locked the door behind Boone and leaned heavily against it. "Wow," she whispered to the empty room. She walked to the table and grabbed the leftover pizza and put it in the fridge. She'd have breakfast *and* lunch tomorrow. Awesome.

She headed to her room, grabbing her vibrator as she climbed into bed. She'd figured it wouldn't take her long to orgasm, not when she could still feel Boone's hard length between her legs as she'd ground herself over him on the couch. And she was right, within minutes she was trembling and shaking as she came, moaning Boone's name. Sated, exhausted, and feeling content for the first time in a long time, Hayden snuggled Ellie in her arms and closed her eyes, knowing she'd sleep better than she had in ages; not even the impending trip home would interrupt her sleep tonight.

Twenty minutes later, Hayden sleepily heard her phone ding with a text. She picked it up and smiled at Boone's message.

Home. Go back to sleep.

She clicked the screen and typed out a response.

Glad. C u tomorrow.

Then she put down the phone, buried her face into Ellie's fur, and was asleep within moments.

13

———

HAYDEN PACED her living room while she waited for Boone. This was a bad idea. A really bad idea. What was she thinking? Bringing him with her for dinner with her folks? Temporary insanity brought on by a really bad day.

She'd slept in that morning and gotten up and done a few errands...grocery store, dry cleaners, and then home to do laundry and eat some lunch. She'd texted Mack just to say hi, liking that they were getting closer ever since the night she and Dax had gone to her place to get some of her things after Dana had drugged her.

Now she'd gotten dressed and was trying to come up with a reason for Boone to not come with her—one that he'd buy and agree to.

Her doorbell pealed and Hayden looked through

the peephole and opened it to see Boone, looking absolutely delicious on her doorstep.

"Hey."

Boone took a step in, shut the door behind him, and took Hayden's face in his big palms. "You look freaked."

"That's because I *am* freaked."

Hayden was honest with him as usual. She'd gripped his wrists as they held her still. Boone could feel her little fingernails digging into his skin. "Do you want me to bow out?"

Hayden sighed and shut her eyes. "Yes, but not because I don't think they'll like you. They're gonna love you. Seriously. But I'm embarrassed for you to see their relationship with me."

Boone studied Hayden as she trembled in his hands. He hadn't thought he'd be meeting her parents this quickly in their relationship, but he relished the chance to get to know her better, by getting to know her parents. Even though Hayden was pretty, she completely downplayed her feminine side, especially when she was out in public. Part of it was because of her occupation, but he'd known other females who worked in typically male-dominated occupations and they didn't seem to have as much issue with it as Hayden did. It might have something to do with how she'd grown up, and meeting her parents might give him a small glimpse into her psyche.

Boone wanted to figure it out. Figure *her* out. "I

couldn't care less about your relationship, except for how it affects you."

Hayden sighed and leaned into him, putting her hands around him, resting her cheek against his chest, and squeezing him tightly. "I'm being a baby about this. I know. But I want you to *want* to keep seeing me and I'm afraid this is gonna put you off."

Boone kept his arms around Hayden, reveling in her reaching out for him and allowing him to provide her the comfort of his arms. "Hayden, this is not gonna put me off. We're adults. While I want your parents to like me, I want them to like me for *you*. But if they don't, I don't give a shit. It has no bearing on the way I feel about you and I hope it has no bearing on how you feel about me. Now, I thought you'd be ready. Go get dressed and we'll go. Whatever happens, happens. It won't affect us one way or another. Okay?"

Hayden pulled back and glanced up at Boone, then down at herself uncertainly. "But I *am* dressed."

Boone looked at Hayden. She had her hair pulled back into a tight coil at the back of her neck, not a strand escaping. She was wearing a polo shirt that looked about a size too big for her, totally hiding her slight curves, and a pair of black jeans with cowboy boots. She looked about like she had when they'd gone out with her coworkers, and definitely not like she had when they'd gone to Cow Town. Masculine, not the beautiful woman he knew her to be.

"Do I not look okay?" Hayden asked her brows drawn together in concern.

"You look fine," Boone soothed. "I just thought you'd dress up a bit more."

"To see my parents?" She sounded horrified, then sighed. "Boone, my dad...he expects me to look like this. He—"

"Come on, let's get this over with," Boone interrupted. He didn't really want to hear what her dad wanted. Whatever it was, would be bullshit, especially if he expected his daughter to dress like a man. "It's like a Band-Aid, Hay. It's better to pull it off quickly. You're all worked up about it. We'll go over there, eat, then come back here and make out on your couch again to take your mind off of the visit."

Boone was relieved to see the smile spread over Hayden's face. He'd almost blown it there. He had no idea why she wanted to look like a boy when she went to see her parents...hell, they were almost dressed alike. She could've passed for a ranch hand on his farm if she wanted to.

She grabbed her cell and put her ID and some bills into her back pocket, not bothering with a purse, and they left. She pocketed her keys and Boone held the door as she got into his truck. He closed the door for her, hoping he'd get more answers about why Hayden was acting the way she was tonight.

Boone clenched his teeth and held back the scathing retort that was resting on the tip of his tongue. He'd been looking forward to the evening and getting to know Hayden's parents, but this was pure torture.

From the moment they'd laid eyes on him, Mr. and Mrs. Yates had practically ignored their daughter.

"You own a cattle farm? How very Texan of you."

"Did you play football in school?"

"I bet you're very popular with the ladies."

And it went on and on. It was obvious the couple was impressed more with the fact that he had a dick than what *kind* of man he was. Shit, he could've been a serial killer, or knocked Hayden around every night and he didn't think her parents would've cared. All they seemed to be focused on was his gender. It was weird and made him feel uncomfortable.

Boone had watched Hayden's personality change before his eyes. She swaggered when she walked, she took on the mannerisms of his ranch hands and the guys she worked with, complete with resting her thumbs in the pockets of her jeans, giving her dad a chin lift when he asked her a question, and drinking a damn beer her dad handed to her without asking if she wanted one, and Boone knew she hated the stuff.

They were now sitting in the family room, with a Dallas Cowboys game playing on the television. Her mom was knitting and her dad was trying to talk to him about the game.

"I'm sorry, Mr. Yates, but I don't particularly care for football."

"Yeah, right. I'll see if I can't find a rodeo...there's bound to be one on the million and one channels we have." He chuckled as he busied himself with the TV.

"Hey, Dad, I had my qualifications the other day," Hayden said suddenly into the silence.

"Mmm hmmm..."

"I beat out all the other guys except for maybe two."

"You should've won. You've never been the best at anything. No matter how much you practiced, it wasn't ever enough. I've told you time and time again— Hey, Boone, look! Found one, and the bull riding is up next!"

Boone looked at Hayden. She was biting her lip and looking down at her lap, picking at her thumb nail. He nudged her with his knee. When she looked up at him, he smiled at her.

Her smile was weak, with no discernible dimple, but she returned it. Boone couldn't stand the sad look on her face anymore. "Mr. Yates, if you don't mind, Hayden said she'd give me a tour of the house."

"Oh, but it's about to start. You don't need to see the damn house; don't understand why Hayden would want to show you a bunch of rooms. Sissy-ass thing to do." He gestured toward the television. "The bulls are on."

Boone stood and pulled Hayden up with him, not letting go of her hand. "We won't take too long."

Boone didn't wait for the man's answer. He pulled Hayden behind him and headed down a hall. "Which one was your room?"

Hayden looked up at him in confusion. "You want a tour of the house?"

"Which one?" Boone's voice was unrelenting.

"Third door on the left."

Boone tugged Hayden along and opened the door. He closed it behind him and took a quick look around, not too surprised at what he saw.

Dark blue comforter, twin bed, a desk in the corner, an empty bookcase—but the posters still on the wall *did* surprise him.

Boone dropped Hayden's hand and wandered over to the wall. One poster had four rows of different types of handguns. Each one had a short description under it, with the caliber bullet it shot, as well as the manufacturer. He moved to the next one. It was of the 1996 Dallas Cowboys Super Bowl-winning team.

There were a few other posters of the football teams from a local high school, obviously from when she was a student. Boone continued to look around the room. If he didn't know better, he'd think this was where a teenage boy lived.

"You have a brother?"

"No."

"This really was your room?"

"Yeah."

"Why are the posters still on the wall?"

Hayden shrugged and threw him attitude. "Because. I don't know. My parents haven't bothered to remove them? What the hell, Boone? You wanna make out on my bed and pretend we're in high school or what?"

Boone ignored her defensive attitude and walked up to her, not stopping even when she backed away from him and hit the wall by the door. "Talk to me, Hay."

"About what?" She tried to act dumb.

Boone wasn't buying it. "About why your parents treat you as if you're a guy, when you're obviously not."

She sighed and sagged. Boone clasped his hands at the small of her back and held her to him. She didn't look up, but rested her hands on his chest, picking at a stray thread on his shirt, and answered him. "They wanted a boy. Mom miscarried twice before she had me. Both boys. Dad had been so excited to have a son. When she carried me to term, they were really disappointed I wasn't male. Mom had wanted to try again, but the doctor advised against it. I got footballs and trucks for Christmas presents as far back as I can remember. I was told to be tough, and to suck it up anytime I got hurt. When I told my dad I wanted to get into gymnastics and ballet when I was five, I still remember the disappointed look on his face and his outright refusal. He signed me up for T-ball the next day."

She tried to change the subject.

"*You're* their dream guy, Boone. Tall, handsome, a cowboy, and you own a cattle farm. Dad's in heaven. I don't think he's ever watched a rodeo in his life, but suddenly you're here and he can't frickin' wait."

"Hayden—"

She ignored him and continued, even looking up at him as she did. "They're proud of what I do, Boone. At least I think they are. Dad enjoys hearing my stories about the stuff that happens at work. I might not be a boy, but he's happy with what I do for a living."

"What did you want to be when you grew up?"

"What?"

"You said your dad is happy with what you do...but are you? Don't get me wrong. You're a damn good cop. You're fucking great at what you do—but are you doing it for you, or for them? What did you want to be when you grew up?"

Hayden looked down again. "You're too fucking observant for your own good."

Boone waited.

She finally answered. "It doesn't matter what I wanted to do. I'm not about to give up what I've spent ten years of my life working toward. I have the respect of my coworkers and my family. If you don't like—"

Boone interrupted her. "You *know* I like everything about you, but I'll stop hounding you. And I hope you know I'm proud of you, Hay. I was serious when I said you were a damn good cop. You took in the situation with Dana that first day, walked around my house for two seconds, then decimated her story when your friends and coworkers were about to handcuff me and haul me in for domestic assault. But, Hayden, I see *you*. I see the beautiful woman under your uniform. I see past your jeans and cowboy boots to the girl underneath who's dying to wear short, silky dresses and high heels."

"I'm not so sure about the heels part."

Boone smiled at her, loving that she could pull herself together and smile at him.

"Okay, maybe small heels then." Boone moved one of his hands down until he rested it on the curve of her ass and pulled her into him until there was no space whatsoever between them. Boone knew his erection was obvious against her stomach, but he didn't give a shit. "You can wear whatever you want, but I know you're all woman under your clothes. Feel how much you turn me on. And yeah, there's definitely a part of me that wants to throw you down on that bed behind us and make out with you just to spite your parents. Bet they never even worried about you meeting curfew or having a boy back here with the door shut, did they?"

Hayden blushed, but kept her eyes on his. "Nope. I didn't have any boyfriends in high school. I was the weird tomboy."

Boone leaned down, waiting for Hayden to stretch up to him and said in a voice thick with lust, "You're not a weird tomboy anymore."

He took her lips with his own and they both groaned. God, he loved the way she felt in his arms and how she lost control with one touch of his tongue to hers. Boone moved the hand that had been at the small of her back around to her front and rested it over her breast. He squeezed at the same time he nipped her lip. She gasped and he drew back. He continued to caress her chest, pinching her nipple through both her shirt and bra.

"Boone?"

He heard all sorts of questions in that one word out of her mouth and he took pity on her. He released her nipple and rested his hand over her now aroused flesh. Boone leaned in and nuzzled her under her ear. "How long do you think your dad is gonna torture me by making me watch that damn rodeo before we can get out of here?"

Loving the giggle that rose out of Hayden's chest, Boone pulled back and smiled at her, moving his hand up to her hair and pulling out the clip holding it in the neat bun at the back of her neck. He ran his hand through her hair, loving how it cascaded over her shoulders and down her back. She might dress like a boy, but he wanted her parents to start to see she was all woman.

He moved his hand, still holding her clip, back to the small indentation in her back.

"He'll probably have adoption papers ready for you to sign when we go back out there," Hayden said, only half kidding.

Boone shook his head. "I'm sorry your dad doesn't see what a wonderful, accomplished woman you are."

She shrugged. "I've always disappointed them, especially my dad. They just don't get me. I'll never be the one thing they wanted most in their life—a boy. I'll never be that close to them. There's too much hurt from the way they raised me."

Boone said nothing, but hugged her tight. "Come on, let's get back out there and see if we can't extricate ourselves."

"Sounds good to me. Boone?"

"Yeah, sweetheart?"

"Thanks for coming with me tonight."

"You're welcome."

"I'm sorry I won't get to meet your parents."

"Me too, Hay. Lord knows they weren't perfect, and sometimes I hated my dad for the blinders he had on when it came to Lizzy and his best friend, but they would've loved you...for you."

"Thanks."

"Come on. Wouldn't want your dad to get the shotgun out," he teased.

Hayden laughed again. "He'd more likely hand you a condom and tell you to have a good time."

They walked hand in hand back to the family room. Boone had no idea why or how Donna and Bob Yates couldn't see what a great *daughter* they had, but it wasn't going to change his mind in the least about her. He wanted her. In his bed, in hers, against the wall of her entryway, in his barn...he hadn't ever waited this long to have sex when he was dating a woman before, but he'd wait as long as it took. Hayden was worth it.

14

———

THE WEEK after Boone met her parents had gone by relatively quickly, all things considered. But after her second twelve-hour shift, Hayden had come home to a dead cat lying on her doorstep. There was no note, nothing to prove Dana had left it there, but Hayden had a feeling it'd been her. There was no outward sign of how the cat had died except for its neck lying at an awkward angle. The only person who could possibly hate Hayden enough to do something like that was Dana.

She'd called it in and Juan had come over to take pictures and take the poor cat carcass in as evidence. Juan hadn't found any sign of who'd left the dead cat on her doorstep, but they both had the same hunch it was Dana.

Hayden hated to put more of a burden on Boone than he already had, but knew there was no way she could keep this from him. He needed to know so he could be even more vigilant, and report anything that seemed out of place. And if the tables were turned, she'd be extremely pissed if he kept something like this from her.

It was late, but she didn't hesitate to call him.

"Hey, Hayden, I didn't expect to hear from you," Boone said as he answered the phone, pleasure easy to hear in his voice.

"Yeah, I wasn't going to call until tomorrow, but something came up."

"Oh shit. Dana?" Boone guessed immediately.

"Yeah." Hayden explained without beating around the bush, figuring he'd appreciate her getting right to it. "Found a dead cat outside my apartment when I got home. There's nothing to prove that it's a gift from Dana or one of her minions, but I'm guessing it was."

"Dammit," Boone swore. "I can't believe this. It's insane. Why isn't she getting the hint?"

"We see this all the time." Hayden tried to keep her voice calm so as not to rile Boone up any further. "Stalkers can't distinguish between what's real and what's fantasy. They have a one-track mind, and want what they want no matter what anyone tries to tell them otherwise."

"She knows where you live," Boone stated unnecessarily.

"Apparently. But I can take care of myself. I already knew she was obsessed with you and figured she'd eventually try to scare me again. And Boone, if I didn't run screaming away from you after she had my drink spiked, this sure as hell isn't going to do it."

"I'm sorry, Hay. I had no idea she'd be so psycho."

"This isn't your fault, Boone. It's not. We'll deal with this just like we've dealt with everything else."

Boone didn't say anything and Hayden knew he was struggling to comprehend the latest threat against her. "Have you gotten any sleep?" He'd been staying up late the last few nights because some of his heifers were giving birth. He'd told her that each one of the calves that were born were worth anywhere from two to eight thousand dollars. He wasn't going to take any chances that the mamas would give birth in the fields on his property. They would do it in the safety of his massive barn, with veterinarians and himself there, in case something went wrong.

"Some."

Which Hayden figured meant little to none.

"I didn't want to add anything else on your plate," Hayden told Boone honestly. "But I also figured you'd want to know."

"Thank you for not keeping it from me," Boone said.

"You're welcome. Will you try to get some sleep tonight?"

He barked out a harsh laugh. "You think I'll be able to sleep after I found out my ex-girlfriend put a dead cat on the doorstep of my current girlfriend?"

It sounded like a rhetorical question, but Hayden answered it anyway. "No. But I was hoping you'd be happy hearing I was home safe from my shift and that I was tucked under my covers warm and sleepy after a hot shower."

That did the trick. "I *am* happy hearing that, Hay." Boone's voice had lost its bite, and was more of the low rumble she loved to hear from him.

"I'll let you go then. Take care of the baby cows, cowboy."

"I will. Stay safe, Hay."

"Always. I'll talk to you soon."

"You will. Good night."

"Good night."

Hayden clicked off the phone and shook her head, pissed at Dana and what she was doing to Boone. At this point, she honestly hoped Dana would confront her face-to-face. She could take care of herself when it came to confronting pissed-off ex-girlfriends. There was nothing she wanted more than to take the bitch down. She'd press charges and make sure they stuck. Dana would regret not simply leaving when Boone broke it off if she made any more attempts to get in Hayden's face.

Hayden hadn't heard from her parents, except for a quick text from her dad asking when she was bringing Boone over again. She'd simply responded with a quick, "I'll let you know," and left it at that.

She and Boone, on the other hand, had texted and

talked every day since he'd left her at her door last week. They'd made out on her doorstep, until Boone pulled back with a deep breath, swearing. He'd told her he had to go or he'd never leave. Even Hayden's, "Then stay," hadn't been enough to convince him. He'd palmed the side of her head and whispered, "Soon," then turned and left.

Hayden knew what he was doing. He was building the anticipation between them...and damn if it wasn't working. She'd have to try to control herself from attacking him when she saw him next. Her sessions with her vibrator and her imagination just weren't cutting it anymore. She wanted the real thing. She wanted Boone.

He'd called after she'd gotten off work each night. They hadn't talked long, or about anything heavy or deep, but it was nice to know he was thinking about her and they could talk about nothing.

But his texts were what made her smile like an idiot. Boone was funny and sweet, and somewhat dirty. She never knew when she heard the ding of her phone what kind of mood Boone was in until she read his text. Brandon had caught her reading one and smiling and had immediately wanted to know what was up. She'd refused to tell him and he'd actually stolen her phone and read what Boone had written.

I woke up from a really sexy dream this morning, you were

wearing a slinky black dress which was hiked up around your waist. You were sitting astride me, dripping all over me, holding your handcuffs and asking if I wanted to try them out. Needless to say, the water in the shower was cold by the time I was done.

HAYDEN HAD blushed beet red at Brandon's whoops and catcalls. He hadn't shut up about it until she'd tackled him and put him in a headlock, promising to tell the other guys he was deathly afraid of spiders if he opened his mouth.

Not all of Boone's texts were explicit as that one had been; most were quirky, light and...nice.

JUST WANTED to check in to see how you were.

Miss you.

Can't wait to see you in forty-three hours and two minutes.

What color panties are you wearing under your uniform today?

HE NEVER FAILED to make her laugh...and to make that spot in her belly fill up. She'd felt so empty inside. Night after night of going home to a lonely apartment with no one to give a crap if she ate, was tired, or if she'd had a hard day, had worn her down until she was just going through the motions of living. But knowing Boone was there, even if it was just by phone, made her feel warm and fuzzy.

Twice since they'd had dinner with her parents, Boone had ordered dinner for her. It'd arrived after she'd gotten home and showered. The first time was pizza; the second time, a huge sub sandwich from the place down from her apartment complex was delivered. The gestures were sweet and made Hayden feel cared for.

Now it was the day of their date. Hayden had braved the crowds and gone to the mall to find a black dress to wear for Boone, as he'd requested. She'd risked going without Mack, as she was busy, and thought she hadn't done half bad. They still had to decide on a day when they'd go shopping so Mack could collect on her bet, but so far they'd both been busy and hadn't been able to come up with a day that worked for both of them.

Hayden ran her hands down her stomach over the silky material of the dress she was wearing and tried to calm her nerves. She'd luckily found a very nice saleswoman who was thrilled to help her find something that would work. She'd tried on about ten different dresses, but the second she'd slipped this one over her head, Hayden knew it was the one.

There was a deep V in both the front and back of the dress, and it hugged her slight curves as if it was made only for her. The bottom flared out over her ass into a flouncy little swirl of material. There were cap sleeves that draped her shoulders and showed off her muscular and toned upper arms.

Hayden felt feminine in it. She imagined the look on Boone's face when he saw her in the dress and it made her bite her lip. He'd like it—at least she hoped so. The saleslady easily talked her into a pair of thigh-high hose with a thick seam up the back of her legs, just like she'd seen celebrities wear. The heels she bought weren't high, still no more than two inches, but they seemed to elongate her legs anyway. The lady helping her had even unearthed from somewhere in the store a small black handbag, which would actually hold her service pistol without being obvious about it. Since she couldn't wear it in her ankle or chest holsters, as she usually did when she went out, she had to carry a purse.

The last thing she'd bought was a black lacy bra that helped make it look as though she actually had some boobs. Seeing herself with cleavage was definitely a rare occurrence.

Now she was sitting at her small table—because pacing was out of the question in her heels—wondering if she was overdressed. Boone hadn't told her where they were going, only that he'd planned a romantic night out for the two of them. Hayden's leg jiggled up and down, and she was just pondering if she had time to run to her room and change when her doorbell rang.

Obviously not. Damn.

Hayden strode to the door and, after making sure it was Boone, she opened it and stared.

She hadn't ever seen him in anything but jeans and his boots. Tonight he was wearing a pair of khakis that had been pressed so the creases along the front were clearly seen. He had on a pair of brown loafers, which shone as if he'd polished them.

His shirt was a rich mahogany that brought out the flecks of gold in his eyes somehow. He'd paired the shirt with a tie with blocks of different color browns in it. He wasn't wearing a Stetson, which was rare for him. His dark brown hair had been brushed back from his face, but a few stubborn tendrils still managed to hang over his forehead. All in all, he looked and smelled delicious.

They stood there looking at each other for a moment before Boone lifted his hand and twirled his finger at her.

"What?" Hayden asked, not understanding.

"Turn." His voice was low and gruff.

So Hayden turned away from him, then faced him again.

"Again."

"Boone," she complained, getting annoyed.

"Please. Again."

Since he said please, Hayden turned again, this time faster, but he caught her hips as she was faced away from him and held her in place. He put one hand on her stomach and pulled her into his front. His other hand ran up and down her arm, starting at her shoulder under the wispy fabric and ending at her wrist, before heading up again.

"You look amazing, Hayden."

"Uh, thanks. So do you."

"Are those thigh-highs you're wearing?"

Hayden had no idea why he was concentrating on her pantyhose, but she answered affirmatively.

"If we didn't have reservations, and I didn't want to take you out and show you off so badly, I'd have you on your back on your kitchen table so fast it'd make your head spin."

"Uh..."

"And just saying, sweetheart...if this night ends up with me inside you, I want to start it out with you wearing this fantastic dress, and those sexy-as-all-get-out hose, and maybe even those heels as well."

"Boone!"

"What?"

Hayden didn't know what. His words were making her melt. She'd never inspired such...lust in a man before, and she liked it. "Nothing," she mumbled lamely, resting her head back on Boone's chest as she reveled in the feel of his hard-on against her back.

He laughed and spun her around, running both hands through her hair. She'd taken the time to use the curling iron on it for the first time in forever. She had thick curls at the ends, which rested on the curves of her breasts. She watched as Boone's eyes followed his hands as he fingered her hair. Hayden swore she could feel the heat from his hands on the skin showing in the deep V of her dress.

"I'd kiss you, but one, it'd mess up your lip stuff, and two, we'd never leave. So come on, we have reservations."

"Where are we going?" Hayden asked, trying to ignore the goosebumps rising on her arms at his words.

Instead of answering, Boone picked up her purse—and then looked down at it in surprise at the weight.

Hayden held out her hand and answered the unspoken question he'd asked with his raised eyebrows. "It's got my service pistol in it. I couldn't exactly wear it." She gestured at herself.

She'd told him she carried it wherever she went. As far as she was concerned, she was never off duty. She'd never ignore a crime that was going down in her presence. She always wanted to be prepared...for anything. Especially when she knew Dana was out there planning something else crazy.

Boone didn't give her a hard time about carrying, just nodded at her and encouraged her to step outside.

Hayden locked her door and dropped her key inside her purse and let Boone lead her to his truck. It'd been scrubbed and detailed by the body shop and he'd told her how glad he was to get his own truck back. The rental was good, but there was nothing like driving around in your own vehicle.

He helped her in, as it was harder to step up in a dress than it was when she was wearing pants. Hayden had to give Boone credit, he was trying very hard to be a gentleman, but she didn't miss the gleam in his eye when her dress inched up her thighs as she sat down. He held out the seat belt to her and Hayden took it with a smile. He shut the door and hurried around to the driver's side. He started the powerful engine and they backed out of the parking space and headed to the main road.

HAYDEN TRIED to calm her nerves as Boone pulled down the long driveway at Hatcher Farms. They'd had a fantastic night. Boone had made reservations at Aldo's Ristorante Italiano...one of the best, and most romantic, restaurants in San Antonio. The meal was fantastic, and they'd talked easily about everything under the sun.

Somehow Boone had made her comfortable enough to open up about how it felt growing up always trying to make her dad proud of her, even though she was female. Boone talked about his parents and how the farm and the business had been their dream, and while he knew his dad had hoped he'd want to take it on someday, he hadn't pressed.

Boone talked more about his cattle business. The pedigree of the bulls was amazing, almost as amazing as how Boone *knew* the pedigree of every bull and cow on his property. He reassured her that his cattle weren't raised for beef, but admitted that when they were sold, he had no control over what other farmers did with them.

Hayden was sad at that, but Boone quickly changed the subject and let her talk about her job. And for once, with someone who wasn't already affiliated with law enforcement, Boone seemed genuinely interested in her stories, and not just to hear the gory details.

After they'd eaten, Boone had led her back to the truck and driven off, once again not telling her where they were going. They'd ended up at the Tobin Center for the Performing Arts, where the San Antonio Symphony was hosting a concert. Hayden hadn't expected it, and she was ashamed of herself for pigeon-holing Boone. The symphony wasn't exactly Hayden's first choice of entertainment, but it went well with her mood for the night. She was dressed up, Boone was dressed up, it seemed right to be attending the symphony together.

They'd sat next to each other and listened to the hauntingly beautiful music, but Hayden was hyper-aware of Boone every second. He'd started out with one arm around her shoulders and had played with her hair. Eventually he'd moved his arm and put his hand on her leg just above her knee. His thumb rubbed back and forth and Hayden tried not to squirm in her chair.

Slowly, his fingers moved until they were resting on her upper inner thigh. Not high enough to be inappropriate, but high enough that Hayden's breathing increased and she could feel her nipples grow taut.

Over the last month and a half, they'd made out several times. Boone's hands had wandered under her clothes more than once. She'd felt his erection against her core, and once they'd even brought each other to climax over the phone while they were both lying in their own beds. She'd never thought Boone would be into phone sex, hell, hadn't thought *she* would be into it, but in the end, it was amazing.

But there was something extremely intimate about Boone's hand resting on her almost bare leg, in public, when Hayden knew darn well what she hoped they'd be doing later that night.

Boone hadn't said a word, but the small smile on his face as he'd pretended to concentrate on the musicians gave him away.

He'd asked when they were back in the truck if she wanted to go to his place, and Hayden had agreed. She didn't have any clothes, or any toiletries, but Boone reassured her he had something she could sleep in if she wanted, and an extra toothbrush. Hayden decided having to wear her black dress home the next day would be the best "walk of shame" she'd ever do if it meant she'd spent the night in Boone's bed.

Boone pulled into his garage and cut off the engine and turned to her. He'd been quiet on the way back to his place, and he made Hayden nervous. "Stay put. I'll come around."

Hayden nodded and watched as he stepped out and shut his door. She kept her eyes on him as he strode around the front of the vehicle with a single-minded purpose. He opened her door and instead of giving her his hand to help her out, he stepped into the space between the seat and the door.

"Turn."

"What?"

"Turn toward me."

Hayden did. Boone stepped back just enough for her right leg to get by him, then he stepped forward again, into her space, so her legs were now spread around his body. He put his hands on her hips and pulled her to the edge of the seat. Her skirt slid up but she ignored it, concentrating instead on the feel of Boone between her thighs. Hayden's hands rested on his shoulders. They were almost eye to eye; with her sitting in the high cab of the truck and him standing, they were a perfect height.

Boone leaned down and buried his face in the side of her neck and Hayden tilted her head to the side to give him room.

"God, you smell magnificent, Hay. You have no idea how hard it was for me to be a gentleman all night. I wanted to drag you under that pretty white tablecloth in the restaurant and flip your skirt up and take you from behind. And at the symphony? I had to physically restrain myself from pushing my hand under your dress and fingering you until you came apart."

He lifted his head and ran one hand over her head. "You're beautiful, and I'm thankful as fuck you're here with me. I want you. Will you let me make you feel good tonight? Let me show you how beautiful and womanly you are."

Hayden gave him a small nod. "I want that. And I had some fantasies of my own tonight as well."

Boone smiled widely at her. "Yeah?"

"Yeah. I thought about how that table in the restaurant was perfect for me slipping under and going down on you right there. I haven't really wanted to do that before, but with you...I have a feeling it'd be a completely different experience. The long tablecloth would've hidden what I was doing, and we were tucked back into that corner..."

"Jesus." Boone's voice was guttural. His hands eased down her body, coming to rest on her thighs, which were spread wide around his body. Without a word, he kept eye contact but eased his hands up and under her skirt, stopping only when he encountered the tops of her hose. He played with the elastic there for a moment before holding his hands still and taking a deep breath.

"Come to bed with me?"

Hayden had no idea why his words sounded

unsure. She hastened to reassure him. "Yes, Boone. Hell yes." She thought he'd step back and give her room, but instead he put his hands at the small of her back and pulled her even closer. Her skirt now barely covering her, Hayden grabbed onto his shoulders and tried not to blush.

"Hold on, Hay."

She wasn't ready when he hefted her and turned away from the seat. She quickly linked her ankles together behind his back and circled his neck with her arms. She felt him move one arm below her ass to hold her more securely against him. He used the other arm to grab her purse, then shut the door of the truck. He easily carried her through the garage and into his house. Without stopping, he went straight for his room. Every step jostled them, and pushed Hayden deeper into Boone.

By the time he got to the master bedroom, Hayden felt ready to explode. Boone eased her down his body until she was standing once again. He ran his hands down her sides once more, pushing her dress back down over her thighs. "Go do what you have to in the bathroom, but don't take off even one piece of clothing. I want you back out here exactly as you are right now. Okay?"

Hayden nodded enthusiastically. She might be unsure about how good she was at the whole sex thing, but she wanted this. Badly. She hurried into the bathroom and did her thing. Before going back out into

Boone's bedroom, she looked in the mirror, almost not recognizing herself.

Her face was flushed with excitement and her hair was hanging wildly around her shoulders. Hayden could see her chest moving up and down with her increased breaths and her cleavage, made possible by the magic bra, made her look at least a size and a half bigger. She was ready, more than ready for Boone.

She opened the bathroom door and had only taken one step back into his room when she stopped dead.

Boone was standing by his bed waiting for her... wearing nothing but a pair of dark gray boxer briefs.

15

<hr>

"OH MY GOD."

Boone smirked, but didn't move except to hold out his hand. "Come here, Hay."

Hayden was frozen to the spot. Boone was absolutely gorgeous. She'd known he would be, but the reality was so much better than what she'd imagined. She wasn't a prude. She'd seen more than her fair share of naked bodies—it was hard not to when you worked in law enforcement—but Boone's body was perfection.

Okay, it wasn't perfect. He was forty, not twenty, but it was obvious he took care of himself.

His legs were long and his thighs were thick and muscular. He had slight love handles, very slight, but it didn't take away from his Greek God looks. He had a light smattering of hair on his chest and she could see the muscles in his upper abdomen clench as he waited for her.

He had well-formed pectoral muscles, no man boobs there, that was for sure. His biceps were large, like his thighs. Probably from wrestling steers and calves all day. Finishing her perusal of his body in general, Hayden's eyes dropped back to his groin.

Dear God in heaven. He was excited, she could clearly see that. The tip of his cock was peeking out over the waistband of his boxers. The briefs left nothing to her imagination and she could even see his balls outlined in the dark material.

"Hayden." Her name was said in a short and amused tone. He repeated, his hand still stretched out toward her. "Come. Here."

Hoping she wouldn't fall on her face, Hayden took a step toward him. Then another, then another. Feeling steadier, she finally looked at Boone's face. His lips were curled into a small smile and she swore if eyes could actually twinkle, that's what his were doing.

A small, wide step stool was sitting on the floor next to the bed, and she took a moment to wonder why, the mattress was tall, but Boone was too. There was no way he needed the extra inches to be able to get into bed.

Her thoughts about the stool disappeared as she stopped in front of Boone and stood still, waiting. Waiting for him to do...something. She felt a bit weird being fully dressed while he was mostly...not.

His hand came up and rested on the side of her neck and Hayden tilted her head almost without thought, trapping his hand against her.

"Remember what I said earlier tonight?"

"You said a lot of things, Boone. What specifically am I remembering?"

He smiled at her snarkiness and his other hand came up and brushed over her hair, as it seemed he loved to do. "When I told you I wanted to take you in this dress."

Hayden nodded, her mouth suddenly dry.

"I know I also told you the first time we'd make love, I'd take my time and learn your body inch by inch, but I've changed my mind. You're too fucking beautiful for me to be able to go slow the first time and I've been fantasizing about taking you in this dress all night. But I swear to you, sweetheart, this isn't like those other assholes you've dated. You're gonna come too. This'll be pleasurable for you. This isn't me rutting against you as if I'm a bull in heat. Do you trust me?"

That was easy. Hayden nodded. She totally trusted Boone.

He stepped out of the way of the mattress and gestured to it. "Face the bed."

Hayden did as he asked without a word. She stepped around him and faced the monstrous mattress. She waited for his instructions.

Boone ran a hand down her back to her ass, then it wrapped around her waist and pulled her to him. He held her against him as his other hand roamed. First it went up to her chest and he squeezed and rubbed her left breast. He moved his hand to the V of the dress, and without warning, reached inside to her right breast and slid his fingers under her bra.

"God, your tits are amazing," he breathed, his warm breath brushing over her neck sending shivers down her spine. She could feel herself get wet with excitement.

"They're small."

He didn't argue with her. "Yeah, but they're so responsive. That beats size in my book any day." Boone's words were said against her ear, tickling as his fingers plucked at her nipple.

"See? All it takes is one touch, one pinch from me, and your nipple is standing up, ready to be sucked...to be played with." Boone tucked his chin into her shoulder and looked over it so he could see what he was doing. He flexed his wrist so it held the material of her dress out of the way. "Look, Hay. Watch."

Hayden looked down and saw, as well as felt, his fingers plucking at her nipple. She groaned at the sight.

"Yeah, beautiful." Boone pushed himself into her backside and Hayden felt his length against her. She pushed back, wrapped a hand around his hip, and smiled when he moaned in her ear.

His hand left her breast and Hayden barely suppressed a whimper. His hand on her stomach hadn't moved, it stayed put, locking her to him. The other moved down to her hip and she felt him slowly gathering the material of her dress as he spoke.

"I've wondered all night what color panties you're wearing. As I fantasized about fingering you right there in the theater seats, I thought about the next time I take you out. If I told you to leave off your panties...I could run my hand up your leg and you'd have no barrier to my touch. I'd bury my fingers inside you and watch you squirm."

Hayden did just that in his arms. "Boone..."

"Yeah, and you'd say my name just like that as I rubbed your clit and spread your juices over your folds."

Hayden could feel the coolness of the room against her legs, and knew Boone had gathered her skirt up until it no longer covered her. He shifted his other hand and took the material in it, leaving his left hand free. She saw him look down over her shoulder again.

"Black lace. Jesus, Hayden, you're killing me. I'm imagining you wearing this pair of undies under your uniform. Straight-laced, hard-assed cop, wearing feminine fuck-me panties."

He didn't ask and didn't hesitate. Boone's fingers plunged under the front panel of her new expensive underwear and explored her soaked folds.

"Ummmm, wet. Wet for me."

Hayden didn't bother agreeing. They both knew it. Her other hand went behind her to clutch at Boone's other hip and she dug her fingers into his skin as he played with her.

Boone ran his fingers through the wetness between her legs and up to her clit. He stroked it once and Hayden bucked hard in his arms. If a man could purr, Hayden would swear that was the sound that escaped his throat.

"In just a second I'm going to bend you over this bed, flip up your skirt and taste you."

When Hayden made a sound of protest, Boone flicked his fingers over the small bundle of nerves again, holding her steady when he thrust his hips into her, hard.

"I know you said you didn't enjoy it, but let me try. Please?"

"It's gross, Boone." Hayden didn't like saying no to him, but she wanted him to understand.

Instead of answering her, Boone brought his hand out of her panties and up to his mouth. Hayden turned her head and watched as he put the fingers that had just been caressing her intimately, into his mouth. He licked up and down each one, making sure to get all of her juices that clung to his skin. Then without a word, he put his hand on the side of her head and brought her lips to his own.

Hayden could taste herself on his lips and tongue. It was tangy and musky, but not entirely unpleasant... at least not in tandem with Boone's unique taste.

He lifted his head and looked her in the eyes, not

moving his hand. "It's not gross. It's fucking awesome. Hayden, some men don't enjoy it. I freely admit that, but I'm not one of those men. You taste divine. I'm dying to experience it all. Your smell, your taste, and to feel your tremors as you come apart under my mouth. I promise, if you hate it, if what I'm doing makes you too uncomfortable, I'll stop." He held her eyes, and whispered, "Okay?"

Hayden found herself nodding. God, when he looked at her that way and spoke to her in that low voice of his, she couldn't say no.

Boone continued describing what he was going to do to her as if she hadn't interrupted him with her uneasiness. His hand went back down the front of her body and under her waistband and again he slicked his fingers through her folds as he spoke.

"I'm going to lick and suck you until you explode. Then when you're still shaking and coming, I'll take you. Slow at first, letting you feel how well I fill you up. Then when you beg me to go faster, I'll speed up. You'll feel so full in this position and I'll use my fingers to make sure you come again before I take my pleasure. Seeing your ass shake as I pound into you will make me shoot off quicker than I ever have before. You ready for that?"

Hayden could only nod. Her mouth was so dry she couldn't have said a word if her life depended on it. She hadn't ever done it doggy style, the position feeling too impersonal, but there was nothing impersonal about what Boone had just described. His hands were suddenly gone and she swayed.

He reached a hand out and moved the step stool she'd noticed earlier closer to where she was standing. "Step up here and bend over, hands on the mattress, Hay."

She did as he asked, because if she didn't, Hayden knew she'd fall over and embarrass herself. The reason for the stool was obvious; it raised her body to just the right height to be able to take him and allowed her to brace herself on the mattress at the same time.

She might've been offended, wondering just how many women he'd done this exact same thing with, but as if he could read her mind, Boone murmured as she got into place, "I wasn't sure it'd work. Thank fuck it does. It's perfect."

She held her breath, waiting for Boone to start. When nothing happened, Hayden looked over her shoulder.

Boone stood tall and proud, as if he'd been waiting for her to look at him. He put his thumbs in the elastic at his waist and pushed. His boxer briefs slid down his legs and he stood there completely nude.

Hayden gulped.

Boone took a step to the side and came up behind her. Hayden shifted until she could see him.

"God, Boone. Are you sure that thing'll fit?"

Boone threw back his head and laughed, squeezing

her sides as he did. "It'll fit, Hay. Promise. I'm a big man. I have big...equipment."

"I'll say," Hayden breathed, looking forward to this, to him, in spite of her trepidation.

"Relax. You're gonna be so wet by the time I get inside that you won't care how big I am. I'll slide right in as though I was born to be there."

"Oh my God." Hayden closed her eyes and rested her forehead on the mattress. She was so excited, she was almost embarrassed. She felt Boone grab the sides of her underwear and ease them over her hips. She shifted her legs together so they could slide all the way down, then kicked them off one foot, then the other.

Boone's hands wrapped around her ankles and he slowly ran them up her calves, then her knees, then her thighs. He stopped once again at the elastic bands holding up her thigh-high hose. She felt him move closer and kiss the back of each thigh. He flipped up her skirt, and Hayden could feel it resting on the small of her back. She blushed, knowing she was fully exposed to him now.

"Freckles," Boone breathed. "I wondered if you had them all over."

"The bane of my childhood," Hayden murmured, not raising her head.

"Fucking beautiful. Spread your legs a bit more." Boone didn't say anything else, but leaned in and nuzzled her inner thigh, encouraging her to widen her stance. When she did, his hands, which had been resting on her thighs, moved up. They squeezed her butt cheeks, and his thumbs spread her folds apart.

"Oh Jesus."

Boone chuckled against her. "Nope, just me." Without giving her any more time to stress about what he was doing, Boone licked from the top of her folds to his thumbs, holding her steady as she jumped. Then he did it again, then again.

He gripped her ass tighter, and spread her pussy lips apart even more with his thumbs and buried his tongue in her as far as he could get it.

"Boone!"

He didn't answer, but continued learning every inch of her flesh. Hayden could feel the wetness seep from her core. When she felt a drop of liquid slide out of her and start to drip down her inner thigh, Boone was there. He lapped it up with his tongue as if it were an errant drip of ice cream escaping from a cone.

As Hayden moaned and squirmed under his expert attention, he moved one finger up to her clit and another eased inside her wet body.

"Boone...oh my God. That feels so good."

Boone nuzzled against the flesh of her ass as he kept up the motion of his fingers. "No, *you* feel so good, Hay. Exactly like I dreamed. Relax and come for me. I want to feel it."

Hayden had never orgasmed with a man before. None of the other men she'd slept with had bothered trying to make her come with them, and she hadn't cared. But now, losing control with Boone at the wheel seemed incredibly intimate. What if she sounded weird? What if she made sounds that turned him off? She tensed.

"Shhhhh, relax, sweetheart. Don't tense up. Just let it happen. I'm right here, I've got you. I can't wait to get in here. You're so hot and wet, I know you'll grab hold of my dick and squeeze until I can't move. I'll feel you trying to hold on to me as I pull out, then we'll both sigh in relief as I get back in there. That's it. Push against me. God, that's sexy as all fuck."

Hayden couldn't think any more. He'd added another finger inside her and he was caressing the walls of her sex as he pushed them in and out. But it was his other hand that was making her move against him. He'd pulled back the hood of her clit and was rubbing directly on the small bundle of nerves. It was as if he'd read her mind and knew just what would throw her over the cliff.

She threw back her head and came up on her hands. She pushed back into him, fucking his fingers for several moments, not caring what she might look like anymore. She could feel the orgasm rising from her depths and froze in place, needing more, but not able to move a muscle. Luckily, Boone took care of her, thrusting into her and rubbing her clit hard at the same time. Hayden squeezed her eyes shut and saw stars behind her eyelids. "Boone! I'm...yes...God."

When Hayden came back to herself, she felt Boone

still kneeling behind her. One wet hand was gripping her hip tightly, and the other was caressing and gently rubbing her soaking wet folds. She felt him kiss her ass. "Fucking beautiful."

He stood up and she heard him tear open a condom wrapper. "Put your legs closer together now, Hay." She did as he requested and Hayden felt Boone's hardness push up against her core. He dipped his knees and his length slid along her folds, coating himself with her juices. Boone didn't waste any more time. The bulbous head of his cock entered her, then pushed inside her with one long, steady thrust.

Hayden came up on her toes in her shoes. "Oh! Boone!" It burned a bit as it had been a long time since she'd had anything other than her slender vibrator inside her, but the burn slowly changed to a full feeling that made her feel consumed by the man standing behind her.

Boone held still and leaned over her on the bed. Hayden could feel his weight along her back and suddenly she wished she was naked so she could feel him skin to skin.

"Am I hurting you?" Boone's voice was low in her ear. He took her hands in his and laced their fingers together, keeping them on the bed.

"N-no. It's just...you're big."

"I am. And you're not. But you feel fucking awesome, Hay."

"Yeah, you feel good too," she admitted.

Boone pulled out slightly, then pushed back in. Hayden flexed her inner muscles against him and he groaned. "Yeah, that feels amazing. Do it again."

She did, and got the same result. He pulled away and came back inside her slower this time. He did it again, and again. Hayden squirmed and tried to push against him as he thrust into her the next time.

"In a hurry?"

"Boone, come on."

"Oh, we'll come all right."

Hayden rolled her eyes, knowing he wouldn't see her. "Please, I'm okay. Fuck me."

"I am."

"You know what I mean."

"I might not have taken my time tasting every inch of your body, but I *will* take my time in this and make it good for you."

"Boone," Hayden whined, trying to push against him as he once again came back inside her slowly and methodically. She wondered what it would take for him to lose that iron control.

"Yes, Hayden?"

She remembered then what he'd told her earlier. If he wanted her to beg, she'd gladly do it if it would make him hurry up. "Please."

"Please what?"

Hayden could hear the smile in his voice. "Please, fuck me. I want to feel you pounding into me like you said you would. Your fingers felt great, but your cock feels even better." She heard the hitch in his breathing this time. Bingo.

He thrust into her harder and didn't wait before pulling back out and doing it again. Hayden groaned. "Yessssss."

Boone released her hands and put his own on her back. "Lean over further, sweetheart."

Hayden did as he asked immediately. Her position put her ass higher up in the air. Boone grasped her hips and pulled her into him as he thrust in that time. They both groaned.

"God, you feel so good. So tight around me. So wet. I can feel your wetness against my balls. You're soaking me."

"Faster, Boone. Please." It should've felt weird to be fully dressed when Boone was naked, but all she could think about was how he felt inside her. All thoughts of being embarrassed or how she was supposed to be frigid left her mind. Boone and his cock were the only things on her mind at the moment.

He went faster. He snuck one hand under her and brushed her clit as he thrust in. "Yeah, Hayden. Yeah."

They worked in tandem this time. When Boone pulled out, Hayden pressed herself against the bed; when he pushed back into her, she pushed toward him, making his thrusts harder and faster. The sounds of her ass slapping against him were loud in the room. He continued to strum her bundle of nerves until he could tell she was close.

"Do it. Come for me, Hay. I want to feel you squeeze me dry."

When Hayden wailed in relief at her release, Boone held himself still inside her, reveling in the feel of her inner muscles contracting against his hard flesh. He enjoyed it for a beat, then thrust in and out of her as fast as he dared and still not hurt her. All it took was four thrusts and he exploded.

Boone couldn't hold back the long groan, as it felt as though he'd emptied every ounce of fluid he had in his body into the condom. He rested his forehead on Hayden's back for a moment, before pulling upright.

Boone eased out of Hayden's body, enjoying the hell out of the groan that left her mouth as he popped free. He put a heavy hand on her back. "Stay put for just a second, Hay. Okay? I'll be right back."

"Mmmmm."

Boone smiled at Hayden's lack of response. He felt like she sounded, but he couldn't collapse on the bed until he took care of her. He went into his bathroom and got rid of the condom. He turned on the water, more glad than he could say for his expensive water heater. He wet a washcloth in the warm water and headed back out into his bedroom, smiling.

Hayden hadn't moved an inch. He stood there for a beat admiring the view. She was sexy as all get out—and all his. Her head was against the mattress and her arms were resting on the bed over her shoulders. Her ass was in the air and her legs in the sexy hose and heels were on display.

Amazingly, Boone felt his dick stir. Jesus, he was forty, not sixteen.

He went over to Hayden and touched her back, making sure she knew he was there. "Let me clean you up, then we'll make you more comfortable, okay?"

Boone watched as Hayden nodded. He put the warm cloth against her folds and almost laughed out loud as she came back to life. She pushed her chest up from the bed and turned her head to look at him. "Uh, I can do that."

"Nuh uh. I've got it. Relax."

Hayden put her hands back on the mattress, but she certainly wasn't relaxing.

Boone ignored the thought that he wanted to clean her up with his tongue, which would end in another round of fucking, so instead finished up with the warm washcloth. He dropped it on the floor, deciding to deal with it in the morning, and helped Hayden stand upright and off the stool. "Arms up, sweetheart."

Boone couldn't believe Hayden was being as docile as she was, but he wasn't going to question it. He lifted her sexy dress up and over her body, leaving her standing there in nothing but her bra and thigh highs. "Holy fuck, Hay. I should've done you this way."

She giggled at him, actually giggled, then lightly smacked him on the shoulder. "Boone!"

He reached behind her and deftly undid the hooks

on her bra, and watched as she lowered her arms and let it fall to the floor. She had marks under her breasts where the underwire had pushed in on her all night. Without thought, he brought his hands up and massaged her breasts. "That has to hurt."

Hayden sighed in relief. "Well, it doesn't feel good, but after wearing a bulletproof vest all day, this is nothing. Besides, I'd say it was worth it the way you were eyeballing my tits all night."

Boone laughed. She never said what he expected her to. "True. Feel better?"

When Hayden nodded, he knelt at her feet again. He unbuckled her shoes and carefully put them to the side so they wouldn't trip over them when they got out of bed in the morning. She put her hands on his shoulders and he knew she watched as he took the first stocking in his hands and rolled it down her well-toned leg. She lifted her foot when he got to the bottom and then he did the same to the other one. Again, she held on to him as she lifted her foot so he could remove the delicate hose.

Finally, they were both completely naked. Boone stood up and wrapped his arms around Hayden's back. One hand rested on the right side of her waist, and the other he put on her left shoulder blade. His fingers wrapped around to the front of her body, and he held on tightly. Hayden wrapped both hands around his shoulders and leaned the side of her head against his as he snuggled into her. They stood like that, their bodies as close as two humans could be to one another, and reveled in the closeness and intimacy.

Hayden felt cocooned in Boone's arms and even though she was smaller than he was, she hoped he felt the same kind of comfort in her arms as she did in his.

Finally, Boone pulled his head back. "You need to use the bathroom?"

Hayden shook her head, so Boone pulled back the comforter and the top sheet and gestured for Hayden to crawl in. She did and he followed. He turned off the light on the side of the bed and pulled her into him. He lay on his back and she snuggled into his side, her head resting on his shoulder and one arm over his stomach.

"You gonna sleep okay without Ellie?"

Boone felt Hayden burrow her head into his shoulder and groan. "I'm so embarrassed you know about her."

He smiled. "It's not a big deal."

"It is to me."

"Tell me about her?"

Boone wasn't sure she would, but after a long moment, he heard her say in a soft voice, "When I was four, I received a baby doll—I called her Molly—in the mail for my birthday. I'm not even sure now who it was from. It might have been mom's sister, but I have no idea. Anyway, I loved that thing. I carried it every-where. Dad hated it. I mean, he *really* hated it. He'd rather I played with the trucks and balls he got me.

One day, Molly was gone. I cried for days. I know it irritated my dad because he kept telling me to get over it already. To man up."

"He said that to you? To man up?" Boone asked incredulously. "At *four*?"

Hayden nodded and continued. "Yeah. Anyway, Mom came home with this ridiculously ugly stuffed elephant to take the place of Molly. Dad allowed it because an elephant wasn't as girly and weak as a doll. Since Molly had disappeared when I was sleeping, I made sure that wasn't going to happen with Ellie. I've slept with her every day since."

"What happened to your doll?"

Hayden shrugged. "Dad threw it out. He despised it."

Boone was pissed for her, but tried to stay relaxed. "It makes sense that Ellie became a security blanket of sorts for you."

"Yeah. And I know it's not normal for me to still have the thing, much less to still be sleeping with it. Hayden, the tough-as-nails cop sleeping with a fucking stuffed animal...but it makes me feel..." Her voice trailed off.

"Secure," Boone answered for her.

He felt her nod against him. "Yeah. I guess. I feel like Linus with his blanket though."

Boone kissed the top of Hayden's head and held her closer to him. "It's cute as all fuck. I don't care. Whatever it takes for you to feel safe and comforted is what *I* care about. If that means you're sleeping with a stuffed animal when you're eighty, and thus *we're* sleeping with a stuffed animal when we're eighty, so be it." Boone felt Hayden's arm jerk against him for a moment, as if surprised by his understanding, and he smiled as she turned her head and kissed the top of his shoulder tenderly. She didn't say anything, but the light kiss said it all.

They lay together in silence and Boone knew the moment Hayden fell asleep. Her arm became dead weight on his stomach and she started breathing deeply through her nose. He smiled and kissed the top of her head. Sexy as hell and cute as fuck. It was a combination that definitely worked for him.

16

———

HAYDEN HAD NEVER BEEN good at "morning afters," but Boone didn't give her a chance to feel weird. She'd woken up to his hands running over her body, and he'd spent forty-five minutes doing just what he'd said he'd do—worshiping her. When Hayden didn't think she'd be able to stand one more second of his lips on her skin and not have him inside her, he'd taken pity on her and made slow, sweet love to her. They'd both exploded and lain there dozing until Boone finally roused enough to get up.

He'd kissed her on the forehead, said he'd get up and shower and find her something to wear, and when he was done in the bathroom, he'd get her up. Hayden had gone into the bathroom later and realized he'd somehow found a size large—instead of the XXL he wore—T-shirt and a pair of running shorts that would work until she could get her own clothes. The shorts obviously were his, but since they had a drawstring, she could tighten them enough so they wouldn't fall off.

She'd showered, blushing at the love bites she'd found on various parts of her body, and gotten dressed. Boone didn't have a hair dryer, so she'd simply combed her hair and put it up in a ponytail. She'd wandered into the kitchen, expecting to feel weird about what they'd done, but found, to her relief, that they were comfortable with each other.

She and Boone had eaten a leisurely breakfast, with Boone explaining that his employees were responsible for the cows that morning, and he'd driven her home. He'd kissed her passionately, his hands roaming her body, when he'd dropped her off, and they'd promised to get together again soon.

Thirty minutes later, she'd received a text from Boone.

Miss you.

Hayden smiled.

Ditto she'd texted back.

You working tomorrow?

Yeah.

A couple minutes went by before Boone texted her again.

Any chance you'd take pity on an old cow farmer and let him spend the night with you tonight?

What time you getting here?

Hayden felt giddy. It was silly, but she really liked Boone and was thrilled he seemed to like her back.

Probably after dinner. I've got a heifer who's going to drop her calf anytime now. I want to make sure she's okay.

Sounds good. See you then.

He hadn't answered, but Hayden wasn't worried. She spent the day cleaning her apartment and making sure it looked all right. She didn't think Boone would care, but she wasn't taking any chances.

Around eight, Boone knocked on the door and the second Hayden let him in, she was in his arms and he was urging her down the hall to her room.

"You eaten?" he asked in between kisses.

"Yeah, you?"

"Uh huh. But I could eat something else." Hayden knew exactly what he meant because of the lecherous gleam in his eye.

Boone eased Hayden's shirt up her body and dropped it as they continued to her room.

"What time do you have to be in in the morning?" Boone said as he used one finger to slide her bra strap off a shoulder.

"Eight."

"Okay, good. We've got all night, and I have plans for this gorgeous body."

Those were the last words they'd spoken for a long while.

∽

THE LAST THREE weeks had been idyllic for Hayden. Most nights she either spent out at the farm with Boone, or he came to her. It wasn't until the week before that Hayden clued into some of the things Boone had been doing for her and called him on it.

They'd been standing in her kitchen and Boone was doing the dishes from dinner.

"You need to stop it, Boone."

He didn't even flinch, just methodically kept putting the dishes into her little dishwasher. "What do you mean? Stop what?"

"This. The dishes. My laundry. Making dinner. Picking me up and dropping me off at work, giving me massages, rubbing my feet...all of it!"

Boone calmly dried his hands on a towel hanging off the fridge, and then put it back and leaned against the counter when he was done. He crossed his feet at the ankles and looked at her. "So you'd prefer if I sat at your table and watched you cook or didn't bother putting your clothes in with mine when I washed them?"

"Well, no, but—"

"And do you hate it when I rub your feet? Are my massages that horrible?"

"You know that's not it."

"Then what's the problem, sweetheart?"

Hayden struggled to put into words what she wanted to say. "I can take care of myself."

"And?"

"And you're not letting me."

Boone had taken a deep breath and pushed off the counter and came to her. "So when you met with all my employees and told them what to do if they saw Dana...that wasn't *you* taking care of *me*?"

Hayden opened her mouth to respond but he continued before she could.

"And when I came in the house after losing that calf, and you ran me a bath, and let me hold you all night long because I was devastated...I shouldn't have let you do that either?"

"Boone—"

"It's called being in a relationship, Hay. We take care of each other. Of course we can take care of ourselves. We're adults. But when you're in a relationship, you do things for the other person because you want to. Because it makes you feel good. Because you *like* them. Do you enjoy looking out for me?"

"Yeah."

"Yeah. And I like looking out for you too. Especially since it seems to me you haven't had that. So let me... okay? If I do something truly out of your comfort zone, let me know and I'll curb it. But, Hayden," Boone leaned down and kissed her forehead and looked her in the eye, "I've never felt this way about someone before. It makes me feel good to take care of you, in bed and out. Okay?"

She'd nodded, and that night he'd shown her just

how well he could take care of her, both in the shower and in her bed.

In appreciation, Hayden learned that she didn't mind getting up close and personal with Boone's cock after all...and taking care of him right back. Going down on him would never be something she loved, but seeing how much pleasure he got out of it, and knowing she was responsible for making him lose some of his tightly held control, made it that much more enjoyable...especially when he reciprocated and made her lose all sense of who and where she was.

They hadn't heard much from Dana, but Hayden suspected she was the one responsible for the petty shit she'd been dealing with. One morning she'd gone to leave for work, only to find all four of her tires were flat. Another night, there had been a pizza delivery man at her door every thirty minutes for five straight hours. The pranks were petty and amateurish. They weren't life threatening, but they were definitely annoying. She'd taken note of each one and put it in a thickening file at work labeled simply, "Dana."

Hayden grabbed the mail from her box and put it under her arm as she unlocked her door and went inside. She dumped it on the kitchen counter as she went to change. She came back after showering, wearing her fat pants and an oversized T-shirt Boone had left at her place. It had a longhorn steer on the front with the words "Hatcher Farms" over the top and his website underneath. It was soft and well-worn from many washes, and Hayden loved it. It was definitely going to be living in her drawers, with the *Think Chicken* shirt, instead of his from here on out.

She opened the fridge and took out a bottled water as she contemplated what to eat for dinner. Hayden wasn't in the mood to cook, as usual, so she popped a microwave meal in and set the timer. She shuffled through her mail as she waited for her dinner to be done.

There was a medium-sized yellow envelope in with the mail, with no return address. Her name and address were handwritten on the front. Hayden opened it and dumped out the contents onto the counter—and froze.

Staring up at her were at least a dozen pictures of herself and Boone, except in every single picture, her face had been scratched out until it wasn't recognizable anymore.

There was no note with the pictures, but Hayden knew who they were from.

Fucking hell.

The last time either of them had suspected Dana's handiwork was when a gate at the back side of his property had been propped open. At least a dozen cows had wandered over to the neighboring property and had to be rounded up. It wasn't a huge deal, luckily the owner of the farm next door was an upstanding and understanding man, but if there were any calves born from the heifers' time with the neighbor bulls, they couldn't be sold. Boone would take a hit from having to wait to breed those cows again.

They both suspected Dana, but there had been no proof. Hayden had even asked the crime scene techs to come out and take a look at the gate, but they hadn't been able to pick up any fingerprints other than Boone's and those of one of the hands, who was responsible for that section of fence. And the cameras that had been installed hadn't operated correctly that night. Boone was dealing with the security company that had improperly installed them, and they'd promised to get them up and running again, correctly this time. He was pissed that they hadn't worked when he'd really needed them to. The owner was apologetic and had refunded half of the cost of the system because of his employee's mistake.

But this. This was different. Hayden looked at the pictures strewn on her counter as if they were blood stains spreading across the surface. The pictures proved Dana was still pissed, and honestly, Hayden could see why, especially since Dana still considered Boone "hers." In the pictures, she and Boone were kissing. Hayden could see his hand on her breast in one, and most of the time in the others his hands were on her ass or lower back. And Hayden's hands were all over Boone in the photos as well.

They would've been sexy if they weren't creepy—and of course, if Hayden's face hadn't been obliterated in every single one. Dana had obviously been following them for some time, letting her anger increase over their blossoming relationship. She probably hoped their growing feelings for each other would fizzle out, but since it was obvious they were flourishing as a couple instead, Dana had felt the need to do something drastic.

Without touching the pictures, and ignoring the dinging of the microwave announcing that the dinner was ready, Hayden called Juan, who she knew was on duty.

Juan arrived with Scott, another deputy who worked at their station.

"There's nothing we can do, Hayden," Juan told her regretfully. "You know as well as I do, this isn't breaking the law."

Hayden paced back and forth in her small kitchen. "Yeah, but *you* know as well as I do it's only a matter of time before Dana snaps and does something crazy. We've *seen* this time and time again."

"He's a guy, Yates. I'm not sure what the problem is. She'll get over it eventually; in the meantime, he can suck it up and deal." Scott's tone was dismissive and bored.

Hayden turned to Scott and got right up into his face. "Have you ever been to a crime scene and seen someone's head blown off?"

Scott took a step back from an extremely pissed off Hayden. "Uh—"

"What about a car wreck where a man's body was

smushed into tiny pieces because his brakes failed or he swerved into oncoming traffic?"

"Look, Yates—"

Hayden again cut him off, on a roll. "Just because Boone is the most masculine man I've ever seen in my life, doesn't mean a woman who feels jilted, even when she wasn't, can't hurt him...*especially* when he's too honorable to fight back. She can blow his head off as easy as *that*." Hayden snapped her fingers in Scott's face and didn't back down when he flinched.

"And it's not *him* she's targeting right now either. It's not *his* face that's been scratched out in every single picture, it's *mine*. Don't ever say that someone will 'get over it' when it gets to this point." Hayden threw her hand out at the defaced pictures on her counter. "This woman is crazy. A fucking piece of paper isn't going to keep Boone, or me, safe. The only thing that'll keep us safe is documenting every single one of her bat-shit crazy actions, and hoping that one will definitively lead back to her and she can be arrested for violating that fucking piece of paper."

"Easy, Yates," Juan said, putting a supportive hand on her back.

Hayden turned to Juan. "You know I'm right, Juan. You *know* it. She's escalating. It's textbook."

"I do know it," Juan said. "That's why I'm going to package up these pictures and bring them in. We'll get them processed. In the meantime, keep an eye on your six, and on Hatcher's too. Got it?"

Hayden turned to glare at Scott and said in a calmer voice, which was all the more effective because she wasn't screaming, "From that first call when she broke into Boone's house, then lied to the cops about him hitting her, to vandalism, to drugging me while I was out enjoying a night with my boyfriend. Then my tires, the fence, the damn pizza deliveries...oh and don't forget the dead *cat* on my doorstep. Textbook escalation, Scott. Next time, don't be a flippant ass to someone who says they're being stalked and are concerned about their safety, or that of someone close to them, when they come to you for help."

"I'm sorry, Yates," Scott told her, sounding contrite. "You're absolutely right. I've seen domestics where the woman is guilty before. Not a lot, but some. I was out of line."

"Damn straight," Hayden nodded, not quite willing to forgive the other deputy yet.

"Keep me in the loop, yeah?" she told Juan, nodding at the pictures he was picking up with gloves and putting into a plastic bag.

"Of course."

"Thanks."

Hayden waited until they left and paced, debating what she should do. Finally, she snatched up her phone and texted Boone.

You up?

They hadn't planned on meeting that night because Hayden worked late, and had to get into work early the next morning. But she then had three full days off and they were planning on holing up at the farm. She'd been looking forward to hanging with Boone while he went about his regular farm day, but more importantly spending as much time as possible with him in his tub, and shower, and bed.

Yeah. What's up?

Hayden took a deep breath and changed her mind. She was going to ask if she could come out to his place and talk, but decided to just wait until the next day. She'd tell him what Dana had sent her then, and they'd figure out what to do tomorrow.

I just wanted to say good night and that I missed you.

You sure you're okay?

Yeah.

Okay. I miss you too. I can't wait to see you tomorrow. Pick you up at 7?

Sounds good.

See you tomorrow.

Hayden headed to her door, double checked it was locked and bolted, then made her way to her room, making sure her pistol was locked and loaded and within easy reach. In her gut, she knew Boone was safe. It was *her* Dana was pissed at. Whatever she had planned would make the GHB incident look like child's play.

All Hayden could think was *bring it.*

17

HAYDEN SMILED at Boone when she opened her door the next evening. She'd had a long talk with the sheriff that day at work. While he wasn't a patrol deputy anymore, she wanted him to know what had been happening and her suspicions. There wasn't anything either of them could do until Dana made her move, but having him know that she suspected Dana was going to do something made Hayden feel better. If push came to shove and she had to protect Boone, or herself, she wanted it on record that she feared Dana would try to hurt one of them.

She was ready to go when she opened the door, so she kissed Boone quickly and shuffled them out of her place.

"In a hurry?" Boone asked with a smile in his voice.

"Yeah, actually." Hayden locked her door and made the decision to tell Boone what Dana had sent her after they'd made love that night. He was usually more relaxed and maybe he'd take it better. He wasn't going to be happy at all that Dana was targeting her again.

Boone leaned into her and kissed the back of her neck as she turned to lock her door. Cognizant of Dana's penchant for taking pictures of them kissing in public, Hayden didn't let Boone distract her. As soon as she'd locked her door, she grabbed up her bag and took Boone's hand and led their way to his truck. She hoped he'd think she was anxious to get him home, but knew he was probably too observant for her to pull the wool over his eyes.

As soon as they were on their way back to his place, Boone said, a bit too nonchalantly, "Want to tell me what that was all about?"

"No. But I will. Later."

Boone didn't look happy, but he didn't push. Hayden put her hand on his thigh as they drove, and she sighed in relief when he reached down and held it in his own. She hated keeping anything from him, but figured that was probably a good thing in regards to any future relationship they might have.

They pulled up to his house and he parked in the garage. Boone grabbed her bag from the backseat and met Hayden at the front of his truck and they went into the house together.

Boone had put together a small dinner, and they ate, discussing nothing in particular. After the dishes had been done and put away, Boone held out his hand to Hayden. She took it and they headed down the hall to his room.

"I thought we'd take a bath before going to sleep tonight. That all right?"

"Sounds heavenly," Hayden told him honestly. She watched as he turned on the water and put the stopper in the tub. He squirted a healthy dollop of bubble bath into the stream of hot water and then turned and crooked his finger at her. "Come 'ere, Hay."

Hayden smiled and went to him.

"Arms up."

She gladly held her arms over her head and smiled as Boone pulled her shirt off. She didn't move, knowing he liked to undress her himself. He looked down and concentrated on undoing the button of her jeans and easing the zipper apart. He gave the denim a push and inhaled sharply at seeing her lack of underwear and that she'd shaved off the auburn curls covering her pussy.

"Really?" His eyes came up to hers, even as his hand went straight to her core as if drawn there by a magnet.

Hayden smiled at him and blew out a breath as his fingers parted her and swiped through the wetness already dampening her skin. "Really."

"Jesus, you're fucking killing me." The words were said under his breath, but Hayden heard them anyway. "If you'd asked me, I would've said not to change a thing. I loved that your hair down here was as red as on your head, but this…" Boone paused a moment to run the backs of his fingers from her soaking wet pussy up to her clit and the smooth skin above it, then back down until he eased a finger inside and held it there. "Damn, you feel good, Hay."

Hayden grabbed hold of his biceps with her hands and held on tightly as Boone teased her. She'd hoped he would like her surprise, and it seemed as if he did. "So do you," she said breathily as he moved his finger lazily in and out of her body.

Slowly he removed his finger and brought it up to his mouth, using his tongue to clean it off as if he was eating an ice cream cone. Only once he was sure he'd cleaned every bit of her musk off his finger did he reach for her. His arms went around her, undoing her bra, smoothing his hands over her breasts and briefly massaging away any soreness from being encased in the constricting cotton all day. Boone ran his fingers over the still fading marks on her sides that the bullet-proof vest left in her skin.

"I can't believe you squeeze yourself into that thing every day."

They'd been over this, but Hayden repeated what she knew Boone was already aware of. He was just complaining because he didn't like to think about her being uncomfortable. "I happily wear it. I've taken a bullet before, and am standing here today because I was wearing the vest."

"I know," Boone murmured before bending down

and kissing the marks lightly. He stood up and quickly stripped off his shirt and jeans, then his boxers, before turning to the tub to check the water.

Hayden squeezed his tight ass cheeks as he bent over and he practically squealed and shot upright. She couldn't help it, and laughed at his girly reaction.

"Laugh at me, huh?" Boone warned, seconds before reaching out and tickling her sides mercilessly until she begged him to stop. They were both grinning when he brought her into his embrace.

Hayden loved when Boone hugged her. He didn't just wrap his arms around her and squeeze, he enfolded her into his body and it seemed as though he tried to absorb her. It was the best feeling in the world.

Finally, he pulled away and turned off the water. He stepped into the tub, not losing hold of her hand as he eased down. He inhaled sharply. "Fuck, it's hot. Hang on, Hay, let me put in some more cold water before you get in."

Hayden ignored his words and stepped in front of him and eased her body down. She sat between his legs and leaned back into him. "Mmmmm, it's hot, but it feels so damn good."

Boone relaxed under her and they lay in the tub together, enjoying the heat of the water and simply being close to one another. At first it wasn't sexual at all. It was just two people enjoying the feeling of skin-on-skin contact.

But eventually, as it did most of the time, with their

naked bodies rubbing against each other, Boone's hands started to roam over Hayden. He had easy access to her as she was lying with her back to his chest. He covered her breasts with his hands and massaged them, making sure to lightly pinch and tease her nipples until they were hard points. Hayden could feel his growing erection at her back and she squirmed against him as he played.

Eventually his hand made its way between her legs and stroked the slick skin there. He used his fingers to tease her clit, then would move down to put one, then two, fingers inside her. His other hand kept busy at her nipples, until she was literally writhing in his grasp and her hips were undulating with his movements. He kept her on the edge until she moaned, "Boone. Please." As if her words were what he was waiting for, he pinched a nipple tightly and used two fingers to roughly strum her clit. As she came apart in his arms, Boone took her mouth and Hayden couldn't do anything but hold on and trust Boone to keep her head above the water as she had one of the hardest orgasms of her life.

When Hayden finally stopped shaking, Boone stood up, holding on to her so she didn't slip. He stepped out and grabbed a towel and slicked it over his body quickly, not taking his eyes from Hayden's body as she not-so-patiently waited for him. He helped Hayden step out of the tub and spent a lot more time making sure every inch of her body was cleared of any water droplets.

Then he picked her up and carried her into the bedroom and settled her on her back on the bed. He took his time showing her how much she meant to him and Hayden did the same right back.

Finally, when they lay naked and exhausted in each other's arms, Hayden brought up the "gift" Dana had left her today.

"I received some hate mail from Dana today."

She'd apparently underestimated Boone's languid mood, because he tensed against her. "What?"

"Hate mail. I can only assume it was from her, as she didn't exactly write me a love letter to go with the pictures she left. She's been following us...taking pictures. She put a bunch in an envelope and sent them to me."

"She sent you pictures of us?" Boone's voice was hard and flat and the muscle in his jaw clenched as he ground his teeth.

"Yeah. But she scratched out my face in all the pictures first."

At that, Boone rolled out of bed and headed into his closet, not saying another word.

Hayden leaped up after him, the relaxed feeling she had after Boone made love to her now gone.

She grabbed a button-down shirt of Boone's that was lying on the floor and quickly shoved her arms into it as she followed him into his closet.

"Boone…"

He'd already pulled on a pair of jeans and was shoving a foot into a cowboy boot. He ignored her, totally focused on getting dressed.

Hayden tried again. "Boone, seriously, I've dealt with this. I called Juan and he came over and got the pictures. They're on it."

"You might have dealt with it your way, but it's time I quit fucking around and dealt with her myself."

Hayden put a hand on Boone's arm, not really shocked when he yanked it away from her and reached for his second boot.

"Look, if you go off half-cocked and race to her right now, you're playing right into her hands. She wants you to come to her. She wants you to get up in her face."

"Oh really? And now you're an expert on crazy ex-girlfriends?" Boone barked, still not looking at her.

Hayden started getting pissed. She'd been trying to deal with this rationally, but clearly Boone was past that. "Yeah, actually, I am. I've dealt with a lot more pissed-off girlfriends, boyfriends, and exes than you have."

"Don't throw your job at me, Hayden. I'm pissed at you," Boone said yanking on the boot to get it on his foot. "You deliberately kept this from me. Do you know how that makes me feel?" Without giving her a chance to answer, he kept talking. "Like you think I'm helpless and a weak, pathetic man. That's how."

"That's not—"

He talked over her, reaching for a shirt on a nearby hanger. "I know it's ridiculous to let myself get beaten by her, I do, but I honestly thought she'd finally get a clue and move on. But it's obvious that's not going to happen until I talk to her."

"Boone!" Hayden said sternly, "You know I don't think of you that way, and this is all on Dana, not you."

When he stood in front of her fully dressed, Hayden started to panic. She had to stop him somehow.

"I didn't immediately tell you what she did because I have a gut feeling she's reaching the end of her rope. She's been spying on us. She's watched us together for a while now. She's losing it. She's gonna break, and we have to be ready for it. I spoke with the sheriff today and gave him a head's up...mostly to cover my ass in case I have to hurt her." Her voice lowered and she hoped Boone was hearing her. Truly hearing her. "Boone, I only received the pictures yesterday. It's not as if I've kept this from you for weeks. I had to talk to my boss, but I also didn't want you to worry. I won't keep things from you; that's not how I work.

"I love you, Boone Hatcher. I'll do anything in my power to keep you safe. If that means keeping you in the dark for a few fucking hours over shit like this, I will. If it means shooting that crazy bitch, I will. Don't you get it? You're *it* for me."

Hayden stood blocking the closet door with her

body. She had her hands on her hips, waiting for Boone to do something.

"That's a low blow, Hayden," Boone said looking over her shoulder, refusing to meet her eyes. "Saying you love me for the first time when you know how pissed I am at you is not cool. And you know why. You *know* I hate it when you keep shit from me, and to know you kept *this* from me shows how much you *don't* care about me."

Hayden's face didn't show the absolute devastation he'd just dealt her. She hadn't been trying to manipulate him in any way. She'd been trying to make her point, but obviously hadn't gone about it the right way. She stood still, waiting for his next move as she had no idea what to say.

"I'll deal with Dana. Get out of my way," Boone bit out bitterly, his hands clenched at his sides.

Hayden ground her teeth together as hard as she could and pressed her lips together. Knowing she'd given him everything she had, and he'd completely ignored her words as if they meant shit to him, she did the only thing she could.

She stepped out of his way and Boone stalked past her as if she hadn't just laid her heart at his feet, and watched as he stomped on it with his size-fourteen cowboy boots.

18

____

HAYDEN SAT in Boone's house in an easy chair in his living room. She'd methodically gotten dressed in her own clothes when she'd heard the garage door close behind Boone's truck. She'd hoped against hope that he'd come to his senses before he left the house, but he hadn't.

She could've gotten any one of his employees to take her home, but she wanted to make sure Boone arrived back at the house all right. It was stupid of her, but she'd been honest with him. She loved him.

She was pretty sure he loved her back, but wasn't a hundred percent sure, especially after he'd ignored her declaration of love and stalked out of the house. He'd been mad because Dana had messed with her...again. If he didn't care about her a little, she didn't figure he would've gotten so upset. So she was gambling on their future.

Sure, she could've acted like a pissed-off bitch, rightly so, but she loved him, and even mostly understood his frustration with the entire situation. That being said, she wasn't going to let him get away with acting like an ass to her. No fucking way. Things were intense, and he was upset when he'd heard about Dana's threat to her, but it was still no excuse to race out of the house in the middle of the night.

So she sat in his chair, feet planted at her ass, knees bent, her legs folded up. Her arms were around her legs and her cheek rested against her drawn-up knees.

Hayden tried to control her temper. The last thing she wanted to do was get up in Boone's face when he got back. But she was pissed and devastated all at the same time. It wasn't in her nature to break down and lose it, so she waited. Hoping like hell Boone wouldn't be able to find Dana and he'd be back sooner rather than later.

It took about an hour, but finally Hayden heard the garage door go back up. She let out a relieved breath, at least Dana hadn't shot him through the heart, but didn't otherwise move. The ball was in Boone's court now.

She kept her eyes on him as he came into the living room and looked down the hall to his bedroom. He ran his hand through his hair and sighed.

"You find her?" Hayden's voice was soft. She didn't want to startle him, but it was better he knew she was here.

Boone twirled around and saw her sitting in the shadows of his living room. "You're still here," he said, surprised.

"Yeah. I'm still here. You drove me here, for one thing."

Boone came toward her and sat on the sofa across from her rather than getting into her space. Smart man. "No. I didn't find her. Shit, Hay, I got about halfway to her apartment before I realized you were right. About all of it. I'm not going to solve anything by getting up in her face. I'd only give her another chance to throw something at me or hit me. She knows I won't hit her back, so going over there would've just been stupid."

Hayden didn't move and stayed silent, waiting to hear what else he had to say.

"I'm sorry, Hay. You didn't deserve that. I was pissed at Dana for what she'd put you through. I can take whatever she dishes out, but you shouldn't have to. I want to protect you, and I feel like I've failed miserably." When Hayden didn't move or say anything, Boone sighed and continued, "You're over there in a defensive ball, and I fucking hate it. But what I really hate is that *I* did that to you. I heard you, Hay. And for what it's worth, I love you too. That's why I was so upset. I know you're a big bad sheriff's deputy and can take care of yourself, but it doesn't stop the Neanderthal inside me wanting to shield you from every danger, and every asshole who is out there. The fact that it was an asshole *I* brought to your doorstep makes me absolutely insane."

When she still didn't respond, Boone let out a huge breath and put his head in his hands and said in a tortured voice, "I'll take you home. I'm sorry I left you stranded here."

"You hurt me, Boone."

At Hayden's soft words, Boone's head came up and he looked at her.

"I bared my soul to you and you tromped on it. That wasn't cool."

"I know," he whispered. "And I'm sorry."

"I've been doing my job for a long time. I deal with this kind of shit every day. Every day, Boone. I know you want to take care of me, and I appreciate it most of the time. But what you did tonight was uncalled for and out of line. Way out of line."

"I know," Boone said again.

"As much as you might hate it, I *can* protect you. It's what I do. I won't ever be the 'little woman' who sits at home while you save the world. I'll never spend all day cooking you a dinner fit for a king. Like it or not, my job isn't safe. I'm gonna be in shootouts, tracking down serial killers, and even dealing with everyday people who have a grudge against police officers. You storming out of here after we'd just made love to each other and not even talking or truly listening to me, was bullshit...and as much as I love you, I won't put up with it. It'll tear me apart and I'm not willing to live like that. I'm sorry I didn't call you the second I realized what Dana had done, but I did what I thought was right for both of us. And I *did* tell you. Just like I told you about the cat, and my tires, and the pizza deliveries. I've loved being with you, Boone, but if you're going to turn into a macho asshole every time you feel like I'm not acting like a helpless female, we might as well end this now."

"You're not a man, Hayden. No matter how much your dad tried to make you into one." Boone said, his voice tight with emotion.

"You're right, I'm not," Hayden agreed immediately. "But I've been practically raised as one, I work in a male-dominated field, and I can kick just about any man's ass if he gets out of line. My point is, I appreciate more than I can say that you want to keep me from harm, but it's just not necessary and frankly, that's not what I need from you. I need your support. I need a shoulder to cry on when I've had a shit day. I need someone to laugh with and to feel like I matter to."

"Hay…"

Ignoring his pleading tone of voice, Hayden hurried to finish her thought. "But that doesn't mean that I don't like the way you see me. That I don't like how you treat me. That I don't like it when you do things for me. But don't ever doubt that I have *your* best interests in mind when it comes to safety. I don't blame you for Dana's actions, just as you don't blame me for anything anyone else might do in regards to us.

We can only control our own actions, and tonight your actions were fucked up and you hurt me."

"You're right. I'm sorry."

"Don't do it again. Okay?"

"I won't. I swear." Boone had heard the hurt as well as the steel in Hayden's voice. He'd been frustrated that Dana continued to harass Hayden, when she'd done nothing wrong, and he'd taken it out on her. It wasn't fair, and he'd been a dick about it. Boone couldn't believe Hayden was forgiving him that easily. *Was* she forgiving him?

He watched as she put her legs down and stood up. She walked toward him and held out her hand. "Come on. We've both had a piss-poor day. Can we please go upstairs and get some sleep now?"

He immediately took hold of the hand she held out to him, sighing in relief at the familiar feel of her slender fingers closing around his own. "Hayden, I have to ask. You're forgiving me for being an ass? Just like that?"

"It wasn't 'just like that.' I sat here tonight before you got back, wondering how I'd go through the rest of my life without you. Imagining the look on your face when I said I was leaving you. In the end, I knew I couldn't do either...live without you, *or* leave. We're gonna fight, Boone. I'm gonna get pissed at you and you're gonna get pissed at me. If I stormed off and ended things with us every time it happened, we'd be living on a roller coaster...and honestly, I've always hated roller coasters at the amusement park. I'd rather yell, get pissed, and talk this kind of shit out than let it fester, or quit on us at the first sign of disagreement. But I'm glad this happened. You now know I won't put up with you hurting me again as you did tonight. And I expect you to tell me if I do or say anything that *you* truly can't put up with. I'm not Dana. I'm not going to go crazy on you. So yes, I can forgive you. We're human. We're gonna fuck things up...but because I care about you, I'm not willing to let it end us. Are you?"

"No! Hell no. I just...I'm not used to this."

"Dana didn't forgive easily, did she?"

Boone shook his head. "Understatement of the century. If I'd done to her what I did to you tonight, she literally would've knocked me upside the head with a skillet and screamed at me for at least half an hour telling me what an idiot and asshole I am."

Hayden winced, knowing he was right. "Again, I'm not Dana. And I'm not any of the other immature women you've apparently dated. I know why you were pissed. I'm not saying you didn't hurt me. But..." her voice dropped and cracked with emotion, "...I love you, Boone. I figured you reacted the way you did because you cared about me. If I didn't think that, I would've been right on your heels, getting the fuck out of your house and out of your life."

"I love you too, Hayden. I more than simply care about you."

"Right, so that's why I waited for you to come back. So we could talk it through like adults. We've done that now. I'm tired, and tomorrow you can make it up to me. Deal?"

Boone smiled and squeezed Hayden's hand as he stood up. "Deal." He pulled her into his embrace, the all-consuming one that Hayden loved. Damn, his arms almost wrapped completely around her back and touched in front. His head was buried in her neck and she could feel his hot breaths against her skin. She snuggled into him and took a deep breath, trying not to cry. She hadn't been sure this was where they'd end up when and if he came home, but she thanked her lucky stars it was.

Boone finally pulled back from Hayden, and took her head in his large hands. He pulled her up to him and kissed her forehead. "I love you, Hayden Yates. You're the best thing that's ever happened to me. If I wasn't so pissed at Dana, I would thank her right now for trying to get me arrested, because it brought you to my doorstep."

Hayden laughed lightly, glad the tension in the room had finally seemed to dissipate once and for all. "That's warped, but I have to say I agree." They smiled at each other and silently moved to the bedroom.

They undressed without a word and crawled into bed and immediately into each other's arms. Hayden fell asleep fairly quickly, happy to be back in Boone's arms, and content now that he was home safely, but it took Boone a lot longer.

He'd been an ass, and he knew it. He recalled the stoic look on Hayden's face when he'd ignored her declaration of love. He swore never to do or say anything again that would put that stony blank look on her face. Because if he'd learned anything about Hayden, it was that she'd hide any hurt or pain she was feeling if she knew it would negatively affect him. It was just one more way he'd take care of her...whether she knew it or not.

19

———

BOONE CAME AWAKE SLOWLY, not understanding what he was hearing.

"Stay here, Boone. I mean it," Hayden ordered in a hiss. "Call nine-one-one and ask for a sheriff's deputy to be sent out. I'd rather deal with my colleagues than the SAPD. Not that I think my friend Quint's people are bad cops, but since the sheriff knows the details, I want his people here."

Boone was wide awake now. "What's going on?"

"If I'm not mistaken, Dana wants that confrontation right this second."

Boone heard it now. Yelling coming from his front yard. Fuck. "I'm coming with you."

"Bad idea, Boone. She wants you there. If you give her that, you're giving her power."

"I'm not hiding up here like a coward while you deal with her."

Hayden sighed. "Fuck. Okay. Can you at least call nine-one-one first?"

They both winced at the increasing cacophony of noise coming from the front yard.

"Yeah, I can do that." Boone wasn't sure if he was glad or pissed that the ranch hands who lived on the property were housed back behind the barn. There was a chance they might not even hear the ruckus, which on one hand would be good, but on the other hand, Boone figured the more witnesses to Dana's crazy, the better.

Hayden leaned over and kissed Boone hard. He noticed she was already dressed and had stuffed her service pistol in the back of her waistband. He wanted to give her crap about that, remembering when they'd watched a television show one night and she'd complained that no "real" cop ever put his pistol in the back of his pants. It simply wasn't safe. "Be smart, Boone. And remember, I'm trained for this kind of situation and know what I'm doing."

Boone kissed Hayden back then nodded. She strode purposefully and confidently out of the room. He quickly dialed emergency services and explained the situation in as few words as possible to the operator. She advised him to stay put, to let the deputy on scene handle the disturbance, but there was no way in hell Boone was following her advice.

He'd heard what Hayden had told him earlier that night. This was what she did, what she was good at, and he'd let her do it—but maybe if he gave Dana some of what she wanted, this could end tonight rather than be dragged out even longer. And there was no way he was going to hide in the house while his girlfriend confronted his ex. No way in hell. That wasn't the kind of man he was, and would never *be* that kind of man.

He hung up, against the operator's wishes, and hurried to put some clothes on. The noise on his front lawn had ceased, but he knew Dana probably hadn't left. They weren't that lucky.

Boone made his way through the dark house to the back door. He opened it and eased out into the yard and made his way silently around the house, wanting to see what was going on but not bust right into whatever might be happening. The last thing he wanted to do was make Hayden's job more difficult. Easing around the corner, he sized up the situation. Hayden was standing at the bottom of the three stairs that led up onto the porch, Dana facing off with her.

His ex looked awful. One of the things he'd been amazed at while they were dating was that she always looked completely put together. Hair done, makeup on, clothes immaculate. The only time he ever saw her without makeup was the few times he shared a bed with her, and even then she made sure to keep the lights dim.

Now, there was absolutely no sign of the put-together woman he'd been dating. Her blonde hair looked as though it hadn't been washed in a couple of days, hanging limp and greasy around her face. She had on a nice blouse, but it was dirty and hanging outside the white pants she was wearing. Actually, those pants *might've* been white at one time, but currently they were almost tan with dirt, and there were grass stains on both knees. She was also only wearing one shoe. Boone had no idea where the other one was.

The car she'd driven to his house was parked haphazardly in his front yard, the engine still running. The front bumper was gone and there was a large dent on the front passenger side. Boone took a second to hope whatever, or whoever, she hit was all right before the words she started screeching rang out through the humid night.

"Move, you fucking bitch! There's no way I'm letting you get your dyke claws into *my* boyfriend. I don't even know what the fuck you're doing in my house. Get out of my way!"

Dana's words seemed to have no discernible effect on Hayden. She was in her deputy mode, unmoving and strong as a concrete pillar. She stood on the grass in front of the stairs with her hands open at her sides, showing Dana she was unarmed. If he hadn't been so concerned about her safety, Boone might've gotten turned on by this side of her.

"Dana, it's the middle of the night and you're violating the restraining order against you. You aren't allowed within two hundred feet of Boone or any of his property," Hayden said in a calm but forceful tone.

"I don't give a flying fuck! He's mine! He'll *always* be mine."

Hayden's voice was still hard, but she lowered it a bit, trying to get through to the distraught crazy woman in front of her. "Dana, Boone broke up with you. He's been broken up with you for months. It's time to move on. Find a man who loves you. He's out there, you just have to keep looking."

It was as if the words bounced right off of Dana. "I *did* find him, bitch. No matter how many times you shove your tongue down his throat, he's still mine! No matter how far down your throat you take his cock, you should know that it was down *mine* first. You'll always come second. It's my cunt, my mouth, and my ass he's taken and loves, not yours!"

Out of the corner of her eye, Hayden saw Boone take several steps toward Dana from the side of the house. Fuck, it really was a bad idea for him to be here.

"Boone!" Dana had finally seen him as well. "Thank God you're here. Get your ass over here! You're mine."

"We broke up, Dana," Boone said in a hard voice with none of the sympathy that Hayden had used in hers.

"No we fucking did *not*! You said you needed some space. I gave it to you. Now I'm taking it back! Get over here and stay away from her!" Dana pulled a knife out of her pocket and waved it in the air manically.

Hayden didn't even flinch at the sight of the knife. She wasn't worried. She'd dealt with perpetrators with knives before. She actually preferred them to guns. In order for a bad guy to use a knife, they had to be up close and personal. She could keep her distance from Dana until backup got there, she just had to keep her talking. "Dana, you need to—"

Before she could get anything else out, Hayden watched in disbelief as Boone took the few steps forward required to put himself between her and his ex, putting him way too close to Dana and the knife she was waving around.

"Boone, what the fuck are you doing? No!" For the first time, Hayden's voice lost its take-charge, calm tone.

But it was too late. Boone was responding emotionally, rather than using his head, and putting himself in danger as a result. Hayden knew he was acting out of concern for her, wanting to protect her, but he'd inadvertently made her job twice as difficult.

Hayden immediately pulled the pistol out of the hollow of her back and pointed it toward the ground, her finger resting near the trigger, her entire body on high alert. Double fuck. This had just escalated past where it needed to. Damn Boone and his protective instincts. She could freely admit that she liked it when Boone was protective of her, but not like this. In this situation, she was way more prepared to deal with Dana than he was.

Especially since they both knew he wouldn't hurt his ex.

As soon as Boone was close enough, Dana lunged and swiped at him with the knife.

Boone jumped back and put up his arm to block her, but he wasn't quick enough. Hayden watched as a line of red bloomed on Boone's arm and realized the bad situation just got worse.

"That's enough, Dana! Put down the knife and let's talk." Hayden put every ounce of power behind her words. It wasn't enough.

"Fuck you! He's a pansy-ass, and he's mine to do whatever I want with!" She turned to Boone. "Aren't you? You'd never hurt me; it's against your religion or some such fuckin' thing. See?" Dana moved the knife to her left hand and balled up her right, swiftly taking a step toward Boone and throwing a punch at him.

Boone easily dodged the blow, but didn't make any move on Dana.

Hayden was beyond furious. At Dana. At Boone for putting himself, and her, in this situation. This had to stop.

"I said, put down the knife, Dana. I'll shoot you if you don't."

"You'll shoot an unarmed woman? I don't think so." Dana dropped the knife. "You can't shoot me. I know the law. Besides...what would the country think about another officer-involved shooting with an unarmed civilian. They'd eat that shit up and your career would be over."

Hayden didn't know what game she was playing now, but she wasn't buying it. Yeah, it would suck to be crucified in the media, but if it meant keeping Dana away from Boone once and for all, she'd do whatever it took. "Turn around and kneel on the ground. Put your hands on your head." Hayden knew she didn't have any cuffs on her, but she could physically subdue the other woman until the deputies got there if she had to.

"You love me, don't you, Boonie?" Dana said in a singsong voice, holding her arms out to Boone and ignoring Hayden. "You know I hit you to try to toughen you up, right? We're good together. You love how I suck your cock. Come on, let me remind you."

"Dana, we were only together a couple of times; you've *never* taken my dick in your mouth or your ass. You're delusional. You need help," Boone said in a reasonable tone, obviously knowing enough not to antagonize her any further.

Dana looked really pissed now. She put her hands on her hips.

"Boone," Hayden said urgently, "get on the porch behind me. Get away from her."

Not surprisingly, Boone ignored her, but he did take a step backward. It was something.

"Not sucked you off? Boone, *you're* the delusional one. You pushed me to my knees and held my head still as you fucked my mouth. You shot off and I swallowed your come. Then you picked me up and threw me on your bed and you fucked me up the ass until I exploded!"

Boone's voice was even and low when he replied, "I'm forty years old, Dana. First of all, there's no way I could get it up again that fast after coming. Secondly, we've never been together in my bed."

"But you've had *her* in your bed, haven't you?" Dana screeched, pointing at Hayden. "She's good enough to have you there, but not me?"

The hair on the back of Hayden's neck rose. Oh shit. Dana was losing it, and Boone either didn't realize it or was past caring. Where the fuck was her backup?

"Yeah, Hayden's more than good enough for me," Boone retorted "I've had her in my tub, in my bed, up against my wall, on my kitchen table and on my desk in the office. I'll take her whenever and wherever she'll have me. She doesn't hit me and she doesn't make me feel like crap whenever I'm around her. She loves me— and I love her back."

Hayden looked on in horror when Dana's arm moved. It was if she were watching a slow-motion training video at work, even as she vaguely heard the sirens from the cavalry screaming down Boone's driveway.

Dana screeched in absolute fury as she pulled a pistol from somewhere; probably from the small of her back, the way Hayden had carried her own pistol into the fray. Dana took a few running steps sideways and instead of pointing the gun at Boone, she pointed it at the object of her hate.

Time seemed to slow.

Boone took quick steps toward his ex and his arm was pulling back even before the loud shot from Dana's gun sounded in the still night.

At almost the same time, Hayden fired her own weapon. Twice in rapid succession.

Dana's head rocked backward from the force of Boone's fist hitting her face. She stumbled as much from his blow as she did from the two bullets from Hayden's gun entering her body.

Blood sprayed from Dana's hand as the first bullet hit it, making her drop the weapon she'd just fired. She was falling toward the ground as the second bullet hit its target just above her knee.

Dana seemed to bounce as she landed, and there was only a moment of silence before she started screaming.

Hayden had no idea if it was because of pain from the bullets, her obviously broken nose, which was oozing blood, or sheer frustration at not getting what she wanted—namely, Hayden out of Boone's life once and for all.

The sound of sirens from the squad cars racing down Boone's driveway was the most welcome sound Hayden had heard in a long time. "Step back, Boone," she ordered unnecessarily; he'd already turned his back on Dana and was headed for her.

Hayden's ears rang from the gunshots as the doors to the deputies' cars opened and "hold your fire" and "put your hands up" were shouted.

Hayden didn't take her gaze from Dana, who was still wailing as she rolled around on the ground nearby.

"I'm a sheriff's deputy. She has an unsecured weapon," Hayden told one of the officers who'd quickly gotten out of his car and was almost to them, gesturing with her chin to Dana.

After the other officer kicked the gun Dana had dropped out of her reach, Hayden slowly bent and placed her weapon on the ground then unsteadily rose and put her hands in the air, showing she was now unarmed. Boone ignored the instructions being shouted into the chaos around them and was frantically running his eyes over Hayden.

"Are you hurt? Did she get you?"

Hayden ignored his question, but stared at him with wide eyes. "You hit her."

"She was trying to kill you!"

"You *hit* her," Hayden repeated.

"Yates? That you?" Hayden heard. She turned her head to the side and saw Jimmy and Juan approaching. Thank God. "Yeah. It's me."

"You good?"

"Yeah, deal with Dana. Two shots fired, both made

contact. She fired at me after assaulting Boone. I hit her in the hand and leg. Boone has surveillance cameras; they should've caught everything that happened." She looked at Boone. "You *did* set them up to record out here, right?"

He nodded at her and told the other deputy, "Yes, and they're definitely working this time. The entire property around the house is covered, as is the inside of the barn, and randomly around the perimeter of the property."

"Good. That'll make things easier. Good job, Yates. Ambulance is on the way for the vic," Juan commented, turning to Dana, who was still crying and carrying on.

Hayden turned back to Boone and said again, "I can't believe you hit her. You don't hit women."

"I don't. But when one is pointing a gun at the woman I love, you better believe I hit women."

She heard his words; they warmed her insides as though she'd just drank a cup of hot chocolate, the impact spreading from her heart out into her extremities until her fingers tingled. "You weren't supposed to come outside." It wasn't really what she wanted to say after his declaration of love, but she was dizzy and felt weird.

"I know, but there was no way I was going to let that bitch kill the best thing that's ever happened to me."

"Okay, well. Wow. Um...Boone?"

"Yeah, sweetheart?"

"You need to get your arm looked at." Hayden nodded at the blood oozing from the small cut on his arm. "With our luck, that knife had poison on it or something."

She could tell Boone was trying really hard not to laugh. "I don't think it was poisoned, Hay, but I'll have the EMTs look at it after they take care of Dana."

"Okay, good, and one more thing."

"What's that?"

"You might have them look at me too. I think she got in a lucky shot…"

Hayden's words fell off and she passed out before she could finish her thought. Luckily, Boone caught her before she hit the ground.

20

HAYDEN ROLLED over and opened her eyes, not surprised to see Boone awake and looking down at her, concern and love in his gaze.

"Hey, what time is it?" she asked sleepily.

"Don't know."

"Boone…"

"Let me rephrase. Don't know and don't care."

"Boone, you have to see to the cows."

"I have staff that's working their asses off to make sure the farm runs with no problems while I'm here with you. You've rid their boss of the wicked witch of the south. The farm is fine," Boone said easily. "Sleep, Hay, you don't have to get up yet."

Hayden yawned and turned over to her back, only wincing a bit when the movement pulled at the stitches in her still healing wound. "I'm not tired anymore. I've done nothing *but* sleep for the last two days. I want to get up. I *need* to get up."

When Boone didn't say anything, she looked over at him. He'd propped himself up on an elbow and was staring at her arm.

"Boone." He still didn't look away from the bandage covering her upper arm where Dana's bullet had grazed her. Okay, it was more than a graze, more like a shallow furrow, but she'd be damned if she'd draw any more attention to it than necessary. Hayden said his name again, louder and more forcefully this time. "Boone!"

He finally looked up at her. "Yeah?"

"I'm okay. Really."

He sighed. "I know. But you scared the shit out of me, Hay."

Hayden knew it. Passing out in his arms wasn't her finest moment, and she knew she'd take a lot of ribbing from the guys at work when she went back, but she had to deal with Boone at the moment. "I'm sorry I scared you, but honestly, I'm fine. I think it was just everything. I had an adrenaline drop and that, along with the pain, made me lose it for a moment."

When the tortured look on his face didn't ease, Hayden sat up and forced Boone to his back and she straddled him. His arms came up to balance her at her hips so she didn't have to put any pressure on her arm. "You need to get over this, Boone. I'm not quitting my job. Dana's not dead—yeah, she'll hopefully be locked up for a good long time and get the mental help she needs, but there's a possibility she'll come back to haunt us. Luckily you'd installed those cameras. Everything was caught on tape. She's going down."

"Jesus, Hay, are you trying to comfort me or make me lose my mind?"

Hayden smiled down at the man she loved. "Comfort. Now listen." She paused. "You listening?"

"Yeah, I'm listening," he said grumpily, flexing his fingers at her waist.

"Are you okay with everything that happened? I get you did it for me, and I love you, but it went against everything that makes you *you*."

"If I had to do it again, I'd do it the same way every time."

"Actually, I'd prefer if you didn't. I don't mean hitting her. That was awesome." Hayden wrinkled her nose, but her lips were tipped up in a small grin. "I mean, she was one hundred percent sure you wouldn't touch her, and the way her head went back when you clocked her was priceless. That was my favorite part of the video. But seriously, you shouldn't have been there at all. She was pissed, but she completely lost it when you showed up. You should've stayed inside."

"No."

"Boone, I had it under control. I disarmed her. There was no reason for you to—"

"If her bullet had landed four inches to the left, you would've been dead."

"Boone…"

He put a finger on her lips, effectively silencing her. "I can't lose you, Hay. I can't. Not now that I've found you. I hit her at the same time she pulled the trigger. I'll believe to my dying day that if I hadn't punched her, her bullet would've hit true and you would've bled out on the ground at my feet, and there wouldn't have been anything I could've done to save you. You weren't wearing your vest. You'd just crawled out of our bed after a hell of a fight. A bullet in the heart can't be fixed, Hay. So yeah, it went against everything I believe in, but if I'm being honest, it felt good. I'd let her bully me for so long that I let my beliefs interfere in what was right. I'm not saying I'm gonna go join an all women's MMA fight club, but Dana taught me a lesson."

"That's good to know," Hayden said softly, torn between wanting to cry and laugh. At the moment crying was winning.

Boone watched as tears sprang into Hayden's eyes. "Don't cry, sweetheart. Dana might've abused me, and that was on me, but there's not a chance in hell I'd let her kill you. No fucking way. I'm hoping that was my one and only time that I have to strike a female, but I'd do it again if it meant keeping you safe."

Hayden sagged further into his hold. "I love you."

"And I love you."

"I think I want to go back to sleep," she mumbled.

Boone chuckled and helped Hayden lay down on

top of him. "Great. Go for it." He stroked a hand up and down her back while the other stayed locked around her waist, holding her against him.

"When are you going to invite me to move in with you? I'm already practically living here," Hayden mumbled into his neck.

"What?" Boone tensed under her.

Hayden didn't even flinch. "I mean, we love each other, right? My parents want to adopt you, and while my dad really couldn't give a shit about me, he loves *you*...so I guess we should make this semi-official."

"Did you just propose to me?" Boone laughed and nuzzled the hair at her neck.

"Uh...I don't think so...but maybe."

"The answer's yes."

"Are you pissed?" Hayden asked, not moving from her comfortable position plastered over Boone's body.

"Pissed you asked before I could? Hell no."

"But in the books I read, the men are always pissed off when their women beat them to the punch."

"Hayden, I don't give a fuck. As long as you end up in my bed with a ring on your finger, I don't care who does the asking." He relaxed as he felt her muscles go even more lax and she melted into him.

"Good, 'cause I've already researched the justice of the peace's website."

Boone snorted when he laughed. "God, I love you."

"Maybe if we're married, Dana will finally leave you alone."

"Go to sleep, Hay. Forget about her. From here on out, it's you and me. Dream of what kind of ring you want and let me know when you wake up."

"Oh, I already know," Hayden sleepily murmured into his throat.

Boone smiled and enjoyed simply holding Hayden as she drifted off to sleep again. He turned his head and looked over at Ellie the Elephant sitting on the table next to the bed. He reached over and grabbed it, eased Hayden to his side and tucked it into her chest between them. She murmured and tucked her head down until her chin rested on the pathetic stuffed toy's body.

Boone didn't know what it was about the old, familiar stuffed animal that gave Hayden comfort, but he didn't give a shit. He had no problem sleeping with her *and* Ellie for the rest of their lives if she wanted it that way. She was a bad-ass sheriff's deputy, and cute as fuck. He loved her with every fiber of his being.

Boone closed his eyes, enjoying the feel of the extraordinary woman curled in his arms. He knew they had a lot to work through; it really was too early to get married, they could have a long engagement. But moving in together? That was definitely happening sooner rather than later. He loved Hayden and she loved him. Nothing was worth losing that.

EPILOGUE

"You know the rule, Yates. If you get shot, you have to buy the beers for an entire night."

Hayden looked around. Not only were Jimmy, Troy, Brandon, Juan *and* the sheriff himself there at the bar, but so were Dax and Mack, Quint and Corrie, Cruz and Mickie, Dax's friend Westin King, and his girlfriend Laine, TJ, Calder, and even Conor had joined them as well.

"Yeah, but not for a thousand people, you morons."

They all laughed at her. "Shut up and pay up, Yates," TJ joked, leaning back in his chair, enjoying Hayden's discomfort.

"I don't know why I put up with you guys," Hayden grumbled as she handed her credit card over to the waitress to start a tab.

"Because you love us," Conor stated calmly.

Hayden looked up as Boone arrived back at the

table with a tray of neon-green drinks. She grinned at him.

"What the fuck kind of drinks are *those*?" TJ asked disbelievingly. "It looks like alien piss or something."

"Midori sours for the ladies," Boone answered easily, handing the drinks out to Mack, Mickie, Laine, and Hayden, and handing Corrie's to Quint to give to her. Since Corrie couldn't see where he'd put the drink down, he didn't want her to accidentally knock it over. He knew Quint would make sure it was secure.

"Oooooh, so now Hayden's a *laaady*," TJ mocked teasingly.

"Stuff it, Rockwell. If I want to drink a frou-frou drink, I fucking well will," Hayden told him, holding up her drink to the group, ignoring TJ's surprised sputtering at her comeback. "A toast..." She paused, waiting for everyone to raise their bottle or glass. "To friendship, love, and our continued safety. May those of you with partners revel in your love, and those of you without," Hayden looked mischievously at TJ before continuing, "find it when and where you least expect it."

Everyone said, "Cheers!" and took long pulls on their respective drinks.

Boone pulled Hayden close and nuzzled her neck, and smiled when she giggled. She'd come a long way from that first night out with her coworkers. She was much more relaxed, and she'd even bought a few skirts to wear. Boone had had to educate her friends and coworkers a few times when they'd treated her inappropriately, and they'd slowly realized just how much they'd treated her like one of the guys when she was, in fact, a beautiful, sensual woman.

Boone knew Hayden's parents would always see her as the tomboy they'd raised, but he hoped, with a little help, they'd start appreciating Hayden as a woman sooner rather than later. Her dad would be a hard sell, but hopefully someday he'd see how successful and wonderful his daughter was—no thanks to him.

The group sat around sipping the occasional beer or drink and chatting for another couple of hours before they started to head home.

"Thanks for the beers, Yates. See you in a couple of days," Juan told Hayden as he headed out.

"We on the same shift?"

"Yup."

"Cool, see you then," Hayden told Juan as he left.

"We need to get together with just us girls," Mack told Corrie, Mickie, Laine, and Hayden. "We see each other here at the bar when we get together with our men, but we need to have a ladies' night out too."

Hayden smiled big, loving that she'd been included in Mack's statement.

"I'll call you all and we'll set it up, okay?" Mack continued, "And Hayden, don't forget, next Saturday I'm calling in our bet. Me and Laine will pick you up at nine, and we'll be spending all day at the mall."

They all agreed to Mack setting up their ladies' night out and Hayden groaned thinking about the marathon shopping trip she was in for with Mackenzie and her best friend. She watched as her new friends left with their men.

Finally, all that was left at the table was TJ, Hayden, and Boone.

"You did good, kid," TJ told Hayden with a smirk.

Hayden rolled her eyes. "I'm older than you, asshole. You can't call me a kid."

They smiled at each other. He'd made his point. He was proud of her actions and glad she was still around. It was enough.

"If you ever get tired of patrolling the streets, give me a call. I'll put in a good word with the sheriff for you," Hayden told him.

"As if I'd get tired of pulling people over. It's interesting as all get out. You never know who you're pulling over. It could be a little old granny driving erratically because she can't see over the dash and is senile, or it could be an escaped convict. I love the adrenaline rush it gives me. It's almost as good as being in the Army."

"You're crazy." Hayden rolled her eyes at TJ. She hated traffic stops.

"Yeah, but I'm good at it. So I'll stick with it a bit longer."

TJ stood up and punched Hayden lightly in her uninjured shoulder and laughed when Boone glared up at him and pulled Hayden closer.

"Go home, guys. I've got an early shift tomorrow, I gotta get home too and get my beauty sleep," TJ teased.

"Sounds good to me. Boone, let me up. I need to go take care of the tab," Hayden said.

"No you don't," Boone said, tightening his arm around her, keeping her right where she was. "I already took care of it."

"You asshole," Hayden said with no heat in her voice, smiling at him. "So me giving the waitress my card when I got here was useless?"

TJ leaned over and kissed the top of Hayden's head. "Yup. We already had a talk with her. She took your card, but never ran it. Glad you're all right, Yates. It wouldn't be the same around here without you." He patted her shoulder lightly and turned and headed for the door of the bar.

Hayden looked up at Boone. "When did you pay?"

"When you went to the restroom earlier with the girls."

"Boone!"

"What?"

"I was supposed to pay."

"Hay, first of all, there's no way the guys who were here tonight would *ever* let a woman pay for their drinks all night. No way in hell."

"But I'm not a woman to them."

"Yes, you are. They might not have seen you that way in the past, but with these legs, how could they miss it now?" Boone stroked Hayden's bare thigh. Her mini-skirt had risen up as she'd sat in the chair. He smiled at her when she blushed.

"And secondly," Boone continued, "you'll never pay when I'm around...remember?"

"You're such a Neanderthal," Hayden mock-complained.

"Yeah, but I'm *your* Neanderthal," Boone countered.

"That you are. I think it's time *my* Neanderthal took me home and to our bed."

Hayden screeched when Boone immediately stood and picked her up. "Boone, my skirt."

"I've got it. I'm not gonna let you flash the entire bar, sweetheart. That's for my eyes only."

Hayden put her arms around Boone's neck and leaned in close. She licked the skin under his ear. "Walk faster. I'm in the mood to try out that new strawberry-flavored lube I bought last week." She laughed as Boone picked up his pace and practically ran out to his truck.

"I love you, Boone."

He leaned over in his seat before starting the engine. "I love you too, Hayden. Now...shut up and let me get us home safely. The last thing I want is one of your friends pulling me over. I'm so ready for you, I can't wait the extra ten minutes it'd take to get a ticket."

Hayden put her head back on the seat of Boone's truck and gazed at him as he carefully drove them back to his farm. She was the luckiest woman on the planet.

AFTER GETTING BACK to work a couple of weeks later, Hayden was sitting in a booth at the small hole-in-the-wall restaurant across the street from Station 7 with Crash, eating lunch. She hadn't thought she'd ever be as close to anyone as she was to her fellow law enforcement friends, but as it turned out, the firefighters in Station 7 were great guys, and because their paths kept crossing, they were getting to know each other better.

She'd gone to the station to talk to Moose, and to thank him for helping take care of her at the bar that night when Dana had drugged her, and found herself staying for over an hour, talking with the rest of the firefighters. Crash had taken one look at her and fallen to his knees, begging her to marry him. Ever since that day, they'd been friends.

He'd also been one of the firefighters who had shown up at Boone's farm after Dana had shot her. He'd been very professional, and not only helped stem the blood oozing out of her arm, but had made sure Boone had been taken care of as well.

Crash was funny. There were times when Hayden thought she saw something in him, something that reminded her of herself before she'd met Boone, but as soon as she saw it, the joking funny guy returned.

"I appreciate you meeting me for lunch."

Crash took a big bite of his sandwich and winked at

her. "No problem. As if I'd turn down a date with a hot cop."

Hayden ignored his blatant flirting. One thing she'd learned about Crash was that he was one of the station's two playboys. It seemed women were drawn to him...and he milked it for all he was worth. After spending time with the firefighters, on the job and after-hours when the cops and firefighters got together for drinks, Hayden realized that most of Crash's behavior was smoke and mirrors. He might flirt with women, but she hadn't ever seen him go home with one from the bars. It was as if he'd cultivated his man-ho reputation to hide his insecurities about something.

"How's Beth doing?" Hayden had been fascinated by Sledge's girlfriend ever since she'd helped find her after the robbery at their house. The woman had been through hell, but with Sledge's help, and appropriate medication, she was beating back her agoraphobia.

"Amazing, really. She loves working for the government. I swear she's lethal though...she can hack anything. I'm afraid to make her mad. The other day, after Sledge did something stupid, she hacked into our TV and the only station we could get was the Disney channel. It was a long day, let me tell you."

Hayden laughed. She could just picture Beth doing that too. She liked her. Hayden opened her mouth to tell Crash that he'd better watch himself, that women always win, when a man's loud voice rang through the restaurant.

"Seriously? You want to leave now? We just ordered!"

Hayden looked over and saw a couple sitting at a booth. There was a black lab wearing a service dog vest under the table, but with its front paws in the woman's lap. She looked shaken and worried. She and Crash watched as the woman said something to the man, but whatever it was, it obviously wasn't what the man wanted to hear.

Crash quickly put his napkin next to his plate and stood up. Hayden was about to join him when he waved her down.

"I'll check it out and let you know if she needs you." Crash's words were brusque and hard.

Hayden relaxed. No, Crash wasn't a cop, but the man the woman had been eating with was already stalking off, so it didn't look like there was any kind of situation that required her presence.

She relaxed into her chair, keeping her eyes on her friend as he quickly headed to the other table and the distraught-looking woman.

CRASH HATED the look on the woman's face. He had no idea why he hadn't let Hayden take care of whatever the situation was, but there was something about the woman and her dog that struck a chord within him.

He didn't talk about his life growing up with his

friends, wasn't even sure anyone knew that he had a sister who had Down syndrome. But he'd seen her being bullied his entire life, and he recognized the signs a mile away.

Laurie was doing great today. She was in a group home in Phoenix, Arizona. She worked in a grocery store bagging groceries, and loved it. Laurie didn't seem to remember anything about how hard her life had been growing up, but Crash wouldn't ever forget.

He turned his attention back to the woman at the table. She was petting her dog and trying to get her things together.

"Are you all right?"

Her head whipped up as if he'd surprised her, which Crash supposed he probably did. "I couldn't help but notice that you seem upset."

The woman looked relieved to see him, or at least his uniform. "You're a firefighter?"

"Yes, ma'am."

"An EMT or paramedic?"

"Yes..." Crash's voice trailed off, not liking where the conversation was going.

"I'm Adeline. I have about ten minutes or so before I'm going to have an epileptic seizure, as Coco," she gestured toward the dog currently panting in her face and pawing at her leg, "has warned me. I need to get to a safe place, I can't drive, and the person who could've taken me somewhere," she paused for a precious moment to glare at the door the man who had been sitting with her had disappeared through, "seems to have ditched me. I'm incredibly embarrassed, but I'd appreciate the help."

The woman's voice was husky. He had no idea if it was her normal tone, or if it had to do with the stress she was currently under, but whatever it was, it struck him hard.

He'd never believed in love at first sight, but Lord, this woman made him think of long nights in bed, bubble baths, and holding hands as they walked down the street.

Crash mentally shook himself. He needed to get her and her dog to safety. He knew never to take epileptic seizures lightly. He had a lot of questions about the type of epilepsy she had and what kind of seizure might be coming, but first things first. She was obviously knowledgeable about her condition, since she had an alert dog and knew exactly what she needed to do, but he still felt the urge to protect her from the prying eyes of the other patrons in the restaurant, and to keep her safe.

Remembering the conversation he'd once had with Beth about his name, and understanding somehow that the instant attraction he had for the woman sitting so bravely in front of him was unique, he made a split-second decision.

Crash held out his hand. "My name is Dean. It's good to meet you. Trust me, I'll take care of you."

He looked into Adeline's eyes as she reached out

her hand and put it in his own, and knew his life would never be the same.

LOOK for the next book in the Badge of Honor: Texas Heroes Series, *Shelter for Adeline*. Available now!

JOIN my Newsletter and find out about sales, free books, contests and new releases before anyone else!! Click HERE

Want to know when my books go on sale? Follow me on Bookbub HERE!

Would you like Susan's Book Protecting Caroline for FREE? Click HERE

Delta Force Heroes Series
Rescuing Rayne
Rescuing Aimee (novella)
Rescuing Emily
Rescuing Harley
Marrying Emily (novella)
Rescuing Kassie
Rescuing Bryn
Rescuing Casey
Rescuing Sadie (novella)
Rescuing Wendy
Rescuing Mary
Rescuing Macie (novella)

SEAL of Protection: Legacy Series
Securing Caite
Securing Brenae (novella)
Securing Sidney
Securing Piper
Securing Zoey
Securing Avery (May 2020)
Securing Kalee (Sept 2020)
Securing Jane (novella) (Feb 2021)

SEAL Team Hawaii Series
Finding Elodie (Apr 2021)
Finding Lexie (Aug 2021)
Finding Kenna (Oct 2021)
Finding Monica (TBA)

Finding Carly (TBA)
Finding Ashlyn (TBA)

Ace Security Series
Claiming Grace
Claiming Alexis
Claiming Bailey
Claiming Felicity
Claiming Sarah

Mountain Mercenaries Series
Defending Allye
Defending Chloe
Defending Morgan
Defending Harlow
Defending Everly
Defending Zara
Defending Raven (June 2020)

Silverstone Series
Trusting Skylar (Dec 2020)
Trusting Taylor (Mar 2021)
Trusting Molly (July 2021)
Trusting Cassidy (Dec 2021

SEAL of Protection Series
Protecting Caroline
Protecting Alabama
Protecting Fiona

Marrying Caroline (novella)
Protecting Summer
Protecting Cheyenne
Protecting Jessyka
Protecting Julie (novella)
Protecting Melody
Protecting the Future
Protecting Kiera (novella)
Protecting Alabama's Kids (novella)
Protecting Dakota

Stand Alone
The Guardian Mist
Nature's Rift
A Princess for Cale
A Moment in Time- A Collection of Short Stories
Lambert's Lady

Special Operations Fan Fiction
http://www.AcesPress.com

Beyond Reality Series
Outback Hearts
Flaming Hearts
Frozen Hearts

Writing as Annie George:
Stepbrother Virgin (erotic novella)

ABOUT THE AUTHOR

New York Times, *USA Today* and *Wall Street Journal* Best-selling Author Susan Stoker has a heart as big as the state of Texas where she lives, but this all American girl has also spent the last fourteen years living in Missouri, California, Colorado, and Indiana. She's married to a retired Army man who now gets to follow *her* around the country.

She debuted her first series in 2014 and quickly followed that up with the SEAL of Protection Series, which solidified her love of writing and creating stories readers can get lost in.

If you enjoyed this book, or any book, please consider leaving a review. It's appreciated by authors more than you'll know.

www.stokeraces.com
susan@stokeraces.com